CASSANDRA'S REWARD ...
FOR FAILURE

~~~

by Nancy I. Young

VICTORIAN WOMEN
OF FAITH

www.nancyireneyoung.com

FriesenPress

One Printers Way
Altona, MB R0G 0B0
Canada

www.friesenpress.com

Copyright © 2025 by Nancy I. Young
First Edition — 2025

All rights reserved.

No part of this publication may be reproduced in any form, or by any means, electronic or mechanical, including photocopying, recording, or any information browsing, storage, or retrieval system, without permission in writing from FriesenPress.

ISBN
978-1-03-832906-6 (Hardcover)
978-1-03-832905-9 (Paperback)
978-1-03-832907-3 (eBook)

1. FICTION, CHRISTIAN, HISTORICAL

Distributed to the trade by The Ingram Book Company

Table of Contents

Chapter 1 1
Chapter 2 10
Chapter 3 24
Chapter 4 33
Chapter 5 42
Chapter 6 52
Chapter 7 61
Chapter 8 76
Chapter 9 91
Chapter 10 95
Chapter 11 104
Chapter 12 120
Chapter 13 133
Chapter 14 142
Chapter 15 152
Chapter 16 158
Chapter 17 163
Chapter 18 173

Chapter 19	185
Chapter 20	203
Chapter 21	212
Chapter 22	230
Chapter 23	238
Chapter 24	242
Chapter 25	252
Epilogue	259
End Notes	263
Coming Next …	265
Author's Notes	269

Chapter 1

Cassandra was tired... No, it was much more than that. She was exhausted. She took off her reading glasses and rubbed the bridge of her nose. The figures were not adding up. She had gone over them at least a dozen times but was coming to the same conclusion. The estate was in trouble. They were out of money.

She had been making do with less her entire life, from the time she was a small girl and through her former marriage. So, she had been ecstatic when her sister-in-law Bethany had offered this home to her and her four boys. The estate was well maintained, and prosperous, largely because of the excellent management of the farm steward, Mr. Wiley. Cassandra had had no money worries for the first time in her life. But that was before the drought had caused the market prices for grain to collapse, and they'd had to buy feed for the cattle and horses.

And then their crops had failed for the second season as the drought continued. They had managed to salvage some of those crops for animal feed that year, but they'd had nothing they could have sold on the market, even had the market process recovered, which they hadn't. These calamities had eaten into the estate funds until there was nothing left. And then today the steward had come to her saying that they needed to buy more feed for the animals or else they would not survive the winter.

Cassandra had been reviewing the books for the last two hours, searching for some area in which they could economise to come up with the needed monies, but she was at a loss. They were broke. She had failed once again, not as a wife this time but as the keeper of Bethany's family estate. She should never have agreed to take this on five years ago. What had she been thinking?

Her key priority, at the time, had been to get her young boys out of London. They had been living in a rented townhouse in a poor area of the city. She had been afraid to even let the boys outside to play because her husband's gambling associates had frequently shown up, demanding money to pay down her husband's debts. She had been terrified that they would snatch the boys away and make them work for the loan shark if her husband Howard did not pay them soon. So, she had hidden all the boys away in the playroom when the older ones were not in school, and prayed that God would keep them safe. Her only reason for living had been her sons.

Howard had only taken her to wife to get his hands on her dowry. And then, once Howard had gambled that away, he'd made her falsely accuse his own stepsister of a theft in order to gain control of her estate. Cassandra had been plagued with guilt for the part she'd played in sending Bethany away to a penal colony in Australia. And so, she had gone to the judge and confessed that she had lied to the court about Bethany having stolen her jewellery. Thankfully, the judge had been lenient with Cassandra and only sentenced her to a year of community service.

During that same year, Bethany, and her brand-new husband Sam, had arrived back in England and done two things for Cassandra: First, they had paid off all of Howard's gambling debts; and second, they'd presented her with the key to Stillwater Estate, asking her to move out there and manage it for them. Cassandra had reluctantly agreed, overwhelmed by their love and generosity, especially after what she had done to Bethany. And so, when she had completed her community service, she and her boys had packed up their things and moved out to the country.

They had loved their first years at the estate. The older boys, Peter and Wendell, started attending a boarding school that was close enough that they could home for the holidays. And Bethany and Sam paid for a tutor for the younger boys, Calvin and Arthur. The tutor lived in a cottage on the grounds and came up to the manor for the boys' lessons each day. Soon enough, though, they too headed off to join their brothers at the boarding school. And now, five years later, Peter was at Eton, and Wendell would soon be joining him there. They were growing up so quickly, and Cassandra couldn't help but wonder where the time had gone.

Before returning to Australia, Bethany and Sam had told her that they would continue to pay all the estate bills, including the educational fees for her sons. The couple had thought the estate would continue to prosper and had told Cassandra to simply use any of the excess funds for her own needs. Of course, they been unaware of the catastrophe lurking just around the corner. And they remained unaware of it even now, as Cassandra still had no intention of telling them about the dire situation at the estate.

There must be a way to buy the animal feed. There must be...

***

As Cassandra was fretting over her finances at the Stillwater Estate, a man she had yet to meet was heading to his own family's townhouse in London. In his mid-thirties, Viscount John Dudley was the oldest son of the Earl of Dudley, and he was hoping to surprise his family with his unexpected return. In fact, he could not wait to see their reactions.

Reaching the Mayfair townhouse in a hired cab, he then walked up the flagstone steps, and grasping the iron ring that was set into the front door, he knocked three times and waited. When he heard no response after about a minute, he repeated his actions. Then he heard someone moving on the other side of the door before it was cracked open by elderly man, dressed in a butler's livery.

"Yes?" the man said as he peered out into the gloom. "Can I help you?"

"Waverly?"

"Yes. Whom may I say is calling?"

"Waverly... It's me, John. John Dudley. Do you not recognise me?"

The old butler opened the door a bit wider, so that the indoor lamps illuminated John's face. Then the light of recognition dawned in the old man's eyes. "John? ... Master John? You are home? You are back from the colonies?"

"Yes, Waverly. I am home. May I come in?"

"Of course," the old man said quickly, moving aside so that John could pass him. "Please come in. I'm sorry that I kept you standing on the porch. Now, let me look at you..."

Smiling, John took a few steps inside, beyond the butler, then turned slightly and struck an elegant pose. "Well? What do you think? Is it me?"

"Oh, yes, sir. But if I may say so, a much-improved version of yourself. You look well."

John laughed. "Yes, it must have been that six months of healthy eating and exercise I got on Sam and Bethany's sheep station. Or else it was just constantly chasing their son, David, all over the yard. He never sits still."

"Is that Lord and Lady Yardley you speak of?"

"Yes, but in Australia, they are just Sam and Bethany Yardley. They prefer it that way."

"Such informality..."

"True, but it is a brand-new country with ideas quite different to our own. Everyone associates with everyone else. If one did not, they would have no social life at all."

"Did you like the country, Master John?"

"Very much."

"Will you plan to return for another visit someday?"

"If I can. But right now, I need to reconnect with my family. Are they in town?"

"No, sir. They are out at the manor. It is not the season for them to be living in the city."

"Ah, yes, The Season. How quickly I have forgotten. In Australia, there is no distinction between the social seasons. You get together whenever you can. But I should have known my parents would be out at Dudley Manor. I shall head there tomorrow. Is there a bed aired that I could sleep in tonight?"

"We can make up your old room. I will alert the housekeeper to do that. In the meantime, do you require any refreshments?"

"Tea and a snack would be nice if it is not too much bother. I have not eaten too much today, so I am hungry. But do not go to any trouble on my behalf."

"I will see what the cook has available. Do you wish to eat in the dining room?"

"No," he said, shaking his head with a slight smile. "Without others around the table, it would be far too formal. I will take tea in my father's study if that is acceptable."

"Certainly. I will have a footman stoke a fire for you while you wait," he said, nodding to a young man who was standing nearby.

"Thank you. I would appreciate a fire. I have yet to reaccustom myself to the cooler northern temperatures."

"Good, sir. Jimmy will get you settled in the study while I speak with the housekeeper and cook. I won't be long."

"Don't hurry on my behalf. I have all evening to relax and enjoy my homecoming. Take your time."

"I'm afraid my hurrying days are over, Master John. I have only one pace now, and that is slow. I still get to where I need to be, though not as quickly as you might remember from when you were younger." He turned away then and strolled down the hall towards the kitchen.

John smiled and headed to his father's den. When he got there, he found that Jimmy had already lit a fire and was putting more wood on it.

"I'll tend to the fire, now," John told him. "I've learned to do a lot of things for myself in the past few years, including building and tending a fire."

"Very good, sir. Is there anything else I can get you?"

"No, I am fine. Thank you."

"Then I will leave you to enjoy your evening, sir. Have a good night."

"I shall. I'll ring if I need your services again."

Jimmy nodded before turning and heading out of the room and back to his station in the foyer.

John sank into the soft leather chair that flanked the fireplace. Then he closed his eyes and let out a contented sigh. It was good to be home.

***

A little while later, the sounds of someone putting a tray beside him startled him from a dream-like state. He opened his eyes to see another familiar face, this one belonging to the cook.

"Mrs. Willings!" he said with a smile, standing to give his old friend a hug. "It is good to see you."

"Master John, I just had to bring the tray myself. I could not believe what Waverly was telling Mrs. Brown and me ... that you were home at last. Stand back so I can get a look at you."

He obliged by taking a couple of steps backward.

"Hmmm. A little on the thin side... Well, I can take care of that," she said, pointing to the tray she'd brought with her, which was covered with sliced meat, cheese, bread, and other goodies. "Starting right now."

"Goodness! You expect me to eat all that?"

"Help to put some flesh on those bones, Master John. Don't want people to think I'm not feeding you."

"I have to admit that I did lose about a half stone on the voyage back to England. But Sam and Bethany fed me well. And Waverly thought I looked good."

"Waverly! Ha! The old fool can't see more than a few inches past his nose now. He has no idea what you really look like. No, if I say you are too thin, you are too thin, and that is a fact. Now, eat up."

"I will. Thank you. Shall I bring the tray to the kitchen when I am done?"

"*You* carry the tray, Master John? No, you leave it, and I will have a maid collect it, either later this evening or tomorrow morning."

"I'll have to remember that I am not in Australia anymore. There, everyone pitches in to help, whether they be servants or the lord and lady of the house. No one is exempt from working."

"Lord and Lady Yardley working like commoners? I don't believe it."

"Believe it, Mrs. Willings. You would not recognise Sam in his dungarees and boots. He has adapted well to his new role."

"Such a strange new land, sir. I don't know how I would cope in such circumstances."

"It is strange and new indeed, but I loved it. It is much more relaxed, and except for the bugs and snakes—"

"Bugs and snakes? No, that definitely would not be for me. Now, enjoy your meal and let us know if you need anything else. Mrs. Brown is airing out your room as we speak."

"I will retire once I have eaten. I am looking forward to sleeping on a bed tonight that does not roll with the waves."

"Then I expect I will see you tomorrow. Have a good night." With that, she exited the room, leaving John to try and make at least a small dent in the heavily laden tray.

***

After consuming as much of the food as he could, John decided it was time to go to bed. Mrs. Brown, the housekeeper, had stopped by while he was eating to welcome him home and let him know his room was now ready. So, with his stomach full, and his eyes closing with the warmth of the fire, he decided to retire. He debated whether he would ignore Mrs. Willings's words and take the tray back to the kitchen, but in the end he decided to leave it alone. He was only planning to be here until tomorrow, after all, so there seemed no point in starting something new.

So, he got out of his chair, headed out of the room, and up the stairs to his bedroom. It was just as Mrs. Brown had said it would be. They had turned the bed down, and there were fresh towels beside a basin of water, which he presumed was still warm. John stripped down, splashed the lukewarm water on his face, and dried it, before climbing into the bed. He had forgotten how far off the floor the mattress was. He had to stretch his long legs just to climb in. Once there, he pulled up the blankets, snuggled down into their warmth, and drifted off to sleep.

***

The next morning, he woke refreshed from a full night of rest. Looking around, he saw steam rising from the basin of water and fresh towels beside it. When had that been done? He must have been in a deep sleep, indeed, to have missed someone coming in and replacing the water. Not wanting to miss out on the heat, he climbed out of bed and gave his face and hands a vigorous wash. *Ah, that felt good.* He dressed quickly in the clothes that had been laid out at the end of the bed. By this time, his stomach was growling again, so he headed to the kitchen for breakfast. He did not know what time it was, but he knew the servants would be up early, as evidenced by what he'd seen in his room. Even a day-old scone would tide him over until breakfast was ready. So, he hurried down the stairs and hallway to see what Mrs. Willings could get for him.

As he had thought, she was already in the kitchen, directing her helpers in preparation for the morning meal and later. She had her back to him when he entered the kitchen, so she was startled when he said, "Good morning, Mrs. Willings. Thank you for the wonderful food last evening. It was exactly what I needed. However, I find myself hungry once more. So, I was wondering if there was something here that I could nibble on prior to breakfast."

"Mr. John! You shocked me!" she said, turning to look at him with one hand pressed to her chest. "I cannot keep up with your new-fangled ideas. First, you want to carry food trays. Then you show up at my kitchen door and ask for food instead of ringing for it. What's next? You helping me cook?"

"Perhaps." He smiled. "But I do not know that my new skills would be of benefit to you. Besides, I plan to leave today for Dudley Manor. So, alas, you will not have time to teach me to cook."

"I am sorry to hear you plan to leave again so soon, but I understand you will want to see your family right away. We can always start the cooking lessons the next time you are in town."

"I look forward to that. Now, about my snack?"

"Head into the dining room, sir. Breakfast is almost ready. We will put it out on the sideboard soon."

"Thank you. I was going to ask to stay in the kitchen for breakfast, but I will do as you ask." John backed out of the kitchen and went to the dining room, where he found they had already set a place for him at the table. A young footman was standing by to assist him.

John approached the sideboard where the food was laid out and selected his preferred dishes: bacon, eggs, and toast, but rejected the black pudding. He had never developed a taste for the dish. The footman poured him a cup of tea and carried it over to the table. John bowed his head and blessed the food before digging in. It was a true English breakfast. He was, indeed, home again.

***

When he finished eating, the footman took his plate and refilled his teacup. Then Waverly walked into the dining room with the day's news-sheets.

"I thought you would like to be brought up to date on the happenings in London, Master John, after so long a time away."

"Yes, that would good, Waverly," he said, taking the papers from the butler. "I received some news from England while I was in Australia, but by the time it reached us, it was months old, if not years. When I was staying in Fremantle with Sam and Bethany's friends, the Tremblants, the papers were newer. But by the time Sam and Bethany received them, the news was older than the surrounding hills. Let me see what the news and gossip these sheets hold today." Spreading out the first one in front of him, he glanced at the headlines and read some articles before flipping to the society-gossip column. He found notices there for weddings and children's births for some of his contemporaries. Obviously, judging by the news, he had missed out on a lot while he'd been away. Time was passing swiftly for all of them.

Once he'd finished reading, he looked up to see Waverly still standing in the room. "I am planning to head out to the manor today," he said to him. "But before I go there, I wish to see my uncle and aunt, the Duke and Duchess of Yardley. Are they still in town, do you know?"

"I believe so. I have not heard otherwise. Would you like me to make inquiries for you?"

"No, that's fine. I am sure you would have heard if they had left the city. I will stop on my way out of town. But I do need transportation. Are any of my horses still stabled here?"

"I believe Black is here, sir. If he is not, we have other horses available for you. When will you be needing one?"

"As soon as possible, thank you. I wish to leave once I have washed and shaved."

"Very good, sir. I will have a horse saddled for you and brought around front."

"Thank you. Now if you will excuse me, I'll head upstairs, do what I need to do, and then come down again."

"Do you need help with shaving or dressing?"

"No, I can do for myself, thank you."

"Then I will be off to prepare your transportation."

John smiled as he watched the old butler shuffle out of the room. Waverly should retire with a lovely cottage in the country, but as long as he could do his duties, he would resist that idea. So, it was better to keep him where he could still live his life productively. Shaking his head, John headed out of the room and up to his bedroom to collect his things and prepare for the day.

As he wondered what he would discover in the hours to come, a Bible verse came to him as he thought about his day: *This is the day that the LORD hath made. We will rejoice and be glad in it.*[1]

Choosing that verse as his day's motto, John leapt into action.

Chapter 2

A short time later, John was on his horse and headed over to see the Duke and Duchess of Yardley, or as he called them, Uncle Douglas and Aunt Margaret. He'd always enjoyed seeing them and had spent a great deal of time playing with his cousin Sam when they were boys. Sam was older than he was, but that had not mattered. Because they lived on adjoining estates, they were often together. Their favourite game had been pretending they were knights of old, slaying dragons and rescuing fair maidens. There had been no fair maidens in either family, so they had dressed up Sam and John's younger brothers and pretended that they were the ladies in need of saving. The young boys only tolerated that for a couple of years until they aspired to be knights as well.

Sam and John had soon grown out of that fantasy in any case. They had moved on to courting the young ladies in London, but neither had found the woman of their dreams while they were there. It was interesting that Sam had found his true love in an Australian prison, and even more amazing that she had been one of the young women they had sometimes seen at parties in London. Now Sam and Bethany were happily married and living their dream on a sheep station in Western Australia. As John had told Waverly, he had thoroughly enjoyed spending time there with them and hoped to go back again soon. But until then, he had family obligations to fulfil, starting with a morning visit to his uncle and aunt.

***

Within minutes, he was at their stables, behind their townhouse, and handing the reins of his horse to the stable boy. "We have only had a brief ride," he said, "so he does not need any feed or currying, only stabling for a few hours."

"Good, sir," said the lad. "I will take care of him."

"Thank you. I don't know how long I will be. Perhaps an hour or two, but only that."

"You can send someone from the house when you are ready to depart, sir, and I will bring your horse to the front porch for you."

"That sounds good to me." He turned to his horse then, stroking its nose. "Now, Black, you be good for the lad. None of your tricks now." The horse neighed and tossed his head before allowing himself to be led off and into the stables with the boy.

John turned then and headed towards the back of the townhouse. He decided to go in through the kitchen, which was a familiar route for him, to not only surprise his aunt and uncle but also their staff. He strode up to the back door, and without knocking, opened it and let himself in. Once inside, he took the few steps up towards the kitchen door, and seeing it standing open, walked in to see the staff sitting at the table. "Are the duke and duchess aware of what lazy servants they employ? I am shocked to see this and have a mind to tell them of your slothful habits."

Everyone looked up. Those who recognised him laughed, before getting up and rushing over to embrace him.

"Master John! You're home!" said Parker, his aunt and uncle's long-time butler.

"I am, Parker. It is good to see you, old man. How are you faring?"

"Well, sir, thank you. And you?"

"No complaints."

Then Parker stepped back to let others greet him and turned back to look at those still seated at the table. "This is Lord John Dudley, a nephew to the duke and duchess. He has been away visiting his cousin, Samuel, in Australia, and has just returned. Am I correct, Master John?"

"You are, Parker. I only arrived yesterday and am on my way home to Dudley Manor. But I wanted to see my aunt and uncle before I left the city. I have packets of letters for them from Sam and Bethany."

"I am sure they will appreciate seeing you, sir, and receiving all of Lord and Lady Yardley's letters. Are they well?"

"They are, indeed. Or at least, they were when I left them several months ago. They love their new home, and their children are thriving."

"How many children do they have now?"

"Two and another one on the way, although I guess it is three by now, as the baby should have arrived about a month ago."

"Well, I won't keep you any longer, Master John," said Parker. "I know you are eager to see your aunt and uncle. She is in the morning room, and the duke is in his den. Would you like me to announce you?"

"No, I want to surprise them," said John. "It was wonderful to see your familiar faces here today, and these new ones as well." He nodded to the others. "Carry on." He laughed before heading out towards the main rooms of the house. Going up another short flight of stairs, he hastened towards his uncle's den. The door was open, but he could not see the duke. So, he knocked. "Lord John Dudley requesting permission to enter, Your Grace."

"John?" said a man's voice from within the room.

"Yes, Your Grace, it is me."

"Get in here, you young scallywag! Let me see you!"

John smiled at the term his uncle used for him. It was true, he and Sam had been scallywags in their youth. He was far past the age of such endearments now, but not too old for a hug. He quickly walked into the room, his arms already held out wide for a hug, and the duke met him halfway across the room, happy to oblige.

"Let me look at you, boy," said the duke a moment later, taking a step back from their embrace to view his nephew. "Hmmm, a little thin, are you not?"

"So Mrs. Willings told me when she greeted me last evening. She then tried to fatten me up all in one meal."

"That is a cook's mission in life, John. But other than being a tad underweight, you look well. Are you?"

"Very well. And you?"

"Older but still healthy, thank you. So, you only arrived home last evening?"

"Yes, but it was too late to call on you and Aunt Margaret. I thought perhaps my parents would be in town, but I hear they are out at the manor."

"Yes, they left about a month ago for the country. Some necessary business has delayed our departure, but we hope to leave soon as well. Are you heading to the manor today?"

"Yes, but I wanted to see you both first before I left."

"That was kind of you. Will you take lunch with us before you leave?"

"I can do that, Uncle, thank you."

"Excellent. Now, I believe your aunt is in her morning room. Shall we surprise her?"

"Please. Parker had wanted to announce me, but I told him that I hoped to surprise both of you."

"Well, you did me, boy. Now, let's see if you can do the same to Margaret." The duke's eyes twinkled with anticipation of her shock.

John agreed, and the two men walked quietly to the foyer, and then down another hall towards the duchess's favourite morning room. When they got there, the duke stayed back, while John moved into the doorway. Then in his best imitation of Parker's voice, he said, "Excuse me, Your Grace, but you have a visitor. Shall I show him in?"

The duchess started to agree before pausing, realising that this had not been Parker's voice, and then looked up to see John smiling at her.

"John Dudley!" she exclaimed, rushing over to hug him. "You almost gave me a heart attack! Don't you know I am an old woman now and cannot take such shocks?"

"You will never be old, Aunt Margaret. You are the epitome of eternal youth," he said, leaning over to kiss her on the cheek.

"Oh, go on with you, young man," she said, blushing with his praise. "Please do go on..."

"Ahem..." The duke had joined them in the room. "That is quite enough, John. I will not have you stealing my lady's heart with your flattery."

Margaret laughed, and the men joined in with her. "But when did you arrive? And Sam and Bethany, how are they? And the children?"

"Slow down, my dear, and give the boy a chance to breathe before he answers all your questions. He has agreed to stay for lunch before heading off to Dudley Manor, so we have plenty of time to question him. Don't we, John?"

"Yes, I will answer all your questions, both yours, Aunt Margaret, and Uncle Douglas's. But first, let me inquire after your health, Your Grace. Are you well?"

"I am, John, and you?"

"Very well, thank you. And before you say it, yes, I am a bit thinner than when you last saw me. Both Uncle Douglas and our cook, Mrs. Willings, have chastised me about my weight. As I told your husband, though, Mrs. Willings tried to remedy that already with one enormous meal last evening. As such, I am sure the weight will be back on very soon."

"I was going to mention it, John, as will your mother, I am sure. But I am glad you are well. That is the main issue, not your weight. However, I will ask our cook to prepare lots of fattening foods for lunch to keep up the work Mrs. Willings started yesterday."

John groaned as the duke and duchess laughed.

"I have already told Parker to set another place for lunch, my dear," said the duke. "Knowing our cook, there will be no shortage of food on the table."

"Thank you, Douglas. Now, John, would you like a cup of tea or coffee? You will need fluids to keep your mouth from drying out while you answer all my questions."

John agreed that a cup of tea would be nice. So, the duchess rang her bell, and when a maid arrived, she asked for another pot of her special tea, along with two extra teacups.

Soon, the maid was back with the tea tray, and after she left, the duchess poured a cup for each of the men. "Now, John ... tell us everything."

***

An hour later, John had reached the end of his tale. "And everything I have said is also likely described in the thick packet of letters I brought with me from Sam and Bethany. I hope their news is not redundant now."

Wiping away tears that had started flowing when John had spoken about her grandchildren, the duchess said, "No, I will read those letters with fresh eyes to see if I missed hearing any of your words. Three little ones, Douglas!"

She turned to her husband. "Three little babies we have yet to lay eyes on! Oh, I hope we see them soon."

"As do I, my love," he said. "Especially our granddaughter. Unless they've since had another girl, she is the only granddaughter we have, and I long to cuddle her."

"Oh, yes. We love our grandsons, but a granddaughter is a special gift from God. I, too, long to meet and hold her."

"I pray that this is no secret, but Sam and Bethany were planning a trip north while I was still with them. They were waiting until the baby was born, and then hoped to bring the children to see you. We can hope they will soon be on their way."

"Thank you for giving us that hope to hold onto, John," said the duke. "We will pray for that as well."

The duchess agreed, and they talked about other news until Parker arrived to call them for lunch.

***

After an enjoyable lunch with his aunt and uncle, John prepared to head out to his family's home. His horse was called for and brought round to the street. The duke and duchess walked out with John to see him off.

"Oh, I almost forgot, John," said the duke. "Would you mind stopping at the Stillwater Estate, Bethany's former home, and inquiring into Cassandra Stillwater's wellbeing? We promised Sam and Bethany we would keep an eye on her, and we have not seen her for several months. Margaret and I will drop in on our way to the country house, but I would appreciate if you could visit, even for a few moments, today. It will not take you out of your way; the estate is on the main road."

"I will do that. In fact, Bethany asked me to deliver letters to Mrs. Stillwater. So, I had plans to stop anyway."

"That is good. It will ease our minds to know the state of her welfare. Will you send us word as to how she is getting along?"

"Certainly. Now, I must be on my way," said John, before kissing his aunt and shaking the duke's hand. "If I do not see you when you retire to the country, I will stop by the next time I am in the city."

"Thank you, dear boy," said the duchess. "Give our regards to your parents."

"I will. Farewell for now," said John as he swung up into his saddle and took the horse's reins from the stableboy.

"Farewell, John," said the duke. "Thank you for stopping by."

John tipped his head, then looked forward, tugged on the reins, and started his horse walking down the street.

The duke and duchess watched him until he was out of sight, then linked arms and walked back into the house, pleased to know that Cassandra would have a visitor that day.

Once John was out of the city, and on the main road to Dudley Manor, he gave Black his head, setting a comfortable pace. Dudley Manor was about a two-hour ride from London, even with a quick stop at Stillwater Estate. A small breeze stirred the grass alongside the road. The sun was shining in a cloudless sky, and the birds were singing in the treetops. It was good to be home. He had enjoyed the vivid colours of Australia's plants, but the muted tones of England's flowers soothed his soul. He had missed these sights.

***

An hour later, he came to the gates of Stillwater Estate. He had never stopped there previously, having had no reason to do so. But now he had a purpose. The gates were closed but did not appear to be locked, so John dismounted and unlatched them. He gave them a push, and they swung inward. Once inside the walls, he turned, closed the gates, and relatched them before mounting his horse again. He had been surprised that the gates were not locked, and that there was no gatekeeper to open them. Anyone, friend or foe, could have easily accessed the estate. He decided this was an issue he would discuss with Mrs. Stillwater and mention to his uncle. Safety was a top priority, especially for a widow living alone in the country.

A short time later, he arrived at the front portico of the house. He admired the Georgian style of the manor: the symmetrical windows on either side of the door, the warm brick façade, and the Georgian columns that supported the covered entranceway. This house had stood the test of time quite well since its construction in the early part of the century, and there were no signs it would not last for many years to come.

Dismounting from his horse, he looked for a place to secure him. The stables were only a short distance away, but he did not think stabling his horse was warranted when he was only going to be there for about an hour. Seeing a hitching post with an iron ring attached to it just to his left, he walked his horse over and tied him there, leaving him enough slack in his reins to nibble the grass. After giving Black a last pat, John reached into his saddlebag and pulled out the letters Bethany had asked him to give Cassandra. He brushed some dust off his coat, gave himself a little shake, and then walked up the steps to the front door. Grabbing the iron ring, he knocked three times and waited for a response, which came swiftly.

A butler in black and white livery opened the door. "Yes? May I help you, sir?"

John smiled. "Good day. Would Mrs. Stillwater be at home?"

"Yes, sir. She is. Whom shall I say is calling?"

"Lord John Dudley."

"Lord Dudley?"

"Yes."

The butler looked uncertain about admitting John into the house and looked him over from top to bottom before apparently deciding that he was not a threat to their household. Then he stepped back. "Please come in, sir. I will let Mrs. Stillwater know you are here."

John stepped through the door and into the foyer. "Thank you."

"You may have a seat while you are waiting." The butler pointed to the chairs off to his right.

"I have been riding for a while, so I prefer to stand, thank you."

"Very good. I won't be more than a minute or two." With that, the butler closed the front door and turned to walk down a hallway on his left.

"Please do not hurry," John said. "I am in no rush."

The butler nodded, even as he hurried away from John.

John scanned the foyer and the impressive oak staircase leading to the upper floors of the manor. The architecture reminded him of his own home, Dudley Manor, which was not particularly surprising as they had been built at around the same time. He loved his home, and this one delighted him as well.

A few minutes later, the butler returned. "Mrs. Stillwater will see you in the morning room, Lord Dudley. Will you please follow me?"

John nodded and followed the butler back down the hallway to a room. Once they reached its open door, the butler stood to the side of it and gestured for John to precede him. John walked in, and the butler followed him into the room before saying, "Lord Dudley, may I present to you Mrs. Cassandra Stillwater. Mrs. Stillwater, Lord John Dudley."

A woman got up from where she had been seated beside a large window. To John, she appeared to be past the first flush of youth, but her face was still free of any signs of aging. *In her early thirties perhaps?* As she walked towards him, he noted her trim figure, not slender but of good proportions. Sunlight flooded the room through the panes of glass and caught the strands of reddish highlights in her coffee-coloured hair quite pleasingly. Reaching his side, Cassandra offered him a small curtsey. "Lord Dudley. To what do I owe this honour?"

John walked over, took her proffered hand in his, lifted it, and pressed a small kiss to the back of her fingers. Then he released her hand and stepped back. "Mrs. Stillwater. The pleasure is all mine."

Cassandra smiled, and then waved him to a chair on the other side of the window. John walked over, flipped his coat tails out of the way, and after she had re-situated herself in the other chair, he sat down as well.

Once they were seated, Cassandra asked John if he would like tea or coffee, explaining that she did not keep any liquor in the house, so as not to tempt the older boys to try drinking when they were home on holiday.

"I am fine, Mrs. Stillwater," said John. "I had lunch with my aunt and uncle in the city before I left, and the road was not dusty, so I do not require anything."

"Very well, but if you change your mind, please let me know. That will be all for now then, Kingsley," she said to the butler, who was still hovering in the doorway.

"Good, ma'am," he said. "Please ring if you need anything."

"I will, thank you."

The butler turned and left the room, returning to his post in the foyer.

Cassandra turned back to John then. "Now, Lord Dudley, I repeat my question: What can I do for you?"

"Before I answer that question, I wish to further introduce myself. I am John Dudley, Viscount. But of what is more importance to you is that I am the nephew of the Duke and Duchess of Yardley."

"The Duke and Duchess of Yardley?"

"Yes. They asked me to stop by and inquire after your welfare, as I am on my way to my parents' country home, Dudley Manor."

"How kind of them to think of me, Lord Dudley. To answer your question, I am well. Please convey that message back to them when you next have contact."

"I am glad to hear that, ma'am. The news will gladden their hearts. They expressed concern that they had not seen you for several months. However, I also had another reason to stop by on my way home."

"Oh, and what is that?"

"To deliver a packet of letters to you from your sister-in-law, Bethany."

"When and where did you obtain such letters, sir?"

"She handed them to me before I left Australia." John smiled, waiting for her reaction to his words.

"You have seen Sam and Bethany? In Australia? When? Lord Dudley, you have been holding out on me. Please tell me all."

John laughed. "I wanted to see your reaction when I sprung that news on you. You did not disappoint me."

"Lord Dudley, I do not know you, but I suspect you are a bit of a jokester. Holding out such precious information from me? Why, I have a mind to send you on your way immediately after such a prank."

"I am sorry, ma'am. That is the last surprise I will spring on you today. I forget you do not know me and would not have seen such a trick coming. My cousin Sam could tell you of all the fun we had as boys, playing tricks on our siblings and the servants. I guess I have not yet grown out of my boyhood ways."

"You are forgiven if you now share everything about your trip, and about Sam and Bethany's life in Australia. You will stay until you have finished relating those tales to me."

"You are most gracious, ma'am. Where shall I begin?"

***

After an hour of telling Cassandra all she wanted to know, John nodded and took a breath. "And now, dear lady, it is time for me to depart. It has been a most enjoyable hour. I hope we may spend time together in the future. May I call on you again?"

"Of course. I, too, have enjoyed our visit. I know you are eager to see your parents, so I will not detain you any longer. Please come again. With my boys away at school, and only the servants here to keep me company, I get lonely at times. I would welcome a return visit."

John stood up. "I will do that. Please do not get up. I can see myself to the door. Enjoy your letters." He bowed his head, and then left the room.

Despite his assertions, Cassandra considered getting up and following him to the door. She had enjoyed his company and was reluctant to see him leave. But she restrained herself and listened as the viscount said his farewells to Kingsley, and then the front door being opened and closed. She wondered if she would ever see him again, or if he had only been polite in requesting another visit in the future. She hoped it would be the former and not the latter. Shaking her head at her fantasies, she reached over and took the thick packet into her lap. These letters would keep her entertained for the next several days. She opened one and began reading.

***

As Cassandra read, John rode on towards Dudley Manor. He, too, had enjoyed his hour with Cassandra. She had been thoughtful, as well as entertaining. Most of the young women he had courted in the past had only his title in mind when they'd agreed to see him. After observing them, he had realised there was nothing behind their fancy hairstyles and ball gowns. He wanted something more if he was to commit to a woman for life. He wanted a companion, as well as a lover, just as Sam had found in Bethany. He would be perfectly happy staying single for the rest of his life if he couldn't find a woman like Bethany. Of course, he had not shared that information with his parents. Being the eldest male in his family, his parents assumed that he would marry one day and settle down to raise another generation of Dudleys. However, as he was now in his mid-thirties, with no prospects in sight, the chances of that happening were starting to dim. Perhaps his younger brothers would have more luck and save the dynasty. He hoped so, as he was running out of time.

Reaching the Dudley Manor gates, John put his maudlin thoughts aside as he prepared to dismount and open the gates. But before he could do that, a man came out of a small hut on the other side of them. "Halt. Who goes there?"

John laughed as he recognized the voice of a man who simply refused to give up his post. Thomas, the gatekeeper, had long said that he would rather die in service than retire and be sent away. And sure enough, he was still here, just as he had been for as long as John could remember.

"Thomas, it's me. Master John."

Thomas peered through the gate's latticework. His face lit up when he could make out John's face. "Master John, is it really you? You are home?"

"Yes, Thomas. It is me. I am back from Australia."

"Praise God! He kept you alive!"

"He did indeed, and now I would like to enter the estate. Would you open the gates for me?"

"Certainly, sir. I am sorry. I was so surprised to see you," said the old man, as he struggled to unlock the chain binding the gates together. Finally, he got it unlocked, and the chain fell slack. Pulling one end off, Thomas pushed the gate outward towards John and his horse.

John backed up a few steps to allow the gate to swing open before riding Black inside. Leaving the reins to trail on the ground for a moment, he turned back, wanting to help Thomas secure the gate, even though he knew it would offend the elderly servant. But as he turned around while dismounting, he saw Thomas already closing the gates and pulling the chain through the latch before locking it again. Then he turned back and reached out to embrace John before stepping back to look at him.

"You look good, Master John. Australia must have been good for you."

"Thank you, Thomas. You are the first person not to tell me that I am too thin and want to stuff my face with food."

"Who has done that, sir? You do not look thin to me."

"The cooks at both our townhouse and the Yardley townhouse, and both within the past twenty-four hours."

"Perhaps it is only the cooks who see you this way, Master John. After all, that is their job, feeding their households well."

"I suppose so, Thomas. Perhaps I will get the same reaction from our cook here at the manor. We will see. Now tell me, old man, how are you?"

"Doing well, sir, thank you. A bit of stiffness in my joints slowing me up somewhat, but other than that I have no complaints."

"I am glad. It would not be the same without you here to open the gates every time I wish to enter or depart."

"I have no plans to leave my post, Master John. You are well aware of that."

"I am, and you will have the job for as long as you want it. I echo my father's thoughts on that issue."

"Thank you, sir. It is good to know that you are not planning to put me out to pasture."

"I would not dream of it." John laughed. "If we did that, you would be here every day, begging for your job back and harassing whoever took your place."

"I would, sir. That I would."

"So, it is better to keep things as they are. Now, tell me, are my parents at home?"

"They are. They will be overjoyed to see you."

"I can't wait to see them either, so I will leave you to your post and head up to the manor now. It has been good to see you."

"It is good to see you as well. May I be the first to welcome you home after your long journey?"

"You can. And thank you for your good wishes. We will speak again soon," he said, before remounting his horse and turning him towards the manor.

Thomas agreed before heading back into his little hut.

Reaching the front porch of the house, John dismounted and tied Black to a post. He knew the stable hands would recognise the horse and stable him. John grabbed his saddlebags and strode up to the door, knocking twice before their old butler, Headley, opened it.

"Hello, Headley," he said, smiling to see another familiar face. "Are the earl and countess at home?"

"They are. And who are... Master John, it that you?"

"It is me, Headley, home after a long time away."

"Welcome home, sir. Please come in." The butler stepped aside so that John could walk into the foyer. "We were saying the other day, the missus and I, *'Isn't it about time for Master John to be coming home?'* And here you are. It is so good to see you. Did you have a good trip?"

"Very good, and I look forward to telling you and Mrs. Headley all about it soon. But right now, I will greet my parents. Do you know where they might be?"

"I believe they are in the back parlour having tea. Shall I announce you?"

"No, I want to surprise them, as I did you, Headley. I will announce myself."

"Good, sir. May I give the news of your arrival to my wife and the other staff while you do that?"

"You may."

"And I will make up another tray and have a maid bring it down, so you can join your parents for tea."

"That would be good. My throat is dry from my ride here. But if you have any coffee, I would like that instead of tea. My tastes changed while I was in Australia; I now prefer coffee to tea."

"I will see what we have available, Master John. Coffee instead of tea. My, you have changed, and not only in appearance."

"Now, don't start in on my appearance, Headley. Two cooks in London have already chastised me for what they see as my deficient weight. And I expect your wife will tell me that as well. I look forward to her attempting to fatten me up while I am home."

"I expect she will, sir." The butler chuckled. "But I will say nothing to her about your appearance. I will let her find out on her own."

"Thank you. Now, I am off to the parlour, and you head to the kitchen. I will see you later, my man."

Headley nodded, and then the two men went their separate ways, one to spread the good news in the kitchen and the other to surprise his parents with his unexpected homecoming.

Chapter 3

John heard his parents' voices as he neared the back parlour. Standing outside the door, he determined how best to surprise them. No plan came to mind, so he decided just to walk in.

"Afternoon," he said, strolling casually into the room. "And how might the two of you be faring today?"

The earl and countess looked up in shock before rising to their feet and rushing over to hug him. "John, you are home!" cried the countess. "When did you arrive?"

"Only a few minutes ago, Mother. You are looking well, as are you, Father."

"It good to see you, son," said the earl. "Why did you not let us know you were coming?"

"Because I wanted to surprise you."

"You did more than that, my boy. You almost gave us a heart attack, didn't he, Mother?"

"He did. In your mid-thirties, John, and still up to your boyish tricks. When will you grow up?"

"I don't know if I ever will, Mother." John laughed, stepping back from her arms. "Life is more enjoyable this way."

His parents laughed with him before ushering him to a third chair near where they had been sitting. Then they started peppering him with questions about his trip, as well as about Sam and Bethany and their children. John answered them as best he could between their rapidly fired questions. Finally, he put up a hand. "That is all I can tell you for right now: My throat is parched, and I see that the tea has arrived. May we continue this conversation at dinnertime?"

"Of course, son," said his father. "I presume you are home to stay, so we have all the time in the world to catch up with your news. If you would like to freshen up a bit after your ride, we will wait on our tea for a few moments. I expect your room is now ready for you."

"If not, John, please let me know, and I will speak to Mrs. Higgins," said his mother.

"I am sure it will be satisfactory, Mother. I have been living the life of a traveller for the past several months, and before that I had a colonial lifestyle with Sam and Bethany, so I don't need much today. A basin of water and a towel. Nothing more."

"I expect those will be the first things Mrs. Higgins will place in your room, John. It sounds as those you have lived quite a simple life since we last saw you."

"Indeed, I have, Father. Sam and Bethany's home is nothing like what you would find them living in here. They have few servants, and they work right alongside them to accomplish the tasks of the day, just as I did."

"Manual labour?"

"Yes. There were no distinctions based on class on their sheep station."

"Did you enjoy that life?"

"Very much. And I slept better than I ever had before in my lifetime."

"You don't plan to go back, do you, John?" asked his mother, a worried frown on her face.

"Not at present, Mother, so you can erase those worry lines from your brow. But it may be a possibility in the future. Now, if you will excuse me, I will head to my room. I will see you again in a few moments." John then stood and exited the room to head upstairs.

***

Back in the parlour, his mother expressed her concerns about his words.

"James, you do not think John is serious about moving to Australia, do you? It was hard enough knowing he was there for a visit, but if he moved there permanently..."

"Now, Martha, don't get upset over a few words. John is a dutiful son, and he knows his responsibilities lie here. The trip has exposed him to a different culture, and from the sounds of it, he thoroughly enjoyed his experience. But once he has been home for a while, he will readjust to British society and find his place again."

"Perhaps you are right. We need to give him time and space. That's all he needs ... time and space."

"Exactly, my dear. He will come around. You will see."

"I hope so, but I don't know, James. I don't know..."

***

If John's parents had been privy to his thoughts, they might have had reason to worry. He was thinking seriously about going back to live in Australia. In fact, while he had visited Sam and Bethany, they had discussed having him join them as a partner so they could expand their sheep station. The present plan was that he would stay in England until they arrived for their next visit and move to Australia with them when they returned there. The only thing John needed to do in the meantime was find a wife.

***

While John contemplated that issue, Cassandra was rereading her letters from Bethany. Her life with Sam in Australia sounded wonderful. A pang of envy shot through Cassandra's heart. Why could God have not blessed her with a husband like Sam? Why had He tied her to Howard Stillwater for so many years? But of course, if her father had not married her to Howard as payment for his gambling debts, then she probably would never have met Bethany. Cassandra had come from a working-class family, whereas Bethany had been raised in a noble household.

Bethany's stepbrother, Howard, however, had only achieved his noble status because his mother, who had been working for the Stillwaters as Bethany's nanny, had married Bethany's father after her mother died when she was only a toddler. At the time of Howard and Cassandra's marriage, Bethany had still been a young girl, but an immediate bond had grown between them, which had only strengthened over the years. Having Bethany in her life, along with her four sons, were the only blessings to come from that wretched union with Howard.

Cassandra shook her head to rid herself of such negative thoughts. She loved Bethany as a sister and was truly glad that she had managed to find love after her legal trials were over. Cassandra only wished... No. There was no point in wishing for what could not be. Her life was here on Stillwater Estate, and here is where she would stay, unless, of course, the estate went under, and they forced her to leave. Somehow, she needed to keep it going, even if that meant selling her mother's jewellery to sustain it. Thankfully, she still was in full possession of it, as it had not been included in the dowry that she had brought with her to her marriage. Otherwise, it would likely have been long gone by now, just like her entire dowry, which had been spent by her deceased husband.

Yes, she decided. *The only way to save the estate is to sell my jewellery.*

That would enable them to buy feed for the animals and sustain them for another year. Hopefully, the next year would bring with it much-needed rains, at last, as well as good prices for the harvest. But that was next year. This year, selling her jewellery was the only way to make money. And to do that, she knew that she would have to head into London and find a buyer.

But where could she go to get the best price for her gems? She knew she could sell them at a pawnshop, like Howard had done when he needed a bit of extra cash for his gambling habits. He had thought she did not know what he was doing, but of course, she had. She had never said anything about it to him though, as he'd always bought them back a bit later. However, she would not go down that route; she needed a more reliable buyer, and one who would give her a fair price. She needed to sell to a reputable jeweller. But where could she find one? She had never bought any jewellery in London. Then a thought occurred to her.

Perhaps she could ask the duchess of Yardley! Cassandra was sure she would know of someone dealing in fine jewellery. But what reason could she come up with for selling her precious jewels? If she told the truth—that it was to sustain the estate for another year—the Yardleys would only step in and give her money to cover her expenses. That was who they were. She also knew that Bethany and Sam had charged them to watch over her and the boys. They were already paying for the boys' education at their fine schools and planned to continue doing so should they wish to go to university later on. No, she could not ask for more money from them, nor let them know that she was failing to manage the estate. She needed to do this on her own, and if that meant visiting the jewellery shops in downtown London by herself, then that is what she would do. She could not involve the Yardleys in her plan.

Having come to this conclusion, Cassandra decided that there was no time to waste. Tomorrow morning, she would head into the city and complete her transactions by early afternoon, so that she could be home by dinnertime. Now, she needed to decide which pieces of jewellery to sell. She knew the sapphire necklace would bring a good price. It was the one she had loaned to Bethany on that ill-fated evening so many years ago.

At the time of Bethany's trial, they had valued the necklace at €500 sterling. But since the trial and Bethany's conviction, Cassandra had never worn it. It was too painful a reminder of what she had done to Bethany. Even though Bethany had forgiven her, Cassandra could not bear the sight of it. Yes, that would be one piece she would sell tomorrow. She would be glad to be rid of it. Wondering what other pieces to sell along with it, Cassandra headed upstairs to her bedroom to review her collection.

***

The next day, after breakfast, she informed Kingsley that she was going into the city for the day but would be back by dinnertime. Although surprised, as Cassandra seldom left the estate, Kingsley did not question her motivation for the trip. It was not his place. So instead, he simply had a carriage brought from the stables, and once Cassandra was inside, he told her to have a good day. Then she was gone. Only then did Kingsley head back into the house to discuss the mistress's strange behaviour with his wife and to let her know Cassandra would not be home for lunch.

***

Cassandra sat back in the carriage and enjoyed watching the passing scenery. She had asked the driver to set a good pace as she had business she needed to accomplish in the city. So, he kept the horses at a canter so that they would not tire before they reached the city limits. Her purpose was to be in and out of the city as quickly as possible. She disliked having to return to a place where she'd had so many terrible memories, not only of her life with Howard but also of her unhappy childhood. Her father had gambled away just about every pence of his meagre income as a lamplighter. Charlotte had never known whether there would be food on the table when she came down for breakfast.

She had often asked her mother why she did not sell her jewels to make a better life for them, but her mother had told her that they were her guarantee that she would never starve. She might go hungry some days, but she would never starve. Having been disowned by her own wealthy father after marrying for what she'd thought at the time was love, though she had soon learned otherwise, Charlotte's mother had kept the jewels as a reminder of her former life, to which she could never return. When she died, she'd willed those jewels to Charlotte, telling her to remember her story and never marry for love, but only money.

Unfortunately, Charlotte never had the chance to fulfil her mother's wishes for her. Howard and her father had seen to that. But since Howard had died, she had experienced the first freedom she had ever known, and if selling her jewellery would allow her to retain that freedom, it was a small price to pay.

***

Soon, they reached the city limits, and the driver slowed the horses to a walk. Cassandra had given him a general destination—the shopping district of London—and so that was where he was headed now. When they arrived in the fashion district, he stopped the horses, climbed down, and inquired of Cassandra where she would like to be set down. Looking around, she could see the signs of several jewellers, so she told the driver that this would be a good place for him to wait. She would walk from here. She could not give him a time when she would be back, only that she hoped it would not be more than an hour or two. The driver agreed to wait at that spot while she shopped. So, Cassandra got out of the carriage and headed down the street, leaving the driver to scratch his head at her behaviour. It was not his place to question her, though, so he found a place to tether the horses in a nearby park and began awaiting her return.

***

Cassandra did not know where to start on her search as there were a series of signs for different jewellers up and down the street. She decided to visit the closest one and have its jeweller appraise her pieces. Then she would proceed to the next shop and do the same. Once she had been in all the stores, she would go back to the jeweller who had offered her the highest price for her pieces. That was only fair, was it not? So, she walked to the first shop, took a deep breath, and opened the door. Then she walked to the back counter and waited for someone to serve her. It was not long before a young clerk appeared behind it. "Yes, ma'am. Can I help you?"

He would not be the one to appraise her pieces, but she nodded in any case. "I hope so, young man. But I need to speak with your jeweller. Is he available?"

"He is, ma'am. Do you have an appointment?"

"No, I was not aware I needed one. Will he see me without an appointment?"

"I will check and see. One moment, please." The clerk then disappeared through a door next to the counter.

Is this going to be a wasted trip? I did not know I would need an appointment. Hopefully, that won't be the case.

Then the clerk returned, accompanied by a slightly bent older man with white hair. The clerk said, "Mr. White will see you now, Mrs...?

Not wanting to disclose her name but deciding it was worth the risk, she said, "Stillwater. Mrs. Cassandra Stillwater."

The clerk retreated, and the older man moved forward to greet her. "It's a pleasure to meet you, Mrs. Stillwater. Your name is familiar. Have we done business before?"

"No, sir. This is my first time in your shop," said Cassandra, realising at that moment that Howard might have been a former patron of this shop.

"Never mind. What can I do for you today?"

"I, uh, have a couple of pieces of jewellery I am hoping to sell, and I was hoping you would appraise them for me."

"Jewellery you wish to sell?"

"Yes."

"We do not operate like a pawn shop, Mrs. Stillwater. Once you sell your jewellery to me, I may sell it as is or make something new with the stones. Are you all right with that?"

"Yes."

"Very well. May I see the pieces, please?"

Cassandra reached into her reticule and pulled out a little velvet bag. Opening the top, she reached in and retrieved the sapphire necklace and an emerald bracelet, which she placed on the glass counter.

"These look to be fine pieces, ma'am. Are you sure you want to part with them?"

"Yes, I have no use for them anymore. Can you give an estimate of how much they are worth?"

"I need to take them to the back and look at them more closely with my eyepiece. Will you allow me to do that?"

Cassandra had hoped the pieces would not leave her sight until she had received payment for them. But she had no cause to think the jeweller would abscond with her necklace and bracelet, so she nodded. "Yes, that would be fine."

"Good. I will only be a few moments. Would you like to take a seat?" he asked, pointing to a pair of chairs near the front of the shop.

Not wanting anyone walking by to recognise her, Cassandra declined his offer. "No, I am fine standing here, sir."

He nodded and said he would not be long, then disappeared into the back room. Cassandra shifted her weight from one foot to the other as she waited for him to return. She was careful to keep her back to the front window, so that no one passing by could see her face.

A few minutes later, the jeweller returned. Setting the pieces back on the counter, he said, "These pieces are of fine quality, ma'am. The sapphire, especially, is beautiful, with a lot of clarity in the stone. The emeralds in the bracelet are not as fine but still quality."

"I am glad to hear that, sir. How much would you give me for both items?"

"As I have to make a profit on what I sell, ma'am, I could give you £350."

"For both pieces together? A few years ago, the necklace alone was worth £500. Has its value decreased so much?"

"Gems increase and decrease in value over time, Mrs. Stillwater. Unfortunately, the market price for sapphires has gone down in the past few years. And, as I say, I need to make a profit to stay in business."

"I understand, sir. Thank you for your time," she said, gathering up the jewellery and putting it back in its velvet bag.

"You do not wish me to purchase them from you today, ma'am?"

"Not at this moment. I see there are several shops in this area. I will have the pieces valued by each jeweller before I decide."

"You will find that we all will give you similar estimations, ma'am, but you are welcome to talk to my fellow jewellers. I will still purchase them from you if they disappoint you in their valuations of the stones. Good day, Mrs. Stillwater," he said, and then returned to his back room.

Cassandra nodded to the young clerk who was standing by one of the other counters, and then headed out of the shop. Two doors down, there was a sign for another jeweller, so she quickly strode there and entered the shop.

After visiting all the jewellery stores in the area, Cassandra had to conclude that Mr. White, the first jeweller, had been right. Her pieces were not as valuable as she had hoped they would be. The other jewellers had offered her similar prices to Mr. White's, with no one of them standing much higher than the rest. So, she decided to go back to White's Jewellery and sell him the necklace and bracelet. It had been a much harder afternoon than she had expected. However, it was almost over. All she had left to do was sell the jewellery to Mr. White, climb back into her carriage, and head back home, knowing that she would now have money to pay for the cattle feed. Straightening her shoulders, she began to walk back to the first shop when she heard her name being called.

"Cassandra? Cassandra Stillwater? Is that you?"

The voice was familiar, and though she dreaded the meeting, she knew she had no choice but to turn and greet its owner. "Your Grace! How lovely to see you. Are you shopping here today?"

Chapter 4

The Duchess of Yardley was right there, not ten yards behind her and accompanied by a young woman.

"Cassandra, my dear!" said the duchess, hurrying to greet her.

"Your Grace. What a coincidence to see you in the middle of London."

"Not truly, my dear," said the duchess. "Beatrice and I are frequently down here shopping. Do you remember Beatrice from the time of Joann's arsenic poisoning?"

"I do," said Charlotte. "You saved Joann's life by giving her that herbal antidote. How could I forget such a heroine?"

"I only did what I could, ma'am. God worked the miracle to save her life."

"Even so, he used your understanding of plants to accomplish it. None of the rest of us would have known what to do. You were a lesson to us all. And now you are here as the Duchess's protégée. Are you enjoying your life in London?"

"I am, thank you," Beatrice said. "The Duke and Duchess have been wonderful to me."

"The feeling is mutual, my dear," said the duchess. "And are you well, Cassandra?"

"I am, Your Grace."

"Now that we have established that we are all healthy," the duchess said, "may I ask what you are doing in London? And why did you not let us know that you were coming?"

"I only planned to spend the day in the city. I had business to attend to this afternoon. Now that I have completed it, I am heading home again."

"But not without a cup of tea, surely. There is a delightful little tea shop only a block from here. Beatrice and I were on our way there when I spotted you. You must join us for tea before you leave. I insist."

Cassandra accepted this invitation as she didn't know how to graciously decline. So, the three women headed over to the café, where the waiter seated them immediately at an outdoor table.

Cassandra looked around. "This is lovely, Your Grace. Have you been here often?"

"Yes. I come here whenever I am in this part of the city. We are shopping for ribbons for Beatrice's new dresses. That is why we are here today. May I ask what business brings you into the city today? I understood that you rarely come in."

"That is true, Your Grace. I love living in the country. The air is so much cleaner than in London, and I don't have to worry about thugs knocking at my door, looking for money. Although, of course, when Bethany paid off Howard's debts, that issue went away. Still, sometimes, like today, I have to come in for personal reasons. Today's business was not something I could delegate to someone else."

"I'm sorry to hear that. Yes, the country air is most refreshing. We will be leaving the city soon and travelling to our estate. We hope to stop by and visit you on the way. It has been too long since we last saw you. But speaking of visitors, did our nephew, John Dudley, visit you recently?"

"He did. We had a pleasant hour together. But he was eager to get home and see his parents, so he did not stay long."

"I'm glad you had the chance to meet him. He is a wonderful gentleman. He and my son, Sam, were close when they were growing up. They used to get into all kinds of mischief as boys." She smiled.

"Yes, he told me that, Your Grace. He also told me a few things about his trip to Australia. It sounded like he enjoyed his visit with his cousins."

"Now, enough of that 'Your Grace' business, Cassandra," the duchess said. "We are not in grand company here. We are only three women enjoying a cup of tea. So, you may call me Margaret or ma'am, but not Your Grace. I forbid it." The duchess laughed, so that Cassandra knew how to take her words.

"Well, uh, ma'am," said Cassandra. "I will do as you ask."

"It makes life easier for all of us, doesn't it, Beatrice?" asked the duchess, turning to the young woman.

"Yes, ma'am. Life is much better when I obey you." She smiled.

"You see, Cassandra, Beatrice has learned her lessons well while staying with us in London. And I hope, when we see you next, that you will remember this lesson as well."

"I will try, Your, uh, ma'am."

"That is all I ask of you. Nothing more. Oh good! I see our tea is arriving. I wonder what treats they are serving us today. Shall I pour?"

Beatrice and Cassandra agreed to have the duchess pour the tea, and then they settled in to talk about Beatrice's new dresses, and the perfect accessories for them.

***

An hour later, they concluded their visit. The duchess tried to persuade Cassandra to come home with them, but Cassandra was firm in her refusal. If she did not part with the duchess, she could not return to White's Jewellers. And she still needed to do that. Fortunately, the duchess's carriage had come round to the café to pick her and Beatrice up. So, Cassandra said her farewells to them, and after they had left, she hurried back to the jewellery store.

When she got there, she pulled on the latch, but it refused to move. She tried again without success. Then she saw the sign. The store was closed now until the following day. She had missed her opportunity to sell the jewels and would have to go home without the money. She should have anticipated having to spend a night in the city, but having failed to properly think her trip through, she now had nothing with her in which she could spend the night. And the cost of accommodations would also be out of her budget. Perhaps if she… No, she would not beg a night's stay at the ducal townhouse. She started lamenting the lateness of the hour but quickly realized the futility of continuing that train of though. It was as late as it was and nothing that she could do would change that. She had failed again and would have to make this same trip again tomorrow. It had been a wasted day.

***

With nothing left to do, she headed back to where she had left her carriage and driver. She increased her pace, and her driver soon handed her back into the carriage. Before taking his seat, he asked if she needed to go anywhere else in the city. She told him she had finished her business and was ready to go home. He nodded his head, closed the door, and after releasing the reins of the horses from their post, he jumped back up onto his seat and started them slowly out of the city.

Inside the carriage, Cassandra was in despair. What was she to do now? The unexpected appearance of the duchess had ruined her well-laid plans. And now, she and the duke were soon going to come by for a visit. Then they would see Cassandra's mismanagement of the estate and most likely dismiss her from her position. *Perhaps that would be for the best. I've never succeeded at anything...*

The atmosphere in the other carriage was much more upbeat. The duchess and Beatrice had found the exact shade of ribbons they'd needed for her new dresses. And they had also had a delightful tea with Cassandra, although the duchess was still perplexed about Cassandra's reason for being in town. From what she knew, Mr. Brown—Bethany's solicitor—handled all financial dealings for the estate. So, Cassandra's business could not have been about that. Then she remembered Cassandra saying that it was personal business. Surely, she was not being threatened by that London loan shark again. He had received everything owed to him six years earlier, so he should not still be in contact with Cassandra. But what else could it be? She needed to speak with Douglas and let him know her concerns. Then he could deal with Cassandra's needs when they stopped at the Stillwater Estate on their way to Yardley Estate. Yes, that was a perfect plan. Douglas would deal with the business whilst she confined herself to looking after Cassandra's other needs, in particular, finding her a new husband.

***

When Cassandra arrived home, she was tired and discouraged. It was also two hours later than she had planned. She was hungry, but all she wanted to do was take a warm bath, curl up in her bed, and cry. However, she knew it would help if she ate something before retiring, so she headed to the kitchen to see what she could find. But, when she got there, she found the Kingsleys sitting at the table and having their evening cup of tea. On seeing Cassandra, Mrs. Kingsley immediately got up to fix a plate of food for her. So, she sat down at the table with them.

"Thank you, Mrs. Kingsley. I will eat something, and then head upstairs. May I have a bath prepared for me? I know it is late but having something to eat, plus a bath, will help me sleep better tonight. I am exhausted, but I know that when my head hits the pillow, all the anxious thoughts from today will crowd into my mind and keep me from sleeping."

"Certainly, you can have a bath," said the housekeeper/cook. "I will arrange it for you now, so that when you go up, it will be ready. Do you need anything else?"

"No, that should be everything."

"Well, then I will get your bath started for you right away."

"Thank you. I am sorry to be such a bother."

"You are not a bother, ma'am. In fact, you so seldom require anything from us that I often find myself looking for things to do to help. Don't you agree, Mr. Kingsley?"

"Yes, I do. We are here to serve you, Mrs. Stillwater, and so don't be apologising for asking for something like an evening bath. But if I may ask, what is it that has brought you to such a state of anxiety?"

"Oh, my plans for today went awry, and now I don't know what to do to solve my problems."

"Is there anything we can do to help you, ma'am?"

"No, it is my problem. I caused it, and I have to fix it. But thank you for offering to help. I appreciate that."

"If it is the estate, you know the Yardley family are more than willing to assist you. You only have to ask."

"I know that, Kingsley, and the duchess reminded me of it today while we had tea together."

"You saw the duchess today?"

"Yes, and that is why I am so late coming home. Having tea with her cost me a precious hour and ruined my plans for the day. She was not aware of my plans, of course, and so did not realise that she destroyed them by inviting me for tea. I could have refused, of course, but how do you say no to a duchess? Especially one as kind as her?"

"I am sure you will find another way to accomplish what you set out to do today, ma'am. In the meantime, while you are having your bath, it is good for you to meditate on the Bible verses that say, *'Be anxious for nothing, but in everything, with thanksgiving, let your requests be made known to God. And the peace of God which passeth all understanding shall guard your hearts and minds in Christ Jesus.'*[2] If you do, I am sure God will help you sort out what you need to do next and give you the peace to sleep well tonight."

"Thank you for those words of encouragement. I will do as you say. Now, I shall head upstairs. Good night to both of you. I will see you in the morning."

The couple responded with smiles before Cassandra headed up the back stairs to her room. Once there, she found a tub full of steaming water and Molly, her maid, waiting for her. Once she was in the tub, her maid laid out towels and her nightgown before Cassandra sent her off to bed. Then she closed her eyes and laid her head against the back of the tub, drowning out her anxious thoughts by meditating on the verses Kingsley had spoken to her. But she continually returned to the same thoughts: The estate was floundering, and it was all her fault. No verses from the Bible could fix that problem.

She needed to find a solution. No longer resting comfortably in the tub, she got out, dried herself off, and put on her nightgown. Then she plopped herself down on the soft mattress and tried unsuccessfully to will herself to sleep. It was going to be a long night.

***

The next morning, Cassandra arose early from her bed. Her predictions of a restless night with little sleep had come true. She wondered if she had slept for even an hour, but no more than that, she was sure. And she still had no solution to her problem. Perhaps she should speak with the estate steward this morning and ask for his advice. If he had none to offer, and she could not sell her jewels, they would be in a disastrous state of affairs in the spring.

Coming down for breakfast, she tried to appear bright, but judging from the expression on Kingsley's face when he saw her, she knew she had failed. In order to avoid his questions, she asked him to find the farm steward, Jack Wiley, and have him come to the manor for a meeting at ten o'clock that morning. Kingsley agreed and left the breakfast room after making sure that she had everything she needed for her meal. Cassandra heaved a sigh of relief when he left. He and his wife were wonderful to her, but sometimes, their concern was a bit of a burden—something she had neither the time nor energy to deal with at present. She ate a little from everything on her plate, but finally left it half full, not able to stomach anything more. Getting up from the table, Cassandra went back upstairs to freshen up for the day before heading to the morning parlour. There, she sat down and just gazed out the window without seeing anything. She hoped Mr. Wiley would have new ideas for her, as she still had come up with an alternate plan to pay for cattle feed this winter.

At precisely ten o'clock, Kingsley ushered the farm steward into the room. Seeing him standing there, hat in hand, Cassandra said, "Good morning, Mr. Wiley. Please, won't you come in and have a seat? Would you like something to drink?"

Walking over, he sat down on one of the small, embroidered chairs, dwarfing it with his size. Perched gingerly on the seat, he shook his head. "No thank you, ma'am. I don't require anything."

Cassandra smiled, hoping to put him more at ease. "Very well. Kingsley, that will be all for now. Thank you."

Kingsley nodded and left the room.

Cassandra then said to the steward, "Mr. Wiley, I was wondering if you had come up with any other ideas to solve our problem of feed for this winter. I have been trying but have not found a suitable one yet."

"No, ma'am, I have not. Are we really in dire straits?"

"Yes, unfortunately, we are. Unless we find another solution, we will have to sell the cattle. We cannot afford to feed them this winter."

"I did not realise things were so bad, ma'am. Uh, do you think we could get a loan from the bank to carry us over?"

"I could look into that, but then I shall have to involve Mr. Brown, my London solicitor. He handles those sorts of details for the estate. That was something I was avoiding though, knowing that he is a close friend of Lady Yardley."

"I understand, Mrs. Stillwater, but I don't see any alternatives, unless..."

"Unless what, Mr. Wiley?"

"Unless you contacted the Duke of Yardley and asked for his help. I am sure he would be more than willing to help you out, considering his daughter-in-law owns the estate."

"I only want to do that as a last resort."

"Yes, but they must know the impact the drought is having on the farming community. After all, they also have an estate in the area, along with tenant farmers."

"You are right, sir, but I will only contact them as a last resort. First, I will talk to Mr. Brown about the situation and see if he can secure a bank loan for us. Thank you for your suggestion."

"I am sorry I cannot come up with anything else, ma'am."

"Do not worry about it. We will survive this winter. Thank you for your time," she said, getting up to shake his hand, even as he stood up as well.

"Thank you for involving me, ma'am. Now, if there is nothing else, I will get back to doing what I do best: looking after the farm."

Cassandra nodded, and after he had tipped his mangled hat to her, the steward left the room. Cassandra sat back down in her chair and stared out the window again. There was only one practical solution: the jewellery would have to be sold. But first, she would consult with Mr. Brown and lay out her failure before him. Getting up from her chair, she went over to her writing desk, pulled out a piece of parchment, and started to write. *"Dear Mr. Brown..."*

***

After she had finished writing to him, she addressed an envelope, put the letter inside, and sealed it. Then she took it to the foyer and said to Kingsley, "Would you see this letter gets posted as soon as possible?"

"I will, ma'am," he said. "It will go out on the next post."

"Thank you. I will be in the morning parlour until lunchtime if anyone needs me."

"Good, ma'am. I will let Mrs. Kingsley know that. How about a cup of tea now?"

"Thank you. That would be lovely," she said, before heading back down the hall to the parlour.

Kingsley watched her walk away, noting that her head was hanging low as she trudged forward. He wondered what was in the letter to Mr. Brown. But, of course, he could not ask her. Only if she chose to share what she had written would he find out its contents. Still, he figured that it must be important for her to want it sent post haste. Kingsley prayed it was not bad news. Shaking his head, he turned and headed for the kitchen. As well as making tea for the mistress, he and Mrs. Kingsley needed to pray for her.

Soon, Cassandra had her tea and was sipping it slowly. She hoped Mr. Brown would be discrete and not contact the duke regarding her request. But it was out of her hands now. She could only wait for the solicitor's reply.

Chapter 5

While Cassandra was contemplating her future, or lack of one, John Dudley was also looking ahead. However, his future appeared brighter than Cassandra's. The decision he had to make, though, was whether he should stay or go. If he stayed in Britain, he knew what lay ahead for him. His father would groom him to become the next Earl of Dudley. Having watched his father throughout his life, John knew what that entailed. The position wasn't flawed; it simply lacked stimulation. Each new day in Australia, working with Sam and his men had excited John. Every day had been different. There had been challenges, but he had loved talking with Sam and Bethany about how to overcome them.

John could see that they were a real team, working together to make a life for themselves and their children. Gender and class didn't matter to them. They laboured for the same goals, right along with their staff. That was what John wanted in his life, not one where he would be the master of the household, only interacting with his wife and staff when he needed to do so. No. He wanted a real partnership with his wife throughout their life together, and he wondered if there was a woman in Britain who wanted the same. Hopefully, there was ... and all he had to do was find her.

***

About an hour down the road, Cassandra was having similar thoughts. She was not contemplating moving to Australia, but she was pondering how nice it would be to have a husband to share the load with her. Mr. Wiley was a competent steward, but it was not his place to come up with solutions to their problems. And she could not share her personal problems with him. She, too, reflected on the partnership she had seen between Bethany and Sam when they were last in England. Everything they did was because they were of one accord. They consulted each other on almost every issue. Bethany was never afraid to challenge Sam when she held a different viewpoint, and vice versa.

If only her marriage to Howard had been like the Yardleys'. But it had been completely different. Howard had looked after everything except the household expenditures, and he had even challenged her on those from time to time. He had been the man about town while she had stayed home and looked after the children. She often wondered if their marriage would have been better if they had shared more of their lives together. But perhaps not. Howard had only married her for her money, not for her looks, her personality, or her brain. So, when the money had run out, so had Howard. But by then, Cassandra had grown beyond caring about her marriage, her sole focus being her sons.

Soon, they would be full grown and living on their own, setting up their own households. Cassandra wondered where she would live when they did. Would she still be living at the estate or in a modest flat in London? If she did not come with a resolution to the estate's problem, she expected it would be the latter. But that was a problem for another day. She already had enough worries for today. Staring out the window, she put on her thinking cap, unaware that help was already on its way.

***

The duke and duchess decided there was nothing further holding them back from heading out to their country estate. They had already purchased all the needed items for Beatrice on yesterday's shopping trip. In their own carriage, they would only take the smaller pieces of luggage, containing clothing they could put on without help, and their staff would follow with the larger trunks.

After breakfast, the duke asked Parker to alert the staff to their plans. Then the duchess and Beatrice headed upstairs to choose appropriate apparel. Within an hour, they were ready to head out. The carriage was brought around from the stables. A driver and footman stowed their bags in the carriage's boot, and then helped the duchess and Beatrice inside. Once the duke had finished giving final instructions to the London staff, he got into the carriage, and soon they were off to the country.

Beatrice was eager to see where the duke and duchess spent their summers. She had been thrilled when the duchess had taken her on as her protégée, buying her new clothes and taking her to her first soirees and balls. But she had missed the country. She let out a contented sigh, relieved to have a break from the dull parties. She longed to breathe clean air again and see entire fields of flowers, rather than the miniscule gardens of the London townhouses. It would be nice to walk around without a maid as an escort, or just sit by a lake to contemplate life and where it was leading her. Even before she'd met the duchess, she had never had the time, nor the energy, for such things. And now her dreams were being fulfilled. She could not wait for the next chapter to begin. Perhaps, this summer, she might even find her Prince Charming, who would sweep her up into his arms and carry her off to their happily ever after.

Beatrice's fantasies brought a smile to her face as she looked towards the future and caught the attention of the duchess, sitting across from her.

"You look happy, my dear."

"Yes, ma'am. I am."

"I'm glad. Do you wish to share your thoughts or keep them to yourself?"

"They are only silly girlish fantasies, ma'am. Nothing worthy of your attention."

"I, too, was once a silly girl, Beatrice," the duchess said, smiling back at her, "though it was many, many years ago. And I had fantasies and dreams of my own."

"Yes, but I am sure you could make your dreams come true, ma'am. I don't know if I can do that."

"Shall we tell her of our past, Douglas, and spoil her vision of us?" asked the duchess, patting her husband's hand.

"It is no secret, my dear," he said. "But if Beatrice wants to hear our story, a long ride in the country seems an appropriate time to tell it."

"Do you want to know how we came to be the Duke and Duchess of Yardley, Beatrice?" asked the duchess.

"I would love to hear it, ma'am. I have often wondered how the two of you met. Was yours an arranged marriage?"

The duke and duchess looked lovingly at each other and laughed lightly.

"Far from it, my dear," the duchess said. "In fact, when I first met my husband's mother, she hated me. Right, Douglas?"

"Absolutely, Margaret. You were the complete opposite of the sort of woman my mother wanted me to marry, and she was not afraid to tell me so."

"She didn't like you, ma'am?" said Beatrice with widened eyes. "I cannot believe that. Why, you are the kindest, most loving woman I have ever met. Why would she not want you to marry her son?"

"Because of whom I was, dear. I was not the woman you see today. I was a simple country girl, raised on a two-acre farm. My father was a tenant of the duchy."

"What?"

"It's true," said the duke. "She was a poor farmer's daughter, living on our land, but the day I first met her, I knew I was going to marry her one day."

"You did not, Douglas."

"Yes, I did. I fell head over heels in love with you the first time I saw you."

The duchess laughed. "Well, it is true that you fell head over heels, but not because of love. It was because of our old boar..."

Entranced, Beatrice sat and listened as the pair across from her told their story of love and marriage, against all odds. And it was a wonderful story...

Perhaps my dreams can come true, even though I'm just girl from a village manor.

***

The duke and duchess's tale of how they met and fell in love took most of an hour to tell. When they finished, the duke looked back out at the scenery. "I believe we are getting close to Stillwater Estate, my dear. Shall we stop and see how Cassandra is getting along?"

"Yes, Douglas, and if you can, will you please try to determine why she was in London yesterday? She was being quite mysterious. She was hiding something from me. I hope she is not in any trouble."

"I will see what I can find out, Margaret. Perhaps Kingsley is aware of the problem. He keeps apprised of everything that is going on at the estate."

"Yes, perhaps while we are having tea with Cassandra, you can make some excuse to slip out and talk to him. I don't think he would say anything in front of Cassandra."

He nodded. "I doubt that he would. He is loyal to those who live at Stillwater. But perhaps, he is just as concerned about Cassandra as we are."

"I hope you can find out. I really am quite worried about her."

"If you are worried, then I am too, dear. You never worry without a reason." Seeing the gates of Stillwater up ahead, the duke knocked on the roof of the carriage.

The carriage stopped, and the footman climbed down and came to the door. "Yes, Your Grace?"

"Tom, we would like to stop at Stillwater Estate for an hour. Would you have the driver take us in?"

The footman nodded, but seeing where the duke was pointing, instead of regaining his seat, he ran up ahead, while the driver walked the horses to the gate. By the time they reached the gates, the footman had them open, and they moved on through them towards the distant manor. The driver stopped once the footman had the gates closed again, allowing him to jump up onto his seat, and then flicked the reins to get the horses going again.

They soon reached the portico of the manor, and the driver halted the horses once again. The footman descended once more, took the reins from the driver, and tied them to a nearby post. Then he moved back to the carriage, opened the door, and put down the footstool before helping the ladies out and onto the porch.

The duke descended on his own, but before going to the estate's front door, he turned to look at the driver and footman. "I expect we shall be here for about an hour. I know you will be welcome to have refreshments with the staff in the kitchen. The door is around the back. I will let you know when we are ready to resume our journey."

"Very good, sir," said the driver, even as the footman nodded his agreement with the plan. "We will see you in about an hour."

The duke nodded, and then extending his arms to the ladies, they walked together up to the door. Instead of using the iron knocker, though, the duke extended his cane and knocked on the door with its brass head. The door opened within seconds of his knock, and Kingsley peered out to see who it was. Recognising the three people standing there, he swung the door open.

"Your Graces, Miss Bunter, what a lovely surprise! Do come in! I know Mrs. Stillwater will be pleased to see you."

The trio moved past him, and Kingsley shut the door quietly behind them. "What brings you out this way today?"

The duke answered. "We are on our way to Yardley Estate and wanted to stop in and see Mrs. Stillwater if she is at home."

"She is, Your Grace. Shall I get her for you?"

"No need, Kingsley. Is she in her morning parlour?"

"She is, Your Grace. Shall I announce you?"

"Again, no need. We know where it is. But could we trouble you for a cup of tea while we are here?"

"No trouble at all, Your Grace. I will have Mrs. Kingsley boil the kettle right away."

"Thank you. Oh, and our driver and footman are probably already at the kitchen door, looking for refreshments. I sent them there. I hope you don't mind."

"Not at all. We will see to their needs as well."

"Excellent. I knew we could count on you, Kingsley, and of course, on your wonderful wife as well. Now, ladies, shall we go down and surprise our hostess?"

They agreed, and while they headed towards the morning parlour, Kingsley went off to the kitchen to alert his wife to the fact they had unexpected guests.

***

A knock on the door startled Cassandra out of her thoughts. Wondering if it was lunchtime already, she looked at her watch, which she wore pinned to her dress. But no, it was only mid-morning. Then she heard a voice that filled her with equal measures of joy and fear. It belonged to the Duke of Yardley.

"Cassandra, may we come in?"

"Of course!" she said quickly, getting to her feet and walking over to greet them at the door. "How wonderful to see you!"

"I hope we are not intruding," said the duchess, coming in and kissing her on the cheek. "We were passing by and had to stop in and see you."

"It is never an intrusion to see you, ma'am," said Cassandra. "And I believe you mentioned you might drop in on your way to your country estate. Only I did not expect you today."

The duke and Beatrice followed the duchess into the room. "Everything is in order in the city," said the duke. "So, there was no reason for us to delay our departure for the country. And here we are."

"Can you stay for lunch?" asked Cassandra.

The duchess shook her head regretfully. "No, dear. We will only be here for about an hour."

"Then you must have tea, at least. I insist upon it." Cassandra moved towards the bell to ring for the servants.

The duke held up his hand to forestall her. "I actually took the liberty of asking Kingsley when we arrived, Cassandra. I hope you do not mind."

"Of course not. Then please come and sit down, and we will await our tea together." Cassandra waved them over to the chairs near the fireplace.

After seating themselves, the duke asked, "How are you, my dear? You look fatigued."

"I had a restless night and got little sleep. So, yes, I am rather tired. But other than that, I am fine."

"I am glad to hear your pallor is only from a poor night's sleep. How are things with the estate?"

Cassandra pondered what to say. She did not want to lie, but neither was she ready to confess her failure. "Everything is fine at the moment, Your Grace. Thank you for asking."

"Do you need any help with anything? You know that we are always available to help you."

"No, I don't believe so. And yes, I know that I can reach out for your help if I need it."

"Please do. Managing an estate can be an enormous responsibility, and we don't want you to think you have to do all of it by yourself."

"I know that, Your Grace. Your family has been more than kind to me."

"And we will continue to be here to support you as long as Bethany holds the estate."

"Do you think she plans to sell it?"

"No, but both her life and Sam's are now in Australia, not in England, so it will likely become at least a possibility. But then again, she may hold onto it with the intention of passing it down to one of her children in the future. That is her decision to make, of course, not ours."

"I had never thought of her selling the estate. Perhaps I should make alternate plans for my living situation, in case she does."

He frowned in concern. "I did not say that to worry you, Cassandra. Only to assure you that we will always be there for you."

"Thank you for your support. I greatly appreciate it. Ah, our tea has arrived," she said as a maid and footman came to the door. "Shall I pour, or would you like to do the honours, Your Grace?"

The duchess smiled. "You are hosting, my dear, so you must pour. We are only your unexpected guests."

"Unexpected but never unwelcome, ma'am. Now, how do you like your tea?"

***

About an hour later, and after consuming several cups of tea, the duke stood up and thanked Cassandra for a lovely time, saying that it would soon be time for them to move on. "If you will excuse me, I will find our driver and footman and have them ready our carriage for departure. No, no, don't get up. I can find the kitchen on my own, which is where I believe they were having their own tea with the Kingsleys."

"I can ring for Kingsley and ask him to relay the message to your staff. You don't need to make the trip down to the kitchen."

"A little exercise will do me no harm, especially after all the goodies I've eaten. When we are ready to leave, Margaret, I will come back and get you."

"We will wait for you here then, Douglas," she said, thankful that he'd found an excuse to seek out Kingsley for a private discussion.

"I won't be long," he said, then left the room and headed down the hall.

After he was gone, Cassandra turned to the duchess. "I always thought people such as yourselves would never do what your husband is doing at this moment, going out of his own way to find a servant. It was once my belief that nobles just sat and handed out orders to the servants, who did all the work. But Your Graces have always disproved that belief."

The duchess laughed. "There are different people in the peerage, my dear. Some are like us, and others are just as you described them. Thank goodness my husband is one who doesn't mind looking after himself. I do not know if I could have lived with him as long as I have if he had been the other way."

"He must have been brought up properly, ma'am, to act as he does."

"If you had known his mother you would not say such things. She was a woman from the old school of peerage." She shook her head. "No, it is only by the grace of God that Douglas behaves in this manner."

"Perhaps it is also your influence. I have only known a rare few who act as you do, the most noticeable of whom is your daughter-in-law, Bethany."

"Thank you for those kind words. I hope I have had a positive influence over Douglas throughout our marriage, but it is entirely mutual. He has had the same influence on me, so we have grown together. And as for Bethany, what can I say? She is the epitome that we all strive for, is she not?"

Cassandra nodded, while Beatrice continued to sit silently beside them, wondering if she would ever meet this paragon of virtue. *To hear them speak of her, one would think she was destined for sainthood.*

***

Soon, the duke was back to inform them that the carriage was ready for their departure, and Cassandra accompanied the duke and the two women out to the porch.

"Goodbye, and thank you again for tea," said the duchess, kissing Cassandra again on the cheek.

"Thank you for providing me with entertainment this morning," she replied.

"Our country estate is only an hour away," said the duke, squeezing Cassandra's hand. "Please come for a visit someday. And contact us if you have need of our services."

"Perhaps I will, Your Grace. And I will keep in mind your offer and reach out if I need you."

"Good," he said, before following the women into the carriage.

The footman pulled up the stool and placed it in the boot, then closed the carriage door, even as the duchess and Beatrice waved through its windows. Then the driver clicked the reins, and they were off.

Once they were out of sight, Cassandra went back into the manor. She hoped she had disclosed nothing that would make the duke or duchess suspicious of her mishandling of the estate. It was still her problem. Not theirs.

Chapter 6

As the Yardley's carriage continued on its way, the duke turned to his wife. "I had an interesting conversation with Kingsley. I think we need to bring in some support for Cassandra. But I don't know who to ask."

"What do you mean?"

"I talked to Kingsley, as you suggested I should, and he, too, is concerned about Cassandra. He said she has not been sleeping, nor has she been eating well. He also said that she has been acting oddly. Usually, she is quite forthcoming with him and his wife about what is happening with the estate, but lately, she has become rather tight-lipped. She has been having more meetings with the farm steward, Jack Wiley, and when they finish those meetings, neither of them appears to be happy. Her trip to the city yesterday was totally unexpected, and this morning, before we arrived, she sent an urgent letter to Mr. Brown. All of those things, plus what you said about your conversation with her yesterday, have the Kingsleys rather concerned about her health and wellbeing."

"Oh, dear! I knew there was something wrong, but I could not put my finger on it. I am glad you could speak with Kingsley. If he said there is cause to be concerned, Douglas, then there surely is, but what can we do unless Cassandra tells us what is wrong?"

"The only thing we can do is pray, my dear."

"Yes, we can do that. But what else?"

"Nothing. Not unless either Cassandra or Mr. Brown contacts us to ask for help. I already feel like I am going behind her back simply by speaking with Kingsley."

"I know, but it is for a good reason: Cassandra's health. Otherwise, I would not have asked it of you."

"I believe John stopped in on his way home. Perhaps he will have some insights as well. We must talk to him once we arrive at the estate."

"That is an excellent idea. We will speak with him tomorrow. In the meantime, we can pray and trust God to look after Cassandra."

"I agree. Now, let's sit back and enjoy the rest of the trip. I am sure Beatrice does not want to hear any more bad news. Do you, Beatrice?"

Beatrice looked over at the duke and duchess. "I am sorry to hear that Mrs. Stillwater may be ill. If you wish to continue speaking about her, that is fine with me. Please know that I will share nothing you have said with anyone else."

The duchess reached over and patted her hand. "Thank you, my dear. We appreciate you keeping this conversation to yourself. Perhaps the duke and I should have waited until we were private to discuss our concerns. However, you are now a part of the family, and as such, you will be privy to most of the conversations in our home. Am I not correct, Douglas?"

The duke nodded. "There are parts of our lives we need to keep to ourselves, but I agree. Beatrice will come to know most aspects of our daily lives. She is not living with us just for shopping and parties but also to learn about healthy family relationships, the good and the bad."

"You are very kind, Your Grace," said Beatrice. "I am blessed to be a part of your family, and to learn how to conduct myself in proper family situations. I now know that I did not have a healthy upbringing. So, it is good for me to see how a true Christian family works."

"We are glad you joined us," said the duchess. "I am enjoying having a young woman to spoil. Now, let us put our concerns behind us, and as Douglas has said, enjoy the rest of our journey. What would you like to do once we arrive?"

That question set the tone for the next hour as the duke and duchess pointed out familiar landmarks to Beatrice as they neared their country home.

***

Soon, they saw the old stone fence that marked the property line of Yardley Estate. It was believed that former Yardleys had built it on a Roman foundation, as some of the base stones were ancient. No one had ever verified their suspicions, but it was something that they liked to point out to guests. And the duke and duchess did exactly that; they directed Beatrice's attention to the fence as soon as they passed by. Then they reached the iron gates. Seeing their carriage arrive, with the ducal crest on the door, the gatekeeper opened the gates immediately so that they could enter. The young man smiled as they passed him, and the smile only widened when he saw Beatrice's pretty face in the window. He then closed the gates behind the carriage as it continued to rumble along the paving stones towards the house.

Beatrice gasped when she saw the house. This was no country manor, such as she had grown up in. This was a mansion. Larger even than the Stillwater Estate manor, the house itself looked to cover almost an acre of land. The stone façade shone in tones of pink and cream, with alabaster columns surrounding a massive porch. It, too, was built in a Georgian style, symmetric in every element of its design. The three stories each had windows, one atop each other. Ivy vines crept up the ends of the building, but the front was clear of all plants save those in massive planters. Green lawns surrounded the building, with trimmed yew hedges separating each of them. In the middle of the front lawn, there was an enormous fountain, with its water cascading down over a multitude of stone cherubs. Beatrice could hardly take it all in. It was so beautiful! And to think that she was going to live here for the summer! She figured that she must be the most fortunate young woman in all of Britain. *No, in all the world,* she thought. It was almost unfathomable how drastically her life had changed since the fateful day when Joann had knocked on their door. It was unbelievable.

The duke and duchess smiled as they watched Beatrice take in the scenery surrounding their home. It was wonderful to see the house and gardens through Beatrice's eyes, and it was going to be a delight introducing her to everything the estate had to offer. They could not wait to begin.

***

The next day, after showing Beatrice around the grounds of the estate, the duke decided to visit his brother, James, at the neighbouring estate. He left the women in the garden, while Beatrice, budding botanist that she was, exclaimed over the multitude of plants that could be used for medicinal purposes. The duke could see that they would be there for hours, so he bid them farewell, and after his horse was brought around from the stables, he rode off to see his brother and family.

It was only a few minutes' ride to their estate. And when he arrived at the gates, Thomas greeted him and opened the gates so that he could ride through. He headed straight up to the manor and tied his horse to a post near the porch. Then after striding across the porch, he used the iron knocker to alert the inside staff. The door opened, and a smiling Headley appeared and greeted him.

"Afternoon, Your Grace," he said, standing aside so that the duke could enter the foyer. "It is good to see you."

"It is good to see you too, Headley. How do you fare?"

"Well, sir. And you?"

"Cannot complain. Is my brother at home?"

"Yes, Your Grace. He is in his study with Master John. Shall I announce you?"

"No, that's fine. I will announce myself, thank you."

"Good, sir. Do you wish your horse to be stabled?" Headley asked, seeing it tied to the post.

"That is unnecessary. I don't know how long I will be here, but it was only a brief ride, so he will be fine for the moment. I'll let you know if my plans change."

"Yes, Your Grace, please do that. Is there anything I can do for you at the moment?"

"I don't think so. I will see myself to the study and see you later," he said, before heading off down a hallway to his left.

Reaching the study door, the duke could hear James and John speaking. Not wanting to stand on ceremony, after all he was the elder brother and the duke, he walked directly into the room. "Good afternoon, gentlemen. How do you fare today?"

Smiles appeared on both faces as the men rushed over to greet him.

"Douglas, you old dog! When did you arrive?" asked his brother as he pounded him on the back.

"Yesterday," said the duke. "Can you not greet me with a little less passion, James? My back will now be sore for days."

"Can't take a little pat on the back, brother? You must be getting old."

"A little pat? Those were more like slaps. And if I am getting old, so are you, dear brother. You are only a year younger than I."

"That is true, and many days now, I feel the weight of those years upon me. They are catching up with me."

"And with me but I try to ignore them as much as possible. Now, John, how are you?" he asked, turning to his nephew.

"Well, Uncle Douglas. I am glad to see you."

"And I you. Have you readjusted to British life yet?"

"No," he said, shaking his head, though he was still smiling. "It has only been a few days, so I still try to do things as I did in Australia."

"And that includes clearing his dishes off the table after a meal, Douglas. Can you imagine that?" said James. The two men laughed at the idea of clearing away dishes after a meal, while John just stood and smiled at them.

"No, I can't. We were never raised in that manner."

"We were not, and neither was John. But he tells me it was commonplace when he stayed with Sam and Bethany in Australia. They all pitch in to help rather than leaving it to their servants."

"It must be a different world than the one in which we live. I don't know how well I would adapt if Margaret and I were to travel there for a visit."

"Any plans to do that?" asked James.

"No, I am hoping they will come and see us instead. When he stopped by on his way here, John indicated that they might visit soon, when the new baby is old enough to travel. We will just have to wait and see if their plans come to fruition. Now, what are the two of you doing today?"

"We plan to take a tour of the estate lands and see how the tenants are faring with this drought. Would you care to accompany us?"

"Yes, that would be a good idea. It will help me in assessing our own tenants' farms. The drought has definitely caused some hardships, hasn't it?"

"It has, and I want John to see for himself what is happening on the farms. Plus, this will give me a better idea of what I need to do to help my tenants survive."

"Were you planning to leave right away?"

"Yes. That was our plan. Are you agreeable to that?"

"Certainly. Are your horses being brought up, or are you going down to the stables to get them?"

"We are going to have them saddled for us at the stables. Did you ride over?"

"Yes, and I left my horse tied to a post by the porch. I can walk him down to the stables with you."

"Good. Then let us be off," said James, motioning for the duke and John to precede him out the door. When they got to the front door, he asked Headley to let the countess know where they were going, and that they would be back in time for tea.

Headley agreed and wished them well for the afternoon, then closed the door behind them.

***

It was a beautiful, cloudless day. In fact, it would have been perfect day for a ride if not for the desperate need for rain. The ground was hard and dusty, and the lawns around the manor were turning brown. But those were not the primary concerns on the men's minds. It was the crops that were of utmost concern, both the hay and the grains. Without the rain, they were not doing well, and although it cost the duke and earl a fair amount, they knew it could cost their tenant farmers far more. It could actually cost them their lives.

The men were caring landowners, unlike some of their peers who only cared about receiving their income from their tenants and nothing more. However, despite their privileged upbringing, the Yardley brothers had learned to respect both their tenants and their hard work. And as such, they knew that they needed to be cared for, as did the animals they were responsible for. Without their help, many would not make it another year.

Soon, the men were going from farm to farm, talking to the tenants, and assessing what needed to be done to help them. While John had done this before with his father, he now saw it through the lens of a new perspective. *If he were to be the next earl, this would be his responsibility. Would he be as caring as his father and uncle? He hoped he would be. But would caring for the tenants be enough to satisfy his thirst for adventure? Of that, he was not so sure.*

The men concluded their tour later that afternoon and had compiled a long list of things that needed to be done. John would be busy over the next while, helping his father attend to these needs. And so for now, at least, he had decided that he would say nothing more about his thoughts of going back to Australia. That was a discussion for the future. Not for today.

***

When they got back to the manor, they found the countess in the front parlour, the tea things set out before her. She greeted the duke with a kiss on his cheek, and then after the men had seated themselves, she poured the tea.

"How did you find things, James?"

"Not good, Victoria. The tenants are barely hanging on."

"Oh dear, that is not good news. What can we do for them?"

"Well, the most crucial issue is feed for their animals. That has to be our priority. We can do nothing about the crops. They will either survive if God sends us rain or die back. If the latter, they can be used for feed, but there will be nothing to grind for flour. That is when we will have to provide food for our people."

"Then let us pray for rain but plan to assist our tenants. That is what we must do."

"I agree. John and I will get on that first thing tomorrow morning."

"Having seen what your tenants are dealing with, James, I am sure ours are in similarly dire straits. I will do the same assessment with my estate steward tomorrow."

"I knew you would, Douglas. As I was not sure when you were coming out, I was going to send John over to assist your steward with the assessment. But now that you are here, our assistance is unnecessary."

"In that matter, yes," said the duke. "But I have another favour to ask of John."

"Yes? What is it, Uncle Douglas?"

"You stopped by Stillwater Estate on your way home, did you not?"

"Yes."

"Did you see anything amiss when you were there?"

"No, not that I recollect."

"How was your visit with Mrs. Stillwater?"

"Quite pleasant. I stayed for about an hour, I believe. We had tea and a lovely chat."

"Did she mention any concerns about the estate to you?"

"No."

"Why do you ask, Douglas?" said James.

"It is only a feeling, James, but Kingsley and Margaret share it. I suspect that things are not as they should be at Stillwater Estate."

"In what way?"

"I don't know, but Kingsley is concerned about Mrs. Stillwater's health, in all aspects. Did you note any concerns while you were there, John?"

"She did seem rather tired, but as I don't know the lady, I cannot say if that was abnormal for her or not."

"Yes, we stopped in yesterday for tea, and she mentioned not sleeping well the previous night. But Kingsley said that such lack of sleep was becoming commonplace for her, and he was worried about her health."

"What could be causing her problems, Douglas?"

"Perhaps personal problems, or perhaps estate problems. We are close to Stillwater, and we saw today the sorts of challenges the tenants are facing. The tenants of Stillwater Estate are facing the same issues, and Cassandra is solving them by herself."

"But does she not have an estate steward?"

"Yes, but his responsibility will be to bring the issues to her, not to solve them, would it not?"

"You are correct. My estate steward was the first one to alert me to our tenant's difficulties, but then he left the problem solving to me."

"As he should. And that might explain why Cassandra, Mrs. Stillwater, made an unexpected trip to London a couple of days ago. And why she sent an urgent letter to her solicitor yesterday. Perhaps she is finding sources of money for the estate."

"But my understanding was that you would assist her with any such problems. Did you not agree to that with Sam and Bethany?"

"I did. But I cannot help her if she does not confide in me. Perhaps she is ashamed to come to me, thinking she has failed."

"You and I both know differently, Douglas. If she is managing the estate as best she can, there is no shame in coming to you, or us, for help. Perhaps it is only her pride that is standing in the way of us assisting her."

"You may be right, James, but if it is, how do we manage to help her without trampling on that pride?"

And that was the dilemma.

Chapter 7

When the duke got home later that afternoon, he sought out his wife. Finding her alone in the front parlour, he asked after Beatrice and her whereabouts.

"Oh, she is with the gardener."

This made a certain amount of sense to the duke. After all, when they had first met Beatrice, she had been running away from home with the strong suspicion that her mother had poisoned Joann with arsenic. As Beatrice had always been interested in the healing properties of plants, she had been instrumental in helping to save Joann's life. And it was not just a passing interest for the young woman. Even once she'd been staying with them at the London estate, she had always been outdoors with the gardener, studying the plants.

"She would like to continue her studies in botany," the duchess continued. "So, the gardener said he would clear a space for her in the potting shed. I believe she will be there until dinnertime. Why do you ask?"

"Only because I was hoping to speak to you alone. I am glad Beatrice has found something that will keep her occupied this summer, and that she does not need to be with you at all times."

"I am glad, too, for her sake. Plus, the undergardener is an affable young man and seemed pleased to assist Beatrice with whatever she needed."

The duke smiled. "It appears that she has cast a spell on our young men. But let us hope it is only for the summer."

The duchess laughed. "I believe I started a summer romance with a young man many years ago that became the romance that would last for the rest of my life."

"So, you did, my dear, and I am most grateful for it. But getting back to the matter at hand, while I was with James and John this afternoon, we may have stumbled upon the reason for Cassandra's recently mysterious ways."

"Oh, what is that?"

"We think she may be having financial issues with the estate."

"Financial issues? But then why would she not come to you and ask for help?"

"Pride, my dear."

"Pride?"

"Yes, one of the seven deadly sins, I believe."

"And what has brought you to this conclusion?"

"I have to assume that Stillwater Estate is facing the same challenges as those I saw on James's land, and that its tenants are facing the same as ours are as well. But I suspect Cassandra is too proud to ask for our help and is trying to solve the problems on her own."

"And what are those challenges?"

"Poor grain crops and no hay again this year will likely lead to us having to buy feed for animals and food for the tenants. If we don't, the tenants and animals alike could very well die."

"Is the situation truly that bad?"

"From what I saw today, I would have to say yes."

"But that's terrible!" said the duchess, bringing her hands up to cover her mouth. "What can we do to help?"

"Well, first, I need to assess our estate tomorrow. Then we will know exactly what we are facing. After that, we must help the tenants, so that both they and their animals can survive the winter. It's as simple as that."

"I am glad we have the resources to help them, as I am sure James is as well. But what of the estates who are lacking such funds. How will they cope?"

"Hopefully, by reaching out to wealthier family and friends for help, or at least applying for a loan from the bank."

"Douglas?"

"Hmm?"

"The other day, Cassandra told me that she was in town on business. You don't suppose..."

"I am not ruling it out, Margaret. Combined with what Kingsley told me about the urgency of her letter to Mr. Brown, it certainly seems like her problem could be financial."

"But how can we help her if she is too proud to come to us?"

A slow smile appeared on the duke's face as he considered his answer. "Perhaps through the attentions of a suitor."

"Are you daft?" the duchess asked. "How would a suitor help her situation?"

"Not quite daft, my dear. Don't you see? The right suitor could get a look at the estate and perhaps find out what we cannot."

"But where would we find such a man?"

"I believe he is living next door."

"John?"

"Yes."

"Why him?"

"For several reasons... First, he is family, and so is aware of our need to assist Cassandra with the estate. Second, from what he said to me today, I believe there was a spark of interest between the two when he stopped for tea the other day. And finally, he could use the guise of wanting to learn different estate-management techniques to better look after his own family estate in the years to come. Cassandra has never been to Dudley Manor, so she will not know just how well managed it is, or that there is no need for John to look for new farming ideas."

"You want him to go there under false pretences?"

"Not exactly. But if James or I were to show up and try to assist her, she would doubtless send us packing. John is the best person for the job. Plus, he could also share what he learned of farming in Australia, and how those techniques might apply to improving the estate."

"I suppose so. Did you speak to John about your idea?"

"No. For the next while, he will be busy helping his father. But after that, he said he would give us a hand if we needed it. That would be the best time to ask him."

"Perhaps you're right. It would also give us time to pray on your plan and see what God has to say about it."

"Yes, that is important too. Thank you for reminding me."

"You are welcome. Shall we take it to Him now and see what He says?"

"Let's do that," said the duke, taking her hands in his and beginning to pray.

"*Dear Father in heaven...*"

***

When they had finished praying, the duke squeezed Margaret's hands. "Have I told you lately how much I love you, Margaret Yardley?"

"Not since this morning, Your Grace."

"I hate to think what would have become of me if I had married one of those empty-headed debutants my mother kept pushing at me. You are the best part of me, my love, and I thank God every day for you."

"Thank you for those lovely words. I am glad to have saved you from those evil debutantes. And I fall deeper in love with you every day. It was worth every day of the trials with your mother to become your wife, and I hope, in God's grace, that He grants us many more years together on this earth."

"I do too, love."

They exchanged a warm kiss and hug then before walking down the hall towards their rooms to prepare themselves for dinner.

***

The next few days, the duke and his estate steward were busy looking after the needs of their tenants, as were James and John on the Dudley Estate. After they finished the initial round of assisting the tenants, James sent John over to help his uncle with his farmers, providing the duke with the opportunity he had been waiting for.

As he was working alongside his nephew, later that day, the duke looked over at John. "So, what are your plans after finishing your assistance here?"

"I have none, Uncle Douglas. Why? Do you have something else you need help with?"

"Well, if your father has no immediate need of your services, I do have one further task I would like you to do for me."

"Of course. What is it?"

"I would like you to go to Stillwater Estate and assist Mrs. Stillwater with whatever she might require to ensure that the estate continues as a viable enterprise."

"Has she asked for your help?"

"No, but I am concerned about both her and the estate. I promised Sam and Bethany that I would look after both for them, and I believe this is the best way to fulfil that promise."

"But if Mrs. Stillwater has not requested any help, how am I to explain my presence?"

"I was thinking that, as the heir to Dudley Manor and its surrounding farms, you could say that you are hoping to see if her farm steward has any new techniques that you could apply to your own estate. Does that sound plausible?"

"I don't know. Even though Dudley Estate is smaller than Yardley Estate, we are still much larger than Stillwater. Would it not seem odd for me to come looking for ideas from her farm steward? If it was the reverse, I would certainly see it in that way."

"Perhaps so," the duke said, then thought for a moment. "I wonder if you could approach it from the perspective of having come from Sam and Bethany's station in Australia. I understand it is always quite dry where they live?"

"Yes. In a normal year, they certainly receive far less rain than we do here."

"Well, then seeing as we are in the midst of an extended drought, it would be the perfect opportunity to apply some of those Australian ideas to our British farms, starting with Cassandra's. How would that suit?"

"Better than your first idea, Uncle Douglas. Perhaps Mrs. Stillwater would agree to that explanation for my presence. But exactly what is it that I will be seeking to learn while I am there?"

"Whether or not the estate is failing, and if that is the case, is Mrs. Stillwater is using her personal funds to keep it afloat."

"And that is what you want me to report to you?"

"Yes. If either, or both, are occurring. I need to know so that I can step in and bolster the estate's finances."

"And if not?"

"Then you will still have had a chance to apply some Australian farming methods to English soil."

"Well," he answered slowly, then nodded his head. "Alright. I will do it. For your sake, and also for Sam and Bethany's. I know they would not want the estate to go under."

"Thank you, John. I appreciate your willingness to do this for the family. After all, you are an integral part of it, both now and for future generations. Someday, as our heirs, you and Rupert will be the head of these estates after your father and I have passed on. So, it will be good for you to take on some additional responsibility, even now."

John reflected on his uncle's words. Just like John's own father, the duke believed that he would be staying in England from now on. But he still did not know whether he actually would, or if he would be relocating permanently to Australia. Either way though, while he was here, he was happy to help in any way that he could. He only hoped that Mrs. Stillwater would receive his help in the way it was intended. Otherwise, their next visit could very well be much tenser than their first encounter.

***

That night, after dinner, John talked to his parents about the duke's suggestion. They agreed that he should do as his uncle requested of him. As the family estates now had all the necessary preparations complete for the coming winter, there was no reason for John not to travel to Stillwater Estate. So, the next day, John packed a small bag and headed back down the road towards London. As he travelled, he prayed that Mrs. Stillwater would be receptive to both his visit and his help. He asked God to prepare her for his arrival.

***

Cassandra, too, was praying. Mr. Brown had written back to her, saying that he would travel out to assess the estate's needs as soon as possible. He also suggested that she contact the Duke of Yardley for his aid, but Cassandra was not yet ready to do that. If Mr. Brown agreed, she would send the sapphire necklace and emerald bracelet back with him to be sold to Mr. White. If not, she would just have to endure another trip into London. She was simply not prepared to accept the duke's handouts and allow him to pay for her mistakes. No, this was her problem, and she would solve it by herself.

***

Approaching the gates of the estate, John prayed that God would provide him with the right words to say, so that Mrs. Stillwater would invite him to stay with her. After all, he was a stranger, even though he bore a connection to the Yardleys. Perhaps, if he told her he had more stories to share of life with Bethany and Sam, she would agree to his presence. That was the only thing he could come up to move himself into the manor. John still felt a twinge of unease about his deception. But it was for a worthy cause. He had to constantly reassure himself of that, and that this was for Mrs. Stillwater's benefit. A verse from Romans came to mind then, which said that God would work all things out for good, for those who were called according to His purpose.[3] Perhaps He was using John to do His work. He certainly hoped so.

Riding up to the now familiar porch, he stopped, dismounted, and tied his horse to a post. Then he walked up to the door and knocked twice with the iron ring. Within a minute, Kingsley opened the door.

"Lord Dudley, what a lovely surprise. Won't you come in?" he asked, standing aside.

"Thank you. Kingsley, isn't it?"

"Yes, sir. It is good of you to remember my name from only having met me once before."

John laughed. "You must have made an impression on me. I am usually not that good with names."

"Yes, sir." Kingsley smiled. "What can I do for you today?"

"I wish to see Mrs. Stillwater if possible. Is she in?"

"Yes," he said, then lowered his voice to a near whisper. "Are you perchance here at the duke's request?"

"Yes."

"*Thank you, Lord,*" said Kingsley, turning his eyes skyward. Then he brought his gaze back down to John. "I have been praying that God would send someone to help the mistress, and here you are. You are welcome here, Lord Dudley."

"I hope your mistress sees my visit in the same light."

"If she does not right now, sir, eventually she will. Please have a seat and I will let her know you are here."

"One more thing before you go. I have only brought a few things with me but left them in my saddlebags in case Mrs. Stillwater turns me out. Would you mind looking after them while I am with her?"

"Of course. But I will have a room prepared for your stay. I cannot see her turning you away. First though, I will announce you."

John nodded, and Kingsley hurried down the hall, presumably to where John had previously met with Cassandra. He was back within a couple of minutes. "Mrs. Stillwater will see you now, Lord Dudley." Then he lowered his voice again. "I believe she is pleased you are here. Her countenance brightened at the mention of your name."

John hoped Kingsley was right. But there was only one way to find out, and that was to see her. So, he followed the butler down the hall to the morning parlour and walked in as Kingsley announced him.

"Lord Dudley to see you, ma'am."

"Lord Dudley," said Cassandra, getting to her feet. "What a lovely surprise. I did not expect to see you again so soon."

"Mrs. Stillwater, it is a pleasure to see you as well. And yes, I hope you do not mind that I am visiting again after such a brief absence."

"Of course not. You are welcome to visit any time, sir. Now, please, come and have a seat. What brings you to Stillwater Estate today?"

John took a deep breath. The time had come, and he still did not know what to say. Luckily, God put the words in his mouth. "Mrs. Stillwater, I hate to presume upon your kindness, but I find myself in the position to, perhaps, assist you with farming techniques for dry lands. I learned much when I was with Sam and Bethany in Australia, and seeing as you are likely in the same predicament as our other country estates, thanks to the drought, I would like to offer my assistance. Will you accept it?"

"Your help, sir? I'm not sure what you could help me with. We are managing well, although I suppose Mr. Wiley, my farm steward, might be open to some suggestions as to how to deal with the drought. I could ask him for you."

"Perhaps I could learn some things from him as well, ma'am, and we could be of mutual benefit to each other."

"I suppose so although I imagine your family estate is larger than mine and managed differently."

"It is larger, but the management would be similar, I expect."

"Well then...why don't you plan to stay for lunch? I will ask Mr. Wiley to join us. Then we can discuss this further with him."

"Thank you for the invitation. I accept."

"Good. Now, I will ring for tea, and we can talk about other things. Shall I?"

"Again, that would be lovely. I was hoping we could visit, and I could share more of my adventures in Australia."

"I will love to hear more, sir. But first, I will let Kingsley know that we require tea. Will you excuse me?" she asked, getting to her feet.

"Of course," said John, also getting up. Then she walked out of the room and down the hall, while he breathed a sigh of relief. He had one foot in the door. Now, he just needed to get the steward's approval of his plan, and he would be in.

***

After a satisfying meal with Cassandra and Mr. Wiley, John became far more comfortable in their presence. They accepted his proposal to stay for a while and discuss farming techniques for dry lands. The steward also was agreeable to John accompanying him on a tour of the tenants' holdings to see what needed to be done to sustain them for the winter. The footman brought in John's bag, and the stable boys fed his horse prior to him riding out with Mr. Wiley. It appeared things were going well. But as John soon discovered, things are not always as they seem.

His first clue came when he and Mr. Wiley, or Jack as he preferred to be called, headed out to the barns before going out to survey the fields. While in the barn, John noted that there was little hay in the loft. At this time of year, it should have been overflowing with it. So, he asked Jack why there was no winter feed in the loft.

"Well, sir, it's because of the drought. Our hay crop failed last year, and we won't get much this year either. In fact, I am letting the cattle graze in the hay fields now; we won't be cutting any for feed this winter."

"So, what will you do for feed?"

"That is a problem, Lord Dudley. I have spoken with Mrs. Stillwater frequently about the issue, but we have yet to come up with a solution."

"Could you not purchase feed from elsewhere in Britain? The drought is not widespread."

"We could, except that... Well, to be honest, there is no money in the coffers to buy feed."

"No money? You mean the estate is floundering?"

"More than floundering, sir. I realize that I am talking out of turn, but we are quite broke."

"Broke? But how could that be, Jack? This estate, from my understanding, has always flourished, even in bad times. I have a hard time believing the coffers are empty."

"Unless Mrs. Stillwater is hiding something from me, sir, that is my understanding. Without financial aid of some sort, we cannot survive past next spring."

"I see... What manner of woman is Mrs. Stillwater? When I mean to say is ... if the coffers are empty, do you suppose—"

"Oh, no sir!" he said quickly, understanding where his question had been leading. "Mrs. Stillwater is an honest Christian lady. She would never do anything untoward or knowingly damaging to the estate."

"That good to know, Jack. I was only checking."

John, too, had gotten no sense that Cassandra was anything but an honest woman during their interactions to that point. But she had lied during Bethany's trial several years ago, so perhaps she was not as upright as Jack believed her to be. John needed to look below the surface to discover if the present mistress of Stillwater Estate was pilfering funds for her own use. *But why would she do that?* he asked himself. *He would have to find out if there was a justifiable reason, assuming she had actually been using that money for her own purpose. In the meantime, though, he needed to continue surveying the farm with the steward.*

"Well, Jack," he said, "now that I have seen the barns, what is next?"

"I will show you the condition of our crops, sir, so you understand what damage the drought has caused us."

"Lead on then, my man," said John, before following him out of the barn to where they had tied their horses.

CASSANDRA'S REWARD ... FOR FAILURE

***

Later that afternoon, John returned to the manor. He agreed with Mr. Wiley that there would be little harvest this year and no hay for the animals. They would have to buy grain and hay, so that the animals were able to survive the winter. He also toured the tenant's farms and found them to be in similar circumstances. They needed cash to help them endure the coming months, let alone survive them. The estate was indeed in dire straits and needed help from the Yardleys. The only question now was how he could convince Mrs. Stillwater to accept that help.

He also still found himself harbouring doubts about her innocence concerning the estate funds. He needed to have a look at the books and see where the money had gone and was still going, before he could confirm her innocence of any sort of theft and clear her name. But would she even allow him to see the ledgers? If not, it would be hard not to take that as a sign of her guilt.

The other person he wanted to speak to was Kingsley. The butler had served the Stillwater family for many decades and would likely know everything, and anything, that was happening in the household. John hoped he would be forthcoming with details and not try to hide the facts because of his loyalty to the family. If they didn't resolve things soon, Kingsley might very well no longer have a family to serve. Perhaps if he put it to Kingsley in that manner, it might help the butler answer his questions truthfully. John could only try.

When he got to the house, he entered through the kitchen door and found Mrs. Kingsley preparing tea. He informed her that he would tidy up a bit before coming down to join Mrs. Stillwater for tea, then asked where he would find her. Mrs. Kingsley told him that she would be in the front parlour. After hearing that, John headed up the back stairs to his assigned room. After a quick wash, he went back down the front staircase to have his afternoon tea.

Cassandra looked up as he entered the parlour. "Oh, Lord Dudley, you are just in time for tea. Will you join me?"

"I will, thank you," he said, walking over to a chair across from her.

"How do you take your tea, sir?"

John informed her of his preference, and once she'd prepared it, he took the cup from her.

"Please, help yourself to something to eat as well," she said. "I am sure you must be hungry after your ride."

"It was a pleasant ride, ma'am, and not too strenuous, so I am not terribly hungry. But these biscuits do look delicious, so I will try one of them."

"Yes, Mrs. Kingsley is a wonderful cook. I am lucky to have her services."

"She and her husband have served the Stillwater family well for many years, have they not?"

"Yes. They came when Bethany was only a baby and have looked after the family for over two decades."

"It is wonderful to have such loyal retainers."

"It is. Whenever I need to know something, I go straight to Kingsley, and he tells me everything there is to know about that issue."

Hearing her say that confirmed John's thoughts that he needed to speak to Kingsley soon about the estate finances. "It is good to have such a confidante within the household, ma'am."

"Yes, I don't know what I would do without them. Now, I am eager to hear what you saw this afternoon. Is the estate in dire straits?"

"From what I saw and heard, from both Mr. Wiley and your tenants, I would have to say that it is."

"Oh dear, I was hoping to hear a different answer from you. But it only confirms my suspicions. What can we do to save it?"

"First, you need a substantial amount of cash not only to purchase feed for your animals but to help your tenants get through the winter. They will not survive without your help."

"Where can I get such an amount of money, sir? We have no crops to sell... I suppose I could sell off some animals, but everyone is in the same situation, so I doubt I would get a decent price for them."

"No, you are right. You would have to transport your animals to markets quite far away and that would require money. You need to cull your herds, leaving you with fewer animals to feed, and gaining you some meat for the winter as well."

"I suppose," she said. "Oh, it is on days like this I wished I had not taken Bethany up on her offer of this home in the country. I have no experience managing an estate. My late husband handled our finances and gave me only a small budget for household expenses each month. I was so eager to have a country home for the boys that I did not consider what responsibilities I would be undertaking on the estate. And now I have failed my dear sister Bethany. I do not know how to tell her, or how to even face her in the future."

"I would suggest that you speak with your solicitor. Mr. Brown, I believe? Perhaps he has some suggestions."

"I have written to him and he plans to come out soon to discuss the financial situation with me. Perhaps, as you say, he will have ideas about how to save the estate."

"You could also speak with the Duke of Yardley, ma'am."

"Only as a last resort. I don't want him to know what a mess I have made of managing Bethany's estate. No, I will only contact him if I am left with no other choice but to do so. And I would appreciate if you would not tell him of my situation."

"I will leave that up to you," said John, nodding respectfully. *But only if you find another way to finance the estate. Otherwise, I will be obliged to let him know what is happening here.*

"Thank you, sir. Now, is there any other news I need to be aware of this afternoon?"

"No, I don't believe so, ma'am. May I entertain you with more stories of my time with Sam and Bethany?"

"Yes, that would be lovely. Anything that does not pertain to the estate would be welcome news, sir. Please, tell me more."

John was happy to oblige and spent the next while enchanting her with tales about the Yardley family in Australia. They did not mention the estate woes again.

Later that afternoon, John talked to Kingsley. Despite his hesitation to speak negatively about Cassandra, the butler couldn't hide his genuine concern and apprehensions about her recent behaviours.

As an example of that behaviour, he told him about her surprising him by coming downstairs early one morning and announcing that she was going to London for the day.

"That was unusual for her," he said, "as she rarely goes to the city. And she said that she was going in on a business errand, but she did not tell me anything about what that entailed. I had a carriage arranged for her, and she left. And then when she arrived back later that evening, well past the hour of her planned return, she looked tired and discouraged. She told me that she had met the Duchess of Yardley for tea but said nothing about how her actual business had gone."

Kingsley shook his head, concern and confusion clear on his face. "Then the next day, after meeting with Mr. Wiley once again, she handed me a letter to post and said that it was an urgent matter. I noted that she had addressed it to Mr. Edwin Brown, her solicitor, but again, she gave me no further details. A letter has since come back from Mr. Brown, and I understand that he plans to come out soon to visit with Mrs. Stillwater. These meetings and letters fill me with a great deal of unease, as you can imagine. So, I was glad to see you today, Lord Dudley. Perhaps you can help the mistress with her problems, whatever they might be."

"I hope to, Kingsley, but she needs to be more forthcoming with me in order for me to do that. You said she has been acting rather strangely of late. Anything else I should know about?"

"Well, she is not eating or sleeping well. When I retire for the night, she is usually in the front parlour, studying the estate books until who knows when in the morning. And she sends half her meals back to the kitchen uneaten, which is of great concern to my wife. I don't know how much longer the mistress can go on like this before she collapses."

"Well, I am here on behalf of the duke to make sure that does not happen. Thank you for speaking with me. I know it was difficult for you to do that, but it is important that I hear from everyone on the estate. One last question though... You witnessed Mrs. Stillwater's testimony at Bethany's trial and later discovered that she had perjured herself. Do you think she could be telling lies again?"

Kingsley paused for a moment. "I don't know what to say, sir. I would like to think that is all behind us, but with all her recent secrecy, I cannot deny, at least, the possibility. But to what purpose?"

"Perhaps she is using the funds for her personal use or storing them away as protection against a day when she might no longer be living here."

"I suppose that is possible, though it would be hard to believe of the woman I've come to know. She does know that it is only by the mercy of

Bethany that she is here. Perhaps she fears that, should she fail in her responsibilities here on the estate, Bethany will look to install another manager and move her out. I hate to even think that she could be feathering her nest from the estate funds, but I suppose I cannot rule it out. She is the only one who sees those books. No one else does."

"I hope to see them myself and review the numbers. If I cannot get Mrs. Stillwater to hand them over to me, where would I find them?"

"Oh dear. This is going from bad to worse, Lord Dudley. Mrs. Stillwater keeps the books in her room. She says it gives her easier access when she needs to look up something during the night."

"That could make it difficult, indeed. If she does not voluntarily allow me to review the books, we will have to access them by stealth."

"We...?"

"Yes, I am sorry, but I will need your help, as well as your silence regarding what we have discussed. You are loyal to the owners of the estate, not to Mrs. Stillwater, are you not, Kingsley?"

"Yes. I hate to even imagine harming Mrs. Stillwater, but my first allegiance is to Bethany. I will assist you in any way I can and hope that what is uncovered only strengthens my belief in the mistress's character."

"Thank you. I hope you do not have to go against her, but I needed to know I had your support to save the estate."

"You can count on me, sir, and of course, on my wife too. She is as devoted to Miss Bethany as I am."

"That is good to know. Now, I have kept you too long and will allow you to go about your duties. You have been a great help to me today. Thank you."

"Let me know if, or when, you need further assistance, sir. I am here to serve," said Kingsley, before heading back to his post in the foyer.

John went up to his room to think about his conversation with the butler and plan his next moves.

Chapter 8

Cassandra, too, was worried. Only now it was not about the estate finances but about Lord Dudley's presence at the manor. *Why is he here? Was he really trying to give them ideas about drought farming, or did he have another purpose in mind?* Cassandra suspected the latter. His close connection with the Duke of Yardley made her apprehensive that he might have been sent to spy on her. She needed to watch her words and ensure that Lord Dudley did not look at the estate ledgers. Not that she had done anything wrong, but she did not want him to see how badly she had failed Bethany. Lord Dudley would be welcome to peruse the books after Mr. Brown came to collect the jewellery. Until then, she would keep the ledgers hidden.

***

That evening at dinner, John confirmed her suspicions when he asked if he might have a look at the estate accounts. Cassandra turned down his request, and that strained their conversation for the rest of the meal. When she asked him to join her for tea afterwards, he declined, saying that he would spend the rest of the evening in his room. Their conviviality from earlier that day had passed. They said goodnight to each other then and parted ways, with Cassandra moving to the front parlour and John retiring to his room.

***

The next day, she received a note from Mr. Brown, who apologised and said that he could not come out to the estate because of some other urgent business he needed to attend to. As such, he asked whether Cassandra would consider coming into the city at her earliest convenience to see him. His letter disappointed Cassandra, but she supposed that it would give her another opportunity to take her jewellery to Mr. White. Instead of sending a message back to him, she informed Kingsley that she would be going to London again the following day, and asked that he please arrange a carriage and driver for her.

***

Kingsley agreed despite once again not knowing the purpose of her trip, and so the next morning, she came down for breakfast carrying a large satchel. When Kingsley accompanied her to the carriage, he spotted a thick ledger protruding from the open latch. Cassandra was taking no chances with the estate books. Frustrated, Kingsley was aware that this news would be an immense disappointment to Lord Dudley.

As soon as Cassandra had left, he sought out John. As expected, he was disheartened to hear that Cassandra had left for the city, taking the ledger with her, but there was nothing John could do about it. So, he headed down to the barns to see how he could help Wiley for the day. The ledgers would have to wait.

***

Cassandra felt foolish, lugging the estate books into the city with her. But perhaps, she reasoned, Mr. Brown would need to look at them during their meeting. It also meant they were out of Lord Dudley's reach. She did not think he would be so brash as to take them from her room, but she was not sure. No, the books were better with her today than left at home.

Arriving in the city, she headed to White's Jewellers before going to see Mr. Brown. This time, she was not going home without selling the necklace and bracelet. However, when she got to the store, there was a closed sign on the window. And there was no specified time listed for when it would reopen. She supposed she could go back to one of the other jewellers, but Mr. White had promised her the best price. Hopefully, his shop would be open later this afternoon when she had finished her business with Mr. Brown.

She got back in the carriage and gave the driver directions to her solicitor's office. Once they arrived, she asked the driver to wait, and he agreed to do so unless or until a police officer asked him to move. Cassandra went into the building then and up a flight of stairs to a door with Mr. Brown's name on it, which she opened, and quickly walked into office beyond.

"Morning, ma'am," said a young man seated at a desk just inside the door. "How can I help you?"

"Good morning. Is Mr. Brown available? If so, I would like to speak with him if I may."

"He is in. Do you have an appointment?"

"No, but he asked me to come and see him as soon as possible."

"Let me see if he has time for you this morning. Your name, please?" The young man got up to head back to the inner offices.

"Mrs. Stillwater."

"Please have a seat, Mrs. Stillwater. I'll check to see if Mr. Brown can see you now."

Cassandra sat down on the wooden, ladder-back chair the young man had pointed to. But almost as soon as she did, she stood back up again at the sound of Mr. Brown's voice as he came out to greet her.

"Mrs. Stillwater," he said, reaching out to grasp her hand for a moment. "It was good of you to come. I am sorry I could not come out to the estate. Please come in." He motioned her to precede him through another open door with his name on it. "Can I get you any refreshment? Tea, perhaps?"

"No, I am fine, sir. Thank you for offering."

"Well, but if you change your mind, please let me know. Now, tell me again what the issue is and how I can help you."

"I am here to see what suggestions you might have to help me save Stillwater Estate."

"Ah, yes. Obviously, you received my reply to your first letter in which I suggested you contact the Duke of Yardley with your concerns."

"I received your letter, but I prefer not to involve him."

"Why is that?"

"Because it is my problem, and I wish to handle it on my own, rather than drag Bethany's family into it."

"I am sure he would be more than willing—"

"I am sure he would, Mr. Brown. But I do not wish the help he would offer, especially if it comes in the person of his nephew, Lord John Dudley."

"What? I don't understand, ma'am. What does Lord Dudley have to do with managing Stillwater Estate?"

"Yesterday, Lord Dudley arrived on my doorstep. He claimed he was there to give my farm steward ideas about how to deal with the drought situation, having just returned from Australia, where he had seen new techniques being used in farming dry lands. But he then started asking a lot of questions of me and Mr. Wiley, which leads me to believe the duke sent him to see how the estate was faring. Lord Dudley even asked to see the estate books, which I refused. I brought the ledger with me today in case you needed to see the facts for yourself, but also to keep it away from him."

"I see," said Mr. Brown, nodding slowly.

"My handling of the estate has been deficient, but I do not want word to get back to Bethany that I have failed her yet again. So, I am looking for ways to sustain the estate for her."

"I understand. You mentioned in your letter that you would like to see if I could secure a loan for you. Is that correct? What collateral do you have for a banker to loan you money? You cannot use the estate as you do not own it. Do you have any property you can offer as a guarantee?"

"Only my jewellery."

"If I remember correctly from Bethany's trial, your jewellery is still... how shall I put this...your lifeline?"

"Yes, it is the only thing of value I own, but I wish to sell at least two pieces to keep the estate viable. I tried the last time I was in the city but could not make the transaction because of an unexpected meeting with the Duchess of Yardley. And today, when I came in, the store was closed. I hope it is open when we conclude our business, so I can sell the pieces to Mr. White."

"Selling your jewellery is a drastic measure, Mrs. Stillwater. Jewellers are not pawn shops; you cannot simply reclaim your pieces when you next have the funds."

"I am aware of that. But these pieces have no special sentimental value for me. The one is the necklace Bethany wore when she was arrested, so I shall never wear it again because of that memory. The other is an emerald bracelet I inherited from my mother, which does not suit me. It will not bother me to never see either of those items again."

"Well, it is, of course, your prerogative to sell them. But perhaps it would be better to put them up as collateral against a bank loan. Would you rather do that?"

"I had not thought of that, but I agree. May I leave them with you to do as you have said?"

"You may. I will go out tomorrow and seek a loan for you."

"Thank you, sir. This takes an enormous weight off my shoulders."

"Don't thank me yet, ma'am. The deal has not yet been made. Once it has been, you can thank me. Now, is there anything else I can assist you with today?"

"No, that is all. I won't take up any more of your time. Thank you for seeing me without an appointment. I look forward to hearing from you soon regarding the loan."

"I will be in touch," he said, standing and reaching out to grasp her hand once more. "Please contact me if you need further help."

"I will," she said, before walking with him to the door. He opened it, and she walked through. "I can see myself out. You do not have to walk me to the street."

Nodding, he watched her walk down the hallway, and then out of sight. He heard her say farewell to his clerk, and then the outer door opened and closed. With a sigh, Mr. Brown went back into his office and sat down behind his desk. He now had two clients to serve, Mrs. Stillwater, with her request to keep the Yardleys unaware of the estate's difficulties, and the Duke of Yardley—as Bethany's representative in England—who wanted to be kept abreast of everything that was happening with the estate in order to protect its viability. Somehow, he would need to serve both interests at the same time. He just did not know how.

***

Cassandra left Mr. Brown's office feeling much better than when she had entered it. Perhaps her troubles were behind her, at least for the moment. But then she remembered that there was still an immense problem at the estate in the form of John Dudley.

Now, what should I do about him...?

John was thinking about Cassandra too. The fact that she had taken the estate ledgers with her to London today only increased his suspicions that she was not being honest with him. But was she actually a thief, stealing funds from the estate for her own purposes? Her manner of dress did not suggest she was spending the money on clothes. He also understood that she had a stash of expensive jewellery, so she would not need any further ornamentation. Was she, perhaps, stashing it away for her sons, thinking they were missing out because they were Howard's sons, and therefore not eligible to inherit the estate? Were the boys pressuring her into skimming money from the estate, or was it her own idea? John needed to see that ledger. It would help him determine Cassandra's guilt or innocence once and for all. But how to get it from her?

***

Cassandra arrived back at the estate later that afternoon. She was tired but pleased with how the day had gone. She was thankful she had not needed to go back to the jewellers and was hoping the bank would accept the jewellery as collateral because she had nothing else to offer. There was nothing left for her to do now but await an answer from Mr. Brown. Unfortunately, waiting was not something she had ever been good at doing.

Kingsley met her at the front door. "How was your day, ma'am?" he asked, reaching out to relieve her of the weight of her satchel..

"It went well, thank you," she said, releasing the satchel into his care but not before retrieving the ledger from its depths.

Disappointed that she would not trust him with the ledger itself, he stepped back. "That's good news. Will you be travelling back to the city again soon?"

"I hope not, but my future travels will depend on what comes from today's meeting. How have things gone here today?"

"No concerns, ma'am."

"That good. Is Lord Dudley still with us?"

"Yes, ma'am. I don't think he has plans to leave. Would you like me to inform him that you are back?"

"No. I am going to head to my room and freshen up. Then, perhaps, I will have tea in the front parlour in about a half hour. Would that be acceptable?"

"Yes, ma'am. I will inform Mrs. Kingsley of your wishes."

"Thank you. Now, if you will excuse me..."

Kingsley nodded and watched her ascend the stairs, with the ledger now tucked neatly beneath her arm. As soon as he heard the door close to her room, he headed out to find Lord Dudley.

***

John was in the barn talking to Wiley. The needed repairs to the tenant's homes were progressing well. There was not much more to do, or discuss, until the duke made funding available to purchase feed, so he was wondering how he could feasibly prolong his stay at the estate without arousing Cassandra's suspicions. And he still needed to get a look at the books. That was his number-one priority. He had to see them. But how?

Kingsley went out to the barn after hearing from a footman that he could locate John there. He found him speaking with the steward, but their conversation ended when Kingsley appeared in the doorway.

"Yes, Kingsley, what is it?" asked John.

"I'm sorry to interrupt you, sir, but I wanted to let you know that Mrs. Stillwater has returned from London, in case you wished to speak to her."

"Thank you. Yes, I would like a word with her. Where might I find her?"

"She will be in the front parlour having tea in about a half hour. Shall I ask Mrs. Kingsley to set a tea tray for two, sir?"

"If you don't mind, that would be good. Mr. Wiley and I have almost finished speaking for today. Unless you have anything further to say?" John said, turning back to the steward.

"No, sir, I don't. I will carry on as usual until I hear anything more from you or Mrs. Stillwater."

"Good. Mrs. Stillwater will discuss further plans with you, Wiley. That is not my place."

"I will wait to hear from her then, sir. Good day to you." The steward left the barn then to continue with his duties.

"I did not want to say anything in front of Mr. Wiley, sir," said Kingsley, "but the mistress carried the ledger in and up to her room. When I tried to relieve her of it, she refused. I don't know how you will manage to look at them."

"I don't either, Kingsley. How was her mood when she returned?"

"Much improved, sir. She was tired but quite pleasant."

"Did she mention any further trips to London soon?"

"No, and I asked her that very question. However, she gave me no further details as to why she went to London today."

"That only adds to my suspicions about her activities. I am sorry to say that to you, but there is something she is not disclosing, and it makes me uneasy."

"And I as well, sir. If Mrs. Stillwater owned the estate, I would not be so concerned, but I certainly want nothing to happen to Bethany's inheritance."

"Nor do I. We shall have to pray that God will soon provide us with a way to view those books. I don't know how much longer I can stay here. The steward has the farm repairs well in hand, so my justification for remaining a guest at the estate is fast wearing thin."

"I will pray too, sir. God will work this out. I am sure of that. In the meantime, I need to get back to the kitchen and let Mrs. Kingsley know that there will be two for tea today."

"Thank you. I'll head to my room for a quick wash before I join your mistress in the parlour for tea. Let's be on our way."

The two men headed back to the manor then, each of them praying that God would show them a way to view the ledgers before John was forced to leave for home.

***

Arriving in the parlour a little while later, Cassandra saw that the tea tray held a setting for two. She had not planned to have tea with Lord Dudley, but she supposed it was inevitable as he was still her house guest. She prayed that, soon, this would no longer be the case. Of course, aside from having him forcibly removed, that might take far longer than she wished. She was uncertain of a polite way to get him to leave otherwise.

When she heard his footsteps approaching the room, she looked up and smiled cooly at him as he stepped in through the doorway. "Lord Dudley, just in time for tea. Won't you join me?"

"I would like that, Mrs. Stillwater. Kingsley mentioned that you were back from London. How was your day?"

"Long and tiring, though successful. And as I accomplished what I needed to do, I am happy. And yours?"

"Good. Mr. Wiley has things well in hand now, so he will carry on with the plans we've discussed."

"That is good news. And you? What will you do now?"

John thought for a moment, but finally shrugged slightly, unable to come up with any idea that might keep him there. "I suppose I will make my way back home, ma'am. I have done what I needed to do here, and there is nothing more for me to accomplish. Unless you had something else for me?"

Cassandra heaved a sigh of relief. He was going home. "No, I don't think so, Lord Dudley. You have been most helpful. But as you said, Mr. Wiley is more than capable now of carrying out your plan for the estate. When will you depart?"

"Tomorrow morning if that is all right with you, ma'am."

More than all right, thought Cassandra. *I would send you on your way this afternoon if such would not be the very height of rudeness.* "That would be fine, sir. Now, would you like some tea?"

John agreed, even while silently hoping that Kingsley was using this time to secure the ledger for him. His time at the Stillwater Estate was quickly running out.

***

Kingsley waited until Cassandra and John had finished eating and were sipping their after-dinner tea before making his move. He felt like a scoundrel, going into his mistress's room to search for the ledger. But he agreed with John. Cassandra was being too secretive of late, especially when it came to her handling of the ledger. So, what was in it?

Kingsley truly hoped that all was in order, but for Bethany's sake, they had to find out for sure. Looking around her room, he could not see the ledger. He did not want to go through the mistress' closet or chest of drawers, but his mission was much too important for him to have such concerns. So, with great reluctance, he examined the wardrobe, then the chest of drawers, searching each one without success.

Where could she have hidden it?

Then he remembered where Cassandra always hid her jewellery. His wife had surprised her one day while she'd been sitting on the edge of her bed, a loosened plank just below her feet and a jewellery case in her hands. Mrs. Kingsley had apologised for intruding, but Cassandra had dismissed her apology with ease, reassuring her that she had no secrets from her or her husband. And so, Mrs. Kingsley had been comfortable in telling him that evening about the hiding place in the floorboards.

If she hid her precious jewels there, what better place to stow the ledger?

Remembering his wife's comments about the loose plank, Kingsley knelt down and felt along the edges of the floorboards. *Ah, there it is!* He pried up the plank and found what he was looking for: the estate ledger. He lifted it out, replaced the plank, and after surveying the room to make sure nothing was out of place, he hurried back to the door. After checking to ensure there was no one in the hallway, he hastened into John's room and placed the ledger under John's pillows. Finally, after again making sure no one was about, he rushed from the room, and then down the hallway and the back stairs.

Once in the kitchen, he plopped down into a chair to catch his breath. He had completed his mission. Now, he only needed to let Lord Dudley know it. But first, he needed to regain his composure.

"Mr. Kingsley?" said his wife. "Whatever have you been doing? You are all out of breath."

"Taking care of some things upstairs, my love. Nothing else."

"Why would you need to be up there?"

"Doing a task for Lord Dudley; that is all."

"Hmmm. The two of you have spent a lot of time together these past few days. I wonder what you have been up to."

"Only looking after the affairs of the estate. Nothing else."

"Well, I understand Lord Dudley is heading home tomorrow, so perhaps things will soon get back to normal. I certainly hope so."

"I do too. But I am starting to wonder, I admit, if we will ever have a normal life again."

"Some days, I think about that too. What with Mrs. Stillwater's strange behaviours and heading off to London every few days, when she never used to leave the estate at all?" She shook her head briefly. "Perhaps our days of normalcy are behind us."

"One part of our normal lives that will never change is your wisdom, my dear. I am grateful God blessed me with a wife such as you."

"Oh, go on with you, Mr. Kingsley." She blushed as she moved to his side and gave him a loving peck on the cheek. "Now, eat your dinner before it gets cold. I need to collect the tea tray from the parlour."

"Thank you, love. Would you give Lord Dudley a message from me?"

"A message?"

"Yes. But he needs to be alone when you tell him."

"Tell him what?"

"That I have delivered the package to his room, and that he will find it when he lays his head down to rest tonight."

She raised an eyebrow but then sighed and nodded her head. "I don't know what that means, but I'll tell him without asking for an explanation. Hopefully, he'll understand your words, at least."

"He will. Just say those exact words to him."

"Men and their secrets," muttered Mrs. Kingsley as she left the room. "Men and their secrets…"

Once she had gone, Kingsley finally managed to relax and began to eat his dinner.

***

A few minutes later, she was back with the tray.

"So, did you pass along my message?" he asked.

"I did," she said. "And he said to tell you thanks. That was all."

"That is all I needed to hear. It is up to him now."

"Mr. Kingsley, the two of you are not involved in something illegal, are you? I will not be a part of anything like that."

"No, dear, nothing illegal. A little… How shall I put this? … A little secretive, perhaps. Yes, that is the best way to describe what we are doing."

"As long as it is not against the law, I will ask no more questions of you. But I do long for days past when everything that was said and done was done openly and without secrets. A return to those days is all that I wish for."

Joining him at the table, she sank down into a chair and shook her head as if to clear away the cobwebs of secrecy and concern.

Kingsley reached across the table and patted her hand. "We will soon put it to rights, my love. Please have a little patience."

***

John could not wait to see what illuminating entries might await him in the ledger. He was thankful for the Kingsleys' help tonight. Without which he hadn't had any idea how he would have managed to retrieve or peruse the ledger. But here it was at last, right in his hands. When he got to his room, the first thing he had done was lock the door, not wanting Mrs. Stillwater to storm in unannounced. He was sure it would not be long before she noticed it was missing from her room.

Where did Kingsley even find it? he thought, then shook his head, realizing that it was irrelevant. All that mattered was what he would find within the ledger's pages. And it was time to find out exactly what that was.

***

An hour later, a relieved John put the ledger down. There was nothing within it to suggest that Mrs. Stillwater was stealing funds from the estate. The documentation simply confirmed her claim that the estate was in financial trouble and would go under if no extra funds could be found. This was exactly what John had been looking for, and what he would soon report back to his uncle, who would then be able to support the estate and bring it back to viability.

Then John could simply go back home and… What? Spend more time learning how to be a future earl and manage his own estate? Was that truly what he wanted to do for the rest of his life? He didn't think so, but how could he tell his father that? He thought about Australia and wondered what was happening on Sam and Bethany's station. Were they planting or were they harvesting? Was it lambing time or sheering time? He had not spent enough time with them to know all the different seasons of their lives. He would love to go back and be a part of it again, but that would have to wait for the future. Tonight, he just needed to get some sleep before he left the next day. *It would be good to get home.*

***

Even as John was drifting off to sleep, Cassandra was turning her room upside down, looking for the ledger after going to review it again before going to sleep. Where could it be? She had searched every corner of the room after discovering it was missing and could not believe that it was gone. Who would have taken it? And how did they know where it was hidden? The only person who knew where she kept her jewellery hidden was Mrs. Kingsley, and that was only by accident. Cassandra had not locked her door that day when she was reviewing her jewellery and wondering which pieces to sell off.

Mrs. Kingsley might have knocked before she entered the room, though Cassandra could not remember her doing so. At the time, it had not mattered. The Kingsleys were upright and loyal in their service to both her and the estate. She would never even suspect them of any wrongdoing ... but if not Mrs. Kingsley, then who could it have been? Lord Dudley had been with her all evening, right until they'd said goodnight and gone to their separate chambers.

She did remember Mrs. Kingsley whispering something to Lord Dudley just before he'd gone upstairs though. She had been too far away to catch what she was saying, but she had noted Lord Dudley's smile and nod, right before Mrs. Kingsley had headed back toward the kitchen. Had the Kingsleys' loyalties changed? Were they collaborating with Lord Dudley and the duke of Yardley now?

If that was the case, she knew that she could not stay. She would never willingly live in a house of lies again. Her life with Howard had been full of deception. She would rather live in poverty than some place where truth was unknown. So, if it proved to be the case here, she would have no choice but to fend for herself in London. Tomorrow morning, she would confront the Kingsleys with her suspicions, and if true, she would start looking for a new home.

With that plan in mind, Cassandra gave up her search for the ledger and got ready for bed. She doubted she would sleep, but she could rest her eyes at least. Her last thought before she fell asleep was that she needed to get her jewellery back from Mr. Brown. Her jewels were the only thing she owned now that might keep her from living on the streets of London. Well, her jewellery, and her dear, wonderful boys...

The next morning, John packed his saddlebags and got ready for the day, leaving the ledger where he had found it beneath his pillow. He had no further need of it. When he went downstairs, he found Mrs. Cassandra Stillwater already in the dining room.

"Morning, ma'am," he said, while going over to the sideboard and selecting several breakfast items.

"Good morning, Lord Dudley, and a lovely one for riding as well."

"Yes, it looks that way. Have you been out yet today?"

"No, but I've seen only clear skies and sunshine through the windows."

"Normally, clear skies and sunshine would indeed be a blessing, but with the ever-worsening drought conditions, I soon hope to wake up to cloudy skies and rain, should God deem it time for such a blessing."

"Well, Lord Dudley, after having experienced this drought for the past couple of years, I must admit that I am beginning to doubt His blessings upon us altogether."

"Never doubt, Mrs. Stillwater. He is still there. Perhaps, He is simply awaiting the persistence of our prayers before acting, wanting to hear them fully rather than simply acting on His own impulses."

"My prayers are few, Lord Dudley. And even when I prayed faithfully, God never did seem to act on my behalf. So, I have given up praying, except for the health and welfare of my sons, of course."

"I am sorry to hear that. I always take comfort in remembering that God's timing is often not the same as ours. So, perhaps, He will still answer your prayers ... in his own time."

"I suppose you are right." She seemed to think on this for a moment before continuing. "And I suppose that He did answer one of my prayers when he allowed my husband Howard to die in Australia, thus releasing me from his control and allowing me to live my life freely."

"And God also provided you with a home in the country, ma'am."

She smiled a bit crookedly at that. "I have found that to be something of a mixed blessing as of late, sir. And as such, I am unsure whether to thank Him for it."

"I'm sorry to hear that. My understanding was that you were happy at the estate."

"At first, I was. Of course, I was. But now that my boys are gone, I am all alone, left with nothing but responsibilities." She cleared her throat then, realising that she had likely said too much, and got to her feet. "But enough of that. I have no wish to weigh you down with my problems. Not when you need to eat and be on your way. Please don't let me delay your departure." She turned away and headed to the door.

Looking at her half-eaten breakfast, John called after her, "Mrs. Stillwater, you have not finished eating... Please come back. I assure you that I will not speak out of turn again."

"I am not hungry, sir," she said without turning back. "I will see you soon."

And then she was gone.

***

John finished eating and headed for the kitchen to say goodbye to the Kingsleys. They expressed sadness at his leaving but wished him a good trip home. While Mrs. Kingsley was in the other room, clearing off the sideboard, John told her husband where to find the ledger and thanked him for getting it for him the previous evening. When Kingsley asked about the entries, John shook his head and smiled. "Everything is in order. There is nothing there to suggest that Mrs. Stillwater is anything but honest. But I hope you understand that I needed to know for certain."

Kingsley agreed, and they said nothing more on the subject. Then John headed upstairs, grabbed his saddlebags, and hurried back down the front stairs. Kingsley had already called for his horse, so it was ready for him as soon as he stepped out the door. Once he was in the saddle, he looked back at Kingsley, and at Cassandra who now stood on the porch with him.

"Safe travels," she said simply.

John tipped his hat, turned his horse, and rode off towards the front gates.

***

Cassandra watched until he disappeared around a bend in the path. Then she turned to look at Kingsley. "I need to have a word with you."

Kingsley paled, understanding in an instant that his clandestine actions had been found out.

Chapter 9

"Where you like to meet, ma'am?"

"In the kitchen?" she suggested.

"I would rather not involve my wife. She had nothing to do with what occurred."

"Really? That is hard to believe, Kingsley. I thought you and your wife shared everything ... that you had no secrets from each other."

"Normally, we don't, Mrs. Stillwater, but in this case, yes, I kept it from her."

"Well... We can talk in the morning parlour, say, in about fifteen minutes."

"Good, ma'am. I'll have the footman stay by the front door, in case we have guests, and I will tell my wife where I am for the next while."

"I will see you then," said Cassandra, walking into the house and up to her room. She needed time to calm her nerves before talking to Kingsley. He had almost admitted his guilt already, but she needed to hear why he had done it. That was all she wanted, an explanation for his disloyalty to her. Once they got past that, she would decide what steps to take next. She knew she could not dismiss the Kingsleys. The estate held their lifetime contract, so she was powerless to let them go. But how could she trust them again if they had gone against her by stealing her ledger and giving it to Lord Dudley? If she could not discharge them, would she need to leave? She would wait to hear Kingsley's viewpoint before considering making such a drastic life change.

A few minutes later, she descended the stairs and went to the morning parlour. Kingsley was already there, standing in an uneasy pose. Cassandra went over to her favourite chair by the window, and then suggested that he sit across from her. He declined, saying he would rather stand.

"Well," said Cassandra with brusque nod, "but if you get tired, you are welcome to sit down."

He thanked her and said that he would keep that in mind, but for the moment, he preferred standing.

"I believe you know why I asked you to meet with me," Cassandra said. "But just to make sure we are talking about the same matter; would you tell me why you think you are here?"

Kingsley drew a deep breath before saying, "Does it have to do with the estate ledger, ma'am?"

"It does."

"I thought so. I admit to taking it from your room last evening and giving it to Lord Dudley to review."

"How did you know where to find it?"

"I didn't at first. But then I remembered my wife telling me about where you hid your jewellery, so I thought perhaps the ledger would be in the same spot. And it was."

"I had forgotten that Mrs. Kingsley surprised me that one morning when I had my jewellery out and was looking at it. I am sure she told you about my hiding place, but why would you look there for the ledger? Why, Kingsley?"

"Because of the way you have been acting of late, ma'am, as if you had something to hide."

"It was because of my recent behaviours?"

"Yes, and also because you are so protective of the ledger. You never allow anyone to touch it, let alone see what is written inside. Begging your pardon, ma'am, but we also have an interest in how the estate is doing financially."

"You are right, Kingsley. I can see how my actions would seem suspicious. But why did you give the ledger to Lord Dudley? He is not a part of our family here."

"No, but he wanted to make sure that everything was legitimate before he left for home. And reviewing the ledger would give him reassurance you were not stealing funds from the estate, which this morning, he was pleased to tell me that you were not."

"Lord Dudley thought I was taking money from the estate?"

"It was only a thought, ma'am."

"Why would he think such a thing of me?"

"Because of the finances of the estate."

"He thought I was stealing money ... for what purpose?"

"That was something neither of us could determine, ma'am."

"I wish he were still here, and I would set him straight, once and for all. But I will tell you, Kingsley, I have not, nor would I ever, steal money from this place. I am hurt that you would think I could do such a thing."

"Well, your past actions with Bethany gave us cause to think you could be lying about needing money."

"So, because I made one dreadful mistake when I lied about Bethany stealing my necklace, I am now branded a liar for all time?"

"It was only a thought, ma'am. You have been acting rather secretive as of late. Even your trips to London were quite out of the norm for you."

"My trips to London were to save the estate, not destroy it, Kingsley. Even though I don't owe you an explanation, I will tell you anyway. I went to London the first time to sell some of my jewellery so we could buy feed for our animals this winter. My last trip was to Mr. Brown's office. He is going to attempt to get us a loan using my jewellery as collateral. I am not my husband. I am trying to save the estate for Bethany, not destroy it."

"You would sell your jewellery to keep the estate from going under?"

"Yes."

"Oh, Mrs. Stillwater, I am so sorry. But why did you not say anything? It would have prevented all of this speculation about your recent actions."

"Because I wanted to do it without involving the Yardleys. It is my problem. I caused it, and I need to fix it, not run to the duke for help."

"Ma'am, you did not cause the problem. The drought has put us in this situation, not you."

"It is my problem, Kingsley. I promised to manage the estate for Bethany and am failing to do so. I want to make it better, not have to tell her that her estate is bankrupt."

Kingsley bowed his head. He had misjudged his mistress. He agreed with her it was a shame Lord Dudley had left the estate. Had he not, they could have cleared up this whole situation. But what could they do now? He was on his way home, likely to tell the duke of his findings. There was nothing they could do but wait until he returned, or they had a visit from the duke. The latter would likely happen soon.

"Ma'am," he said, "is there anything I can do to make up for misjudging you?"

"No, I don't think so. We cannot undo what has been done. We will now have to wait and see if we receive a visit from the duke. Also, we cannot do anything about our finances until we hear about the loan. Hopefully, that news will come soon."

"I agree, ma'am. Is there anything else you wished to speak to me about before I go back to my duties?"

"Only this. The next time you suspect something, either from my words or my actions, come to me. Please do not go behind my back again."

"I won't, ma'am. You have my word on that."

"Good. That is all for now."

"Thank you. I will return to my post now," he said, turning and walking out the door.

***

Cassandra took a deep breath. That had been a hard conversation, but a much needed one. Now she knew what had been transpiring in the past few days. If only Lord Dudley were still here. She would have a few choice words for him as well. But he had left, and now all she could do was wait—wait for the duke to arrive, which she was sure he would, and wait on the news from Mr. Brown. There was nothing else she could do. She had to be patient.

***

She received the letter from Mr. Brown a few days later. But when she started reading, it was nothing she had expected...

Chapter 10

Dear Mrs. Stillwater,

I am sorry to be the bearer of ill tidings, but such is the case today. I took your request for a loan to several reputable establishments, none of which will loan you the funds you require. Your jewellery cannot stand as collateral, only land and buildings are admissible. I told the bank managers you could not put up the estate as collateral because you were not the owner of the property. They still declined to do business with me.

So, unless you are willing for me to find another source of funds, such as, I even hate to write the words, a loan shark, we have no further options. Given your late husband's experiences with them, I do not think you wish me to go that route, but I am your servant in this matter.

Please advise me how you would like me to proceed.

Your servant,
Edwin Brown
Solicitor

Cassandra shuddered at the thought of approaching a loan shark for money. She had had far too much contact with them while Howard was alive. No, she would never consider going that way, even to fund the estate. It devastated her that the banks would not loan her money. She understood their reasoning but had hoped for a positive outcome. Now, what was she to do? She was running out of options, and she was sure the duke would arrive soon to offer his support. It looked now like that was the only way to save the estate from her mismanagement. Perhaps when he arrived, she would ask him to secure another manager, so she could leave and head back to the city to live. But first, she needed to reply to Mr. Brown and inform him what to do next. So, she went to her desk, pulled out a piece of parchment, inked her quill, and wrote,

Dear Mr. Brown...

Finishing the letter, she put it in an envelope and sealed it. She would give it to Kingsley when she went for lunch, along with the news, so there would be no more secrets between them. She was sure he had seen the envelope from the solicitor, and so would be waiting anxiously to see what the letter had said. The contents would disappoint him as well.

***

She was not wrong about Kingsley's reaction. It shocked him when she revealed what Mr. Brown had written to her.

"What will you do now, ma'am?"

"I don't know. Perhaps go back to my original plan and sell some of my jewellery. That would at least give money to look after the bills over the winter."

"Sell your jewellery? But that is your security, is it not? To ensure that you would never be without funds?"

"If I don't help the estate survive, Kingsley, I won't have a home. So, if it is a choice between saving my jewellery or saving the estate, I prefer to do the latter."

"Uh, my missus and I have been talking, ma'am. We have a bit of money saved up. We could help you."

"No, I could not take your money. You need to save it. There may come a day when you need it."

"What is the difference between you selling your jewellery or us giving you money, ma'am?"

"The difference is that I am responsible for this issue. Therefore, I need to look after solving it."

"I have said this before but it bears repeating: You are not responsible for the drought. God has allowed it for reasons of His own. We don't know what those are, and may never know, but we can trust in His goodness. We need to pray and ask Him for a solution that hopefully does not include you selling your security."

"Are we not to put our security in God, and not in wealth, Kingsley? If I hang onto my jewels, am I not saying that they are my refuge, instead of trusting in Him?"

"You are right, ma'am. I had not thought of it that way."

"Perhaps this is a test of my faith. God wants to see if I trust His promises or am I still managing everything on my own. I am afraid that often, even today, my faith is weak, and I look for human solutions rather than giving my problems to God and asking Him to fix them."

"I see what you are saying. Yes, prayer is the answer. Let God deal with the issue and fix the problem."

"Thank you, Kingsley. You have opened my eyes. Even if I end up selling my jewellery, it will be because of my trust in God to look after my future and not my lack of faith in His ability to look after the estate. I have instructed Mr. Brown to send my jewellery back to me, rather than take them to Mr. White. So, let's wait on God and see what He has for us."

"I agree, ma'am. Mrs. Kingsley and I will pray with you for God's solution. I look forward to seeing His answer."

Cassandra nodded, and they parted ways, she to go up to her bedroom to pray and he to join his wife in the kitchen for prayer. Hopefully, the prayers would bring answers from above.

***

The answer came in the person of the Duke of Yardley. He arrived a few days later to meet with Cassandra and the farm steward. From his perspective, there was only one solution: He would bear the cost of shoring up the estate until it was viable again.

Cassandra had known that this would be his answer, and perhaps it was God's answer as well. But she only had one request: If he was going to finance the estate, then he needed to find a new manager. She did not want to continue in that role. Her request shocked him.

"Cassandra, are you sure?"

"Yes. I am not capable of managing such a large estate. That has become obvious to me over the past few months."

"A situation such as this does not reflect upon your management skills. It could happen to any of us."

"Has it happened to your estate, Your Grace?"

"No, but we are fortunate that God has blessed us in other ventures, so we have the means to weather this crisis."

"Well, we do not, and I am exhausted. I do not eat, and I do not sleep. My whole life revolves around this issue. I need to be relieved of my responsibility as soon as possible."

"If you insist. I will search for a suitable manager once I return home. In the meantime, I will have my banker release funds to you so you can purchase whatever you need for the estate. I will send a note to London and ask them to come out and meet with you soon. Is that satisfactory?"

"Yes, Your Grace. I will await their visit. Thank you for taking my request seriously."

"I am only doing it because you ask it of me. I have no doubts about your abilities. But it is a tremendous responsibility, as you say, and perhaps needs another manager."

"I look forward to handing over the estate management. I hope you can find someone soon to replace me."

"Very well. If you are set on this action. Now, if you have paper and an inked quill, I will send a message to my bank regarding funds. Do you have someone who can take it in, so we don't have to rely on the post?"

"Yes, one of our footmen can ride in this afternoon if you give me the direction of your bank. I will find the writing items for you now." Cassandra then headed upstairs to get a sharpened quill, an inkpot, and some parchment for the duke. Coming back downstairs, she directed him to a small writing table in the corner of the front parlour where they had been meeting. Before he sat down to write his note, she asked, "Will there be anything else?"

"No, I don't believe so. You are free to go about your own activities now."

She thanked him, and then dismissed the farm steward. After that, she headed to the foyer to ask Kingsley to find a horse and rider to take the duke's message to his London bank. He agreed and sent a footman to the stables to saddle a horse and bring it back to the front porch. While the footman was gone, Cassandra updated Kingsley on her conversation with the duke.

"So, is he going to get the funds, ma'am?"

"Yes, we should expect a visit from the banker soon."

"That will be good, will it not? Now, you don't have to worry about selling your jewellery."

"Or you and Mrs. Kingsley giving up some of your savings for the estate."

"God's answer was good, was it not?"

"It would not have been my way, Kingsley, but His wisdom is far greater than mine, so we shall have to accept His answer."

Kingsley was about to reply when the duke emerged from the parlour, sealed envelope in hand.

"Ah, Kingsley, the person I needed to see. Can you see this letter gets to London today?" he asked, handing him the envelope.

"Yes, Your Grace. Mrs. Stillwater has already told me that your letter needs to go post haste to London. A horse is being saddled at this moment, and a footman will ride immediately to the city."

"Excellent," said the duke. Then he turned to Cassandra. "My dear lady, your worries should soon be over. And as per your request, I will begin looking for an estate manager as soon as I get home. Is there anything else I can help you with today?"

"No, Your Grace. Thank you for your generosity. I will sleep better at night now that I don't have to worry about the estate."

"You should never have had to worry about it. We should have installed a farm manager as soon as your husband passed away; it was our fault, not yours. Soon, you will just be the lady of the manor. You can enjoy your life in the country without the extra responsibilities. Now, if there is nothing more, I will head back to Yardley. It has been good to see you, Mrs. Stillwater, and you too, Kingsley. We will stay in touch." With that, the duke took his leave of them, and soon his carriage was rolling down the lane towards the gates.

After it was out of sight, and the footman was on the way to London with the letter, Kingsley turned to Cassandra. "Ma'am, what did the duke mean when he said he would look for an estate manager? Is he replacing you?"

"Yes, but only at my request, Kingsley. Otherwise, things will remain the same."

"You requested it?"

"Yes. It is not a role suited to me. I aspire to be rid of the responsibilities."

"Do you know who he has in mind to replace you?"

"No. He said he would look into it as soon as he returned home. Perhaps he plans to ask someone living there to move over."

Kingsley frowned. "Someone like Lord Dudley, perhaps?"

"Oh, I hope not. I had not thought of him."

"From the duke's perspective, he would be the perfect candidate. He is unattached. He knows the estate. He is—"

"A thief and a liar."

"Mrs. Stillwater!"

"All right, perhaps that was a bit harsh, but I have no sympathy for the man. If he comes, I am leaving."

"Perhaps the two of you got off to a poor start, ma'am. I am sure this time would be different."

"Maybe. But if we pray, mayhap God will send another man, someone I can tolerate."

"He answered our prayers for the estate monies. Now, we will pray for the new manager."

"Yes, I will," said Cassandra, before she walked back into the house. "I will pray that he is short, fat, and ugly. Oh no, that was what Howard looked like. I only pray he is not tall, dark, and handsome of face. Yes, that should rule out Lord Dudley. Please, God, make it so!"

Kingsley followed behind her, shaking his head. *A new manager...* That was something he had not seen coming. Now, what would Mrs. Stillwater do?

***

An hour later, instead of going straight home, the duke decided to visit his nephew at Dudley Manor. Throughout his trip, while mulling over candidates to manage Stillwater Estate, the only potential person he could come up with was John. It made sense. John was presently unattached to any of the family holdings. He had a working knowledge of the estate after his recent stay there. He got on well with the staff and the tenants, or at least, that is what he had told his uncle when he'd returned from his visit. And he and Mrs. Stillwater were ... well, if not on the best of terms, they were at least speaking to each other. John had not been sure if she would invite him back if she ever found out about the ledger. Hopefully, that would never come to light. So, other than that bit of disheartening information, the duke thought John will be an ideal choice to take over as manager. *Now, to convince John of that.*

Arriving at Dudley Manor, Heddington informed him that John was at home, and that he would ask him to attend the duke in the front parlour. A few minutes later, John came in.

"Uncle Douglas, what a pleasant surprise. You wished to see me?"

"Yes, John. Please come in and sit down. I have a proposal for you."

"A proposal? Of what sort? Has some young lady asked for my hand in marriage?" He laughed.

His uncle chuckled at that. "No. Not that kind of proposal. A business proposal."

"A business proposal? You have me intrigued. Please go on."

The duke told him of his visit to Stillwater Estate earlier that day, and Cassandra's request to be replaced as the estate manager. "I have been mulling over candidates for the position, and the only suitable one is you, my boy. Would you consider taking on that responsibility?"

"Me? Why me?"

The duke started listing off the reasons John would suit the position, ending with, "And your father can manage Dudley Estate without your help. So, what do you think?"

"I don't know. I don't know if Mrs. Stillwater will accept me. Do you think she would?"

"She was the one who asked for a new manager, John, leaving it up to me to choose one. If she does not wish to continue in the role, I don't think she has a say in the matter."

"I suppose not. May I talk it over with Father this evening and get back to you tomorrow with my answer?"

"You may. I have no plans to be away tomorrow, so you will find me at home."

"Good. I will pray about it and talk to my parents tonight. Then I will give you my response tomorrow."

"Thank you, John. I appreciate you even considering this. I know that you are still finding your place now that you are back in England. Perhaps this will help you decide."

"Perhaps. It would surely give me some practical experience for the future when I take over from Father."

"It would. Now, I must be off home. Margaret will be expecting me. I look forward to seeing you tomorrow." The duke got up from his chair and headed for the door, followed by John.

"It was good to see you, Uncle Douglas," he said. "Say hello to Aunt Margaret for me."

The duke said that he would, and then headed to his waiting carriage. John waited by the door until the carriage had rolled away. Then he went inside and headed upstairs to his room. He needed time to think and pray before speaking to his parents. This was a major decision, much more so than agreeing to visit Stillwater for a few days. If not a lifetime commitment, this would certainly be a long-term one. But what would that mean for his plans for Australia? If he took the job, would he have to put off moving there? That thought did not sit well with John. He wanted to get on with life sooner rather than later, and a hiatus at Stillwater Estate had not been in his plans. But maybe it was in God's plans for him. The only way to find out was to pray. So, he closed his eyes and did that.

***

That evening, after dinner, he told his parents what the duke had requested of him. While surprised about Cassandra's decision to relinquish the role of manager, they were in favour of him taking on the responsibility. John said that he would do it for a time, but not for the rest of his life. Perhaps while he was there, he could search out a new manager, one who would stay for the long term, but it would not be him.

His parents agreed with his plans. After all, soon he would take over Dudley Estate. He did not need to be managing two properties that were many miles apart.

John did not mention his plans for Australia. Nothing was in place yet, so he did not want to upset his parents. The time for that would come soon enough.

With a settled heart and mind, he went to bed that night, thanking God for His wisdom in guiding him to this decision. It was the right one. At least for now...

Chapter 11

The next day, John rode over to give the duke the news. When he arrived, the duke was in his study. Instead of having the butler announce him, John strode to the study and knocked on the heavy, oak door.

"Yes?"

"Uncle Douglas, it's me, John."

"Come in, my boy!"

John walked in, and the duke came from around the other side of the desk to grip his hand. "Please, have a seat," he said, gesturing to the large, dark leather chairs beside the fireplace. When they both were sitting down, the duke got to the point. "Well, shall I presume you are here to give me an answer?"

"Yes, I am," he said. "I will manage the Stillwater Estate for the next year, but I will not commit past that time."

"Thank you. Much can happen in a year, so even that length of time suits me. You, of course, will receive the same salary as Mrs. Stillwater does. Is that satisfactory to you?"

"Does that include my room and meals, or am I to pay out of pocket for them?"

"Your meals and accommodations are not your concern. They will come out of the estate funds."

"If they come out of the monies from the estate, where is my salary coming from?"

"From me. I suppose you could say I am paying for everything. I have instructed my bank to forward any necessary funds to the estate, to buy animal feed, flour, and other necessities for the manor and tenants, and seed for next spring's planting. Those funds should arrive within the next week so that you can get on with the needed purchases."

"You are a generous man, Uncle Douglas. I applaud you."

"I am only doing what the Good Book tells me to do. The Bible contains many references that tell the blessed ones to share their blessings with the less fortunate. I would not be faithful as a Christian if I did not do my part to help others."

"I will remember those words and hopefully emulate your actions in the coming years."

"Read the Bible and follow Christ's commands. That is all God asks of you."

"I will. Thank you for the lesson."

"You are welcome. Now, getting back to your new role. When can you start?"

"I will go soon, perhaps in the next day or so. I aspire to be there when the funds arrive, so I can be involved right from the beginning."

"That's a plan. Would you like me to send a message to Mrs. Stillwater and let her know our plans?"

"No, it is better she is unaware of my arrival date. Because of my previous words and actions, she might not be too happy with your selection of new manager. Better for me to tell her myself when I get there."

"Whatever you think is best. Let me know if there is anything either you, or the estate, need in the future. Contact me with any concerns."

"I will. Thank you for putting your trust in me. I hope I don't let you down."

"I am sure you will do a fine job. And I will pray that you and Mrs. Stillwater find a rapport during your tenure."

"Please do pray. I'd appreciate it."

"Good. Now, do you have time for a morning coffee with me? It is just about time," said the duke, looking at the wall clock.

"I do. Perhaps Aunt Margaret would like to join us. Is she aware of what I am going to do?"

"I said nothing to her in case you turned me down. But I am sure she would like to see you and hear about your plans. Let's go find her."

The two men left the study and headed down the hall towards the morning parlour where they were sure they would find the duchess. Passing by a footman, the duke asked for a tray of tea and coffee to be brought down so that the three of them could enjoy a lovely visit—perhaps one of the last ones before John left for Stillwater.

***

John was busy the next few days, getting his belongings together. This time, he needed a trunk full of clothes. When he had gone to Australia, he had left all his more formal attire behind. But seeing that he would now be meeting with bankers, solicitors, etc., when he was occasionally in town, he would need to dress up a bit. Sorting through his clothes, he found that many of them did not fit well, either in the shoulders and chest, where his muscles had developed, or in the other regions where he had slimmed down. He found a few outfits he could still wear, but it looked like he would need to head to the tailor in London soon to refit his wardrobe. He also needed more clothes suitable for helping Mr. Wiley, as he did not intend to be a hands-off manager. He anxiously hoped that they would feel at ease, considering his suspicion that neither Mrs. Stillwater nor her deceased husband, Howard, had operated in such a manner. Sam and Bethany managed their station that way though, and John wanted to copy this practice and see how it went over in England. It would be an interesting experiment if nothing else.

Soon, he had packed his trunk and was ready to leave. He put a few things in his saddlebags to tide him over until the carriage with his belongings arrived. Saying goodbye to his parents, he headed out the gate and started down the road. It might not be the beginning of his new life in Australia, but at least he was doing something worthwhile. He was on his own. He hoped he didn't mess it up.

***

Cassandra, too, was moving on, though her moves were much more subtle, so as not to alert the Kingsleys to her plans. At night, when the house was quiet, she would pull her dresses out of the wardrobe to assess their worthiness to travel with her. Most of them were satisfactory, so she put them to one side, and left the others hanging as they were. She did the same with her slippers and accessories. Of course, her jewellery would come with her. That was a given. But she sorted everything else based on its suitability to a new life in London. She did not know what she would do there or where she would live. The rented townhouse she had shared with Howard and her sons was not a possibility for a couple of reasons: first, because other tenants had moved in as soon as she'd moved out five years ago; and second, because she did not want to go back to that neighbourhood and all the terrible memories attached to it.

No, she would have to find somewhere else to live, somewhere genteel but not ostentatious. She did not need that. It would be best if she could both live and work in the same house. Perhaps she would qualify as a housekeeper. She knew how to manage a home and a household budget. That she could do. She was too old to be a housemaid. Most of them were young girls with lots of energy. If she had to, she would do that, of course, but she doubted anyone would hire her for that position. As soon as she got to London, she would settle in at the YWCA before heading out and looking for a job. Now, if only that new manager would arrive so that she could get on with her new life.

***

The new manager was close. In fact, he was just down the road. John stopped his horse at a nearby creek to let him drink while he looked after his own needs. After that, he tethered the horse to a tree, and after spreading out a blanket to cover the dirt, lay back with his hands under his head to stare at the sky. Why was he stalling? If he was honest with himself, it was because of the way he had left the estate only a few weeks earlier. He had deceived Mrs. Stillwater, and he was not feeling happy about that. He would have to confess what he had done, as soon as he arrived, so they could start their working relationship with a clean slate. God had forgiven him when he repented of his sin and asked for forgiveness. Now it was time to do the same with Mrs. Stillwater. *Hopefully, she will be as forgiving as God was.* If not, they would be off to a rocky start in their new relationship.

But time was a-wasting. So, John jumped up, brushed himself off, shook out the blanket before refolding it and putting it in a saddlebag. Then he untied his horse, remounted, and started down the road once more. It was time to begin anew.

***

John arrived at the manor within minutes of remounting his horse. He tied his horse to the post, quickly climbed the steps, crossed the porch, and knocked on the door.

It opened soon after his knock, and Kingsley appeared in the door frame. Seeing who it was, he smiled. "Lord Dudley, what a lovely surprise. Please come in," he said, opening the door to its full extent.

"Thank you, Kingsley. How are you today?"

"Well, sir. And you?"

"Can't complain."

"Excellent." He noted John's saddlebags then, hanging from his shoulder. "Are you here for another visit?"

"You could say that. It all depends on your mistress and how she reacts to my presence. My visit could either be short or extended. It is all up to her."

Not sure what to make of John's words, but knowing it was not his place to question him, Kingsley just nodded. "In that case, can I relieve you of your bags and take you down to see Mrs. Stillwater?"

"Perhaps we will leave the bags here until Mrs. Stillwater and I have talked. Then if things go well between us, you can have a footman take them up to a guest room for me."

"I will do that, sir. Do you wish to be announced?"

"No, I presume, at this time of day, that she is in the morning parlour?"

"She is. I took a tray of tea down to her. Would you like me to have Molly bring an extra cup for you?"

"In a few moments, perhaps. I wish to test Mrs. Stillwater's reaction to me before I may have tea with her."

"Good, sir. I will be in the hallway if you don't mind. Then I will know what to do for tea."

"That sounds like a plan, Kingsley. How have things been since my uncle visited?"

"There is an air of tension, sir, which was not there previously. I don't know if it relates to your uncle's visit or to what the mistress determined just after you left for home."

"Oh, what was that?"

"That you and I conspired against her to obtain the estate ledger without her permission. Mrs. Stillwater confronted me as soon as you had ridden through the gates. I had no option but to confess what we had done."

"I am sorry you had to endure her displeasure, Kingsley, when you were only aiding me. Was she angry?"

"Quite. But her temper cooled quickly after I apologised for my actions."

"I am glad she did not retain her anger. That gives me a sense of what kind of reaction I can expect when she sees me. Perhaps it is good that I announce myself to her."

"It has been a while since the incident, sir, so perhaps she has forgiven you. But we will soon know."

"Yes, we will. Wish me luck, Kingsley. I am going to need it if I am to remain here."

"I will pray for you, sir."

"Thank you. I can use God's help." John grimaced, then turned and walked down the hall towards the parlour, with Kingsley following close behind him.

When he reached the parlour door, John took a deep breath before striding in. "Good morning, Mrs. Stillwater. Isn't it a lovely day?"

***

Cassandra gasped. Her nightmare was now her reality. He was here. What was she to do now?

"Lord Dudley... What a ... uh, surprise. I did not expect to see you this morning. Have you come for another visit?" Cassandra got up, walked across the room, and extended her hand.

John took her hand and shook it gently before releasing it. "That depends on you, dear lady."

"Me? Whatever do you mean?"

John took another deep breath. This was the moment of truth. "I am here as the new estate manager ... if you will accept me."

He had just confirmed her worst fears. The duke had appointed his nephew to oversee the estate, and everything connected to it, including herself. Did she really have any choice in the matter?

"I see," she said. "The duke acted quickly to relieve me of my duties."

"I understand it was upon your request, Mrs. Stillwater. Otherwise, he would not have done so."

"That is true. I asked him to find another estate manager, and now, here you are. Well, we will get you settled so you can begin your duties." Cassandra started to move past him, but John held up a hand.

"Before we do that, ma'am, we should talk about some issues, so we can begin with a good working relationship."

"What issues, Lord Dudley?" Cassandra retreated a couple of steps.

"I am sure you are aware of what I am speaking about, but I will clarify my words to you. May we sit and have a cup of tea while we talk?"

"If you wish, sir," she said, moving to pull a cord beside the small table.

Kingsley immediately appeared in the doorway. "Yes, ma'am. What can I do for you?"

Suspicious about his quick appearance, but not wanting to say anything about it, Cassandra said, "Lord Dudley is joining me for tea. Would you have Molly bring another cup for him?"

"Yes, Mrs. Stillwater. I'll get on that right away," he said, before turning and leaving the room.

Cassandra directed John to a chair across the small table from where she had been seated. Then she said again, "Now, Lord Dudley, what issues do we need to discuss?"

Not knowing exactly how to start this difficult conversation, John plunged right in. "It's about what I did when I last visited here, Mrs. Stillwater."

"Oh, and what was that?" she asked, knowing full well where he was heading.

"I got your estate book in a rather unethical way and reviewed it."

"Is that how you describe theft, Lord Dudley?"

"I don't know if I would put it that way, Mrs. Stillwater. I always planned to give the ledger back to you once I had reviewed it."

"Theft is theft, sir. You stole the book from my room. For what purpose did you need to see it?"

"To convince myself that you were not skimming money from the estate for your personal use."

"Did I look, or act, like someone who would do such a thing, sir?"

"No, but looks can be deceiving. Also, you were so secretive about the ledger that it made me wonder why that might be."

"Perhaps I acted in such a way, sir, but you had no reason to see the book. You were only here to observe and perhaps give suggestions regarding dryland farming. You had no right to review the ledger."

"I know. I am here to apologise for my actions and ask for your forgiveness. Will you do that for me?"

"As a Christian, I must forgive you, sir, but my trust in you is gone. I no longer consider you a worthy man."

John winced. *That hurt ... and it does not bode well for our relationship in the future. I will have to work to earn her trust once more.* "Thank you for your forgiveness, Mrs. Stillwater. I will endeavour to regain your trust in me."

I won't be here long enough for you to do that, thought Cassandra. *As soon as I can, I will head into London and start a new life, far away from you.* "You will have to work hard, Lord Dudley. I don't trust easily, and it's difficult to rebuild that trust once it is broken."

John nodded. At least now they had said the words and could go from here. He had nothing more to say.

Neither did Cassandra, who simply wanted out of his presence. "Is there anything else, Lord Dudley? If not, I will have Kingsley show you to your room. Will the room you previously occupied be satisfactory for a long-term visit?"

"Yes, ma'am. Thank you for hearing me out. I did not want to start our working relationship with that issue hanging over our heads."

"It is good to have the conversation out of the way. Now, if you will excuse me," she said, getting up from her chair, "I need to inform the staff of your presence and your new position within the estate. Or did you want to do that?"

"No, I am fine with you telling them, ma'am." John also rose to stand with her.

"Good. I will also let Mrs. Kingsley know that there will be another person dining with me today, and in the future. Do you have any preferences as to where we take our meals?"

"I will leave the household matters in your capable hands. My primary responsibility will be outside these walls."

"Then I will leave you to unpack," she said, heading towards the door. "I will see you at lunchtime."

"Good. My trunk will arrive by carriage soon. I only have a few things with me in my saddlebags. But I will take this time to store them away in my room."

"The footman could do that for you. You only have to ask for help."

"I am used to doing for myself, Mrs. Stillwater. There were few servants on Sam and Bethany's sheep station, and I quite enjoyed looking after my own needs."

"Whatever you prefer, Lord Dudley. It is up to you. Now, please excuse me," she said, before turning and walking out of the room, leaving John to wonder how the two of them would get along. A chill ran down his spine. While the lady had claimed to have forgiven him, her actions in no way matched her words. His new life at Stillwater Estate had begun with an icy reception indeed.

***

Kingsley was waiting for John when he exited the parlour. "How did it go, sir? Are you staying?"

"Yes, I am staying. As to how it went, let's say that Mrs. Stillwater and I talked about my previous behaviours, and she has forgiven me, at least in word. Her attitude says otherwise, though, so we will have to see how we get on."

"I am glad you will be with us and managing the estate. It has been a burden on the mistress, especially during the past year. She will be relieved that someone else is now shouldering the responsibility."

"As it was her decision to step away from the position, she should be, Kingsley. I am not sure if that is how she is feeling though, especially with me taking over."

"But you are the perfect one for the job. You know the estate, and the issues, so I cannot think why Mrs. Stillwater would have a problem with you managing it."

"I think it relates to my past behaviour and the fact that I am closely connected to the Duke of Yardley. She seems to have a problem with both."

"Well, hopefully, that will diminish when she sees what a fine job you are doing, sir. In the meantime, I will continue to pray for her acceptance of you."

"Thank you, Kingsley. Now, I will take my saddlebags upstairs and get my things stowed away. Then I will head out to the barns, find Mr. Wiley, and let him know about the change in leadership."

"I am sure he will be delighted to hear the news. I believe Mrs. Stillwater was going to inform my wife of your presence, so I will stay at my post, unless you have need of my services upstairs."

"No, there are few things in my bags," John said. "I can put them away. My trunk will arrive by carriage later this afternoon. If the footmen can put it in my room, I will also put those clothes away myself. I am used to looking after my own needs."

"Good, sir. I will keep an eye out for the carriage and do as you request," said Kingsley when they reached the foyer. Then he took up his post beside the door once again, and John headed upstairs to unpack before he headed to the barns.

***

After sending a message to the manor at noon, John ate lunch with Jack Wiley. The farm steward smiled when he saw John and was delighted to hear that he was the new estate manager. Not that he had anything against Mrs. Stillwater, the steward was quick to assure John. It was just easier for him to speak with another man. That way, he did not have to mind his speech or manners. John told Jack he understood and that it would not offend him if either Jack's speech or manners slipped while they were together. That set the stage for a friendly hour of conversation. Jack offered to share his lunch with John, which he was pleased to accept as he was reluctant to head back to the manor and eat with Mrs. Stillwater. Dinner would come soon enough.

***

Cassandra, too, was pleased to eat alone. It gave her more time to think and plan her future, or lack thereof. John's surprising arrival that morning had only confirmed her need to leave. She had most of her clothing sorted, so it would not take long to pack. She believed that she could be ready to leave the next morning. There was no point in staying. Regardless of what Lord Dudley thought, they would never have any kind of relationship, working or otherwise. And so, it was best for both of them, and for the estate, that she left. This evening, after dinner, she would ask Kingsley to have a carriage readied for her tomorrow morning. With all her recent trips to the city, it should not surprise him at yet another venture to London. Tomorrow morning, she would come down after breakfast, say her farewells to Lord Dudley and the staff, and be off. Yes, that would work.

Then she would have the driver take her to the YWCA boarding house. If they had a room available for her, she would stay there until she found suitable employment and accommodations elsewhere. Once that was done, she would let her sons know where she was situated, so they could visit her. She knew they would have a lot of questions, but she also knew they would honour her request for privacy and not tell anyone where she was living or working. Until she found a position, she could always sell some jewellery to Mr. White. The money from those sales would keep her for quite a while.

Having solidified her plans, Cassandra spent the afternoon, as usual, in the front parlour. Only now, she did not work on the estate ledger; that was now Lord Dudley's concerns. So, she did what most ladies of a manor did: She sat and worked on her embroidery. When her eyes tired, she went upstairs and lay down on her bed to rest, something she had not done in a long time. As soon as she lay down, she fell into a deep and dreamless sleep, only awakening when someone knocked on her bedroom door.

"Mrs. Stillwater?" It was Mrs. Kingsley, calling from the hallway. "Are you all right, ma'am?"

"Yes," Cassandra responded. "What time is it?"

"Past teatime. Half four o'clock."

"Half four? Oh, my goodness, I did not mean to sleep, only to rest my eyes a bit. Thank you for waking me up, Mrs. Kingsley. I will be down for tea shortly."

"Good, ma'am. I will get the kettle boiling."

Cassandra listened to the woman's footsteps fading as she hurried to the kitchen staircase.

Half four? I have not napped that long in ... well, I can't remember if I have ever done that, thought Cassandra. She got up, splashed some water on her face, and straightened her wrinkled gown. When that did not work, she went over to the wardrobe and pulled out one of the gowns that she planned to leave behind. *Might as well get one more day's use out of it.* She quickly changed into the new gown, and after fixing her hair, she left her bedroom and walked down to the front parlour. When she got there, she found Lord Dudley already seated beside the small table, upon which sat the tea tray. She wondered if her last memories of this place would now always include him.

She pasted on a smile. "Good afternoon, sir. I am sorry you had to wait for your tea. You could have started without me."

"I arrived only a few moments ago. I have been out with Mr. Wiley all afternoon, so I have not been waiting on you."

"That's good. I was resting my eyes for a few minutes and did not realise how late it was. Now," she said as she settled herself across from him, "shall I pour?"

John agreed. Kingsley had given him a different reason for Mrs. Stillwater's late appearance for tea. He wondered why she could not admit that she had taken a nap, as there was no harm in it. She had changed her gown, but her hair seemed to have been hastily put up. However, none of this was his affair, so he would not call her out on her small deception.

They took their tea largely in silence. They occasionally commented on the estate or the weather, but then the conversation would quickly die again. John was glad when he took the last sip of his tea and finished his biscuit. He hoped this sort of tense silences would not become a trend for all their meals together. If it did, he would be better off eating on his own, either in his room or with Mr. Wiley. Anything would be better than this silence.

As soon as he had finished, he excused himself and headed upstairs. Cassandra breathed a sigh of relief. She, too, had felt the tension in their silence. But she only had one more meal to endure with him, and then she would be free. *Only dinner tonight.* She frowned slightly, wondering why that thought brought a tinge of sadness as opposed to joy. Perhaps because she was still shaking off the last vestiges of her sleepiness. Yes, that was it. It could be nothing else. Cassandra got up, shook herself, and then she too headed upstairs until dinnertime.

***

Dinner that evening was a repeat of teatime. The only sounds were those of the footman serving or removing plates from the table. Kingsley stood in the room, mystified as to why Mrs. Stillwater and Lord Dudley were not speaking to each other. Hadn't they reconciled their differences earlier that day? So, why did they have no conversation to share? It was not a good start to Lord Dudley's tenure in the household. But there was nothing Kingsley could do about it, so he did his job, watching over the footman and the maid as they went about their duties. He was thankful when the meal was over, and the couple declined to have tea in the parlour. Kingsley did not think he could have handled any more of their company. He was about to go into the kitchen for his own dinner when Cassandra stopped him and asked for a private moment. Lord Dudley raised his eyebrows at her request but left them alone in the dining room. After dismissing the maid and footman, Kingsley said, "Yes, ma'am. What can I do for you?"

Cassandra replied, "Would you have a carriage readied for me right after breakfast tomorrow? I wish to travel into London."

Another trip to London? Why is she going this time? But he did not voice his questions. Instead, he said, "Very well, ma'am. I will do that for you."

"Thank you. That is all. I will retire to the morning parlour now, as I believe Lord Dudley plans to use the front parlour as his office. Good evening, Kingsley."

"Good evening, ma'am. I will see you in the morning," he replied, before heading out of the dining room.

And that will be the last time you ever set eyes on me, she thought. One of the hardest parts of leaving Stillwater Estate would be leaving the Kingsleys. They had shown nothing but kindness to her over the past five years. Cassandra did not know how she would cope without them. But it had to be done. So, she straightened her shoulders, took a deep breath, and left the room for her parlour—again, for one final time.

***

The next morning, Cassandra was up early. She finished packing her last items into her portmanteau before heading down for breakfast. She prayed that Lord Dudley would not be in the breakfast room when she arrived. God answered her prayer. When she inquired as to John's whereabouts, the footman informed her that he had already eaten and left for the barns. He had said not to expect him back before teatime. Cassandra heaved a sigh of relief. She would not have to see him before she left. That was one less burden for the day. She enjoyed her breakfast, savouring every delicious bite of Mrs. Kingsley's cooking. Then she headed back upstairs, made sure everything—including her jewels—was secure in her portmanteau, and went down the back stairs to the kitchen.

Seeing both of the Kingsleys at the table was a bonus. Now, she only had to say her goodbyes once. And there was no time like the present. "Good morning to you both. I hope you are both well today."

They told her they were and asked about her welfare. When informed that she, too, was well, Kingsley said, "I have asked for the carriage to be brought around to the front porch for you, Mrs. Stillwater. It should be there now."

"Thank you, Kingsley. In a moment, would you have a footman go up and bring down my portmanteau? It is sitting on my bed."

"You are staying in London overnight, ma'am?"

"No, I am leaving Stillwater today and won't be coming back."

The Kingsleys gasped at her news. Then Kingsley said, "I don't believe I heard you correctly, ma'am. You did not say you were leaving us, did you?"

"Yes, I did. But leaving the two of you is the hardest part. You have been wonderful to me over the past five years. I cannot thank you enough for all you have done."

Getting over her shock, Mrs. Kingsley said, "But why, ma'am? Why are you leaving?"

"There is no longer a place for me here. You have a new estate manager, and I am no longer needed."

"But isn't that what you wanted? To be relieved of your duties in the estate?" asked Kingsley.

"Yes, and if they had hired another manager, someone with whom I could get along, I would think of staying. But as it is, I cannot stay here with Lord Dudley."

"Is he aware of your plans?"

"No, and I don't wish him to be informed until after I am gone, Kingsley. Please grant me this one final request."

"Well, but where will you go? Where will you stay?"

"I am hoping to stay at the YWCA boarding house if they have a room available, but only until I find employment in the city. Then I would like to live where I work. But until then, I shall be at the YWCA."

"It sounds like you have planned this out, Mrs. Stillwater. This is not a hasty decision, is it?"

"No. Ever since I asked the duke to replace me, I have been planning to remove myself from the estate. And Lord Dudley's arrival yesterday has hastened my departure."

"Is there nothing we can say to change your mind, ma'am?"

"No. Now, if you would have my bag brought down, I will be on my way."

"Very well, ma'am," said Kingsley, before leaving to get a footman to carry out her wishes.

"The house will not be the same without you, Mrs. Stillwater," said Mrs. Kingsley. "I will miss you terribly."

"And I you, Mrs. Kingsley. But it is the right thing for me to do. I need to move my life along."

"I understand. I only wish you and Lord Dudley could have been compatible, but if not, perhaps this *is* best for both of you. My prayers will be with you."

"Thank you. Now, the time has come for me to say goodbye. No, don't get up and hug me. I will burst into tears if you do."

Mrs. Kingsley sank back onto her chair, her own eyes filling with tears as she choked out her farewell: "Goodbye and God be with you, ma'am."

Cassandra echoed her words back to her, and then fled the kitchen. When she reached the foyer, she found the door open and could see Kingsley standing by the carriage. She hastened out to him. "Thank you, my dear friend.

I know you do not understand my actions, but you will see that it is for the best. Take care and God bless you."

He harrumphed to clear his throat. "Please return if things do not work out for you. You will always have a home with us."

Cassandra nodded, unable to speak for the tears clogging her throat. She stepped forward, and the footman assisted her into the carriage. Once she was inside, he picked up the step, put it into the carriage, and then closed the door. Cassandra looked out the window at Kingsley and the manor for a long moment, before tapping on the roof to signal the driver that she was ready to leave. He clicked the reins, and they moved away from the porch and down the lane.

Never to return.

Chapter 12

John was out in the paddocks when Cassandra's carriage rolled past him. He saw her profile in the window. She was looking straight ahead and did not appear to notice him as the carriage passed by. He wondered where she was going. Did she have more personal business in London today? She had said nothing about leaving at dinner last night. In fact, she had said hardly anything at all. It had been an awkward meal. They were going to have to get past whatever was bothering her if their relationship had any chance of success. If dinner tonight was a repeat of last night's, he was going to say something. They could not carry on like this. But if she was heading for London, he could have lunch in the manor and talk to Kingsley about his concerns. Until then, he would give his full attention to his work. At least that was satisfying and uncomplicated. Unlike the lady of the manor, Wiley was a straight talker, with no hidden meanings or layers to his words.

***

Having not seen the carriage return while he was in the fields, John decided it was safe for him to have his lunch in the manor. So, after coming through the back door and slipping unnoticed up the back stairs to his room, he descended them a few minutes later, hungry for his meal. In the kitchen, he found the Kingsleys eating their lunch.

As soon as he saw John, Kingsley jumped up from his seat. "Oh! Lord Dudley, we were not expecting you. But now that you are here, it will not take any time to set a place for you at the dining table."

"Is Mrs. Stillwater not having lunch at home today? I saw her carriage leave this morning, but I have not seen it return."

An uneasy silence pervaded the room before Kingsley said, "No, sir, Mrs. Stillwater will not be home for lunch. In fact, she will not be having any more meals at the estate. She has left us."

"What do you mean 'left us,' Kingsley?"

"What I said, sir. She has gone to London and will not be returning."

"Why?"

"She feels she is no longer needed here now that you have arrived to take over as estate manager."

"But it was her decision to give up the role. She asked the duke…"

"I know, sir."

"Why then would she leave? Were you aware of her plans?"

"No. I knew she wanted a carriage for this morning, but I thought she was making another day trip to London. It was only when she came down and asked me to have a footman bring her bag to the carriage that the missus and I found out about her actual plans."

"Why didn't you tell me, Kingsley?"

"She asked us not to say anything to you, sir. I had to respect her wishes for privacy."

"Yes, you are right. But I still don't understand her sudden need to leave."

"If I may be so bold, Lord Dudley, I believe it had something to do with your arrival and instalment as the estate manager. She said that if someone else had taken the position, she might have stayed at least for a while to see how things worked out. But when she saw you yesterday, she knew that she had to leave."

"That is ridiculous. I would have been happy to have her stay. I know she was not happy with me after my actions on my last visit. But I thought we had put that behind us. Her distrust of me must run much deeper than I had thought." He sighed in disappointment and frustration. "But now I can't even work to change her opinion of me. Did she say where she was going?"

"To the YWCA boarding house."

"Then that is where I shall go this afternoon to bring her back."

"I would not advise it, Lord Dudley."

"Why not?"

"For whatever reason, she needs time away from here, and particularly from you. If she has that time and space, perhaps she will reconsider her actions and come back to us. But if you drag her back…"

"I suppose you are right. That would only make things worse. No, we need to let her be for a while, and then, perhaps, like you say, she will see reason and come back. But if she doesn't—"

"Then we can talk about bringing her home, sir, but only then."

John nodded. His hunger pangs had almost disappeared with the news of Cassandra's leaving, but knowing that not eating would solve nothing, he said, "Would you mind if I joined the two of you for lunch? I do not want to eat alone in the dining room."

The Kingsleys agreed to his request and invited him to sit down. Then Mrs. Kingsley bustled around, gathering up a plate and eating utensils for him, before serving him a large portion of the beef stew. Talk then turned to what John had been doing that morning, but Cassandra was never far from their minds.

***

The Kingsleys and Lord Dudley were also on Cassandra's mind as she sat down with the other women for lunch at the YWCA boarding house. She had been fortunate to find a room available, so she had sent the carriage back to the estate. After checking in, she had put her few belongings in a rickety wardrobe before heading to the common room to meet the other women. There were only a couple of ladies in the room, as most of the women were off working for the day. After greeting the others, Cassandra found a daily newssheet on a table and immediately started looking at the ads for employment. Only a couple of them suited her skills.

She asked the other women if she could take the sheet with her to her room, and they told her it was permissible. So, that is what Cassandra would do, determining that she would start looking for work first thing tomorrow morning. But first, it was time for lunch. The food was nourishing but not as flavourful as Mrs. Kingsley's cooking. Cassandra wondered if they were missing her as she was missing them. And whether they had yet told Lord Dudley of her departure, or if he was currently eating lunch in the barn with Mr. Wiley. She shook her head. It did not matter. They were out of her life, and she was out of theirs. She needed to look to the future, not the past, and her future was in London.

***

The days passed, and Cassandra did not return to the estate. Her absence frustrated John. He still wanted to ride into London and bring her back. He knew that he had no right to do that, though, so he continued to take Kingsley's advice and wait. But he did not know how much longer he could do that. Perhaps he would ride in and check on her welfare. Yes, that would be acceptable. Then if she was agreeable, he would bring her home, but if not, at least he would know that she was well. So, the next morning, as he breakfasted with the Kingsleys, he said, "I am going to ride into London today. No, perhaps I will take a carriage. I need to see my tailor and get some new garments. I expect I will be gone most of the day. Do either of you need anything from the city?"

Both the Kingsleys shook their heads. Then the butler said, "Is that all you plan to do, sir? Will you perchance be making a stop at the YWCA boarding house?"

"I might, if only to check on Mrs. Stillwater's welfare."

"Not to bring her home?"

"Only if she wishes to come, Kingsley. Otherwise, I will leave her to her new life in the city."

"That sounds like a plan. We will pray for your wisdom in speaking with her."

"I assure you that I will not kidnap her. If she does not want to return on her own volition, I will come back alone."

"Then have a good day, Lord Dudley. We will await news of Mrs. Stillwater upon your return."

"I shall be happy to report on her wellbeing. Now, would you mind having a carriage brought round for me?"

"Not at all, sir," said Kingsley, getting up from his chair.

John also rose, thanking Mrs. Kingsley for the meal, before heading up the stairs to prepare for his trip. He prayed it would be a successful one, in all ways.

***

Soon, he was back downstairs and striding out to the front porch. A carriage was waiting for him, along with a driver and a footman. Seeing the footman, John dismissed his services, saying that he could get in and out of the carriage without assistance, demonstrating that skill by ably climbing into the conveyance and closing the door after himself. Once he was inside, he tapped on the roof, and they left the manor behind.

As they travelled, John thought about what he would say to Mrs. Stillwater to persuade her to return to the estate. He could not come up with anything other than that he missed her company, as did the Kingsleys. That was a weak reason for her to return, so he pondered what else he could say. Nothing came to mind, so he prayed God would give him the right words to say when he next saw her. Then he turned his mind to his other reason for travelling to London: the purchasing of new clothing. He spent the rest of his journey determining what he needed to purchase to meet the needs of his new position.

***

Arriving in London, John directed his driver to take him first to his tailor. It was still mid-morning, not the time to visit a single lady at her dwelling, especially without prior notice. No, that would not do. It was better to see to his clothing needs, have lunch, and then visit Mrs. Stillwater. That would still give him time to return home in plenty of time for dinner.

Having not seen his tailor since he had returned from Australia, the man was both delighted to see him and amazed at the changes in his physique. The tailor spent a great deal of time taking his measurements and comparing them to his previous ones. As John had suspected, his shirts and jackets needed to be larger in the chest and arms, and smaller at his waist. His hips and thighs were also more muscled, from the months of physical labour in Australia, and now on the estate, so his trousers had to be refitted as well.

John ordered several pairs of work trousers and shirts, with a couple of more formal shirts, waistcoats, and trousers also. He asked the tailor to prioritise his work wear, as he knew that was what he needed most. The other garments were not as important; they could wait. If he had still been a man about town, and only that, he would not have cared about work garments, only looking fashionable. He smiled absently at how drastically things had changed for him over the past few years.

Once he completed the garment order, John exited the shop and invited his driver to join him at a local pub for lunch. This invitation took the driver somewhat aback, as he had never lunched with a peer before, but John insisted, so they left the horses and carriage secured to a post and enjoyed a tasty lunch together. After lunch, John gave the driver the directions to the YWCA, and they headed off in that direction. John still did not know what he was going to say to Cassandra. But he needn't have worried. When they arrived, she was not there.

***

"You say that Mrs. Stillwater is not available to speak to me," he said to the woman, who had introduced herself as the housemother.

"That is correct, sir. She is away, and I do not know when she will be back."

"Do you have any idea where she might have gone?"

"No, and even if I did, I would not share that information with you. I respect the privacy of my boarders."

"That is good to know, but I am only in town for the day and wished to assure myself of her wellbeing."

"You appear to be a gentleman, sir, but I do not know you, and Mrs. Stillwater has not spoken of you, so I will say only that she is well."

"I am glad to hear that. Could I leave a message for her?"

"Certainly. I will give it to her when she arrives."

"Do you have parchment and an inked quill I could use?"

"No, but there is a stationery shop only a couple of blocks from here where you could purchase what you need. I can give you their address."

"Thank you, ma'am. I will proceed there now and come back once I have written my note to Mrs. Stillwater."

"Good, sir. Their address is…"

***

John repeated the address and direction to himself, so he could tell his driver. Then he thanked the housemother for her time and headed back to the carriage. Upon arriving, he gave the driver the directions to the shop, climbed in the carriage, and set off to get the needed writing implements. It disappointed him that Cassandra was not at home. He wondered where she could be and what she was doing. This was not the best area of the city for a woman to be out on her own. He hoped she would return to the boarding house soon, for her own protection.

Within minutes, the driver stopped in front of the stationery shop. John hopped out of the carriage, went inside, and was soon back out with his purchases. Then he asked the driver to head back to the boarding house and park near it—not in front of it, but close enough that they could watch for Mrs. Stillwater's arrival. He would still write his note, but he would rather talk to her in person, if that proved possible, as he only had a couple of hours before they needed to head back to the estate. In the meantime, he would relax in the carriage and await Cassandra's return.

***

One hour passed, and then another, and still she had not returned. John watched as the sun began its descent, and the shadows lengthened. The activity around the boarding house changed as well. He watched young women start returning to the house in groups of two or three. But he was disturbed to also see single men strolling along the street, tipping their hats to these young women as they passed. Some men appeared to be gentlemen, but others had a rougher cut to them. John also noted that, sometimes, after passing the women, the men would look back at them, as if admiring their figures. It was not a glance, but a slow perusal of their silhouettes. John hoped Cassandra would return with another lady or two. He did not know what the men would do if they spied a lady on her own. *Please, Lord,* he prayed, *bring her back while I am still here to protect her.*

Finally, a few minutes later, John saw her coming down the street. She was alone. Her head was down, her shoulders rounded, and her steps slow. She kept looking to the path rather than up ahead or off to her sides. And as such, she did not see her assailant until he grabbed her arm, though fortunately, John did.

"Hello, pretty lady," the man said. "You are looking sad. Can I cheer you up?"

"No, thank you, sir," she said, trying to pull her arm out of his tight grasp. "Please let go of my arm."

"A gentle lady like yourself shouldn't be out here alone. You need an escort to keep you safe. Allow me to do that for you."

"I don't need your help, sir. Now, let go of me, or I shall have to call for a bobby."

His hand tightened even more. "Do you see any bobbies around? I don't, so I guess you will have to come with me."

Cassandra struggled harder to free herself from his grip. But it was no use. He was too strong. He started pulling her towards a grove of trees when another male voice said, "If you know what is good for you, my man, you will listen to the lady and let go of her arm. Do it now, and you can leave without being harmed."

Cassandra looked towards the voice. It was Lord Dudley. *What was he doing here?* She looked again and saw another familiar face, one of the carriage drivers from the estate. She pulled again, and the assailant's grip slackened slightly, though he did not let go of her.

"Only offering the lady some company. Why don't you find your own lady?"

"Afraid I can't do that, sir. I am responsible for this lady's welfare, and I take my job seriously. So, I will tell you one more time: Let go of her arm. And do it now."

"Or what? You'll hurt me? Why, from the looks of you, I bet you're one of those uptown gents, aren't you? Never thrown a punch at anyone, except perhaps one of your friends at Gentleman Jack's. I, on the other hand, have to take care of myself every day. So, you don't want to mess with me, mister. Please go away and leave us alone."

"Sorry. I can't do that," said John, before he took a step forward. Throwing his walking stick at the assailant's legs then, John followed this up with a punch to the right side of the man's jaw.

The man dropped Cassandra's arm and rushed towards John, throwing a wild punch at John's face. The swing missed when John ducked down beneath it, and then rammed his head into the man's abdomen before kneeing him in his groin. The man collapsed on the street, screaming in pain.

John quickly moved Cassandra away, asking the driver to keep an eye on the downed ruffian, while he made sure Cassandra was not hurt. As he walked her over to the steps of the boarding house and sat her down, she assured him that, except for a bruised arm, she was only shaken up.

"Are you sure?" he asked again.

"Yes, I am fine, Lord Dudley. But why are you here?"

"I came to town to see my tailor and thought I would stop in and inquire as to your welfare. I am glad now that I did."

"Thank you for coming to my rescue. I was later getting back than I intended to be. Usually, this is a safe street for women."

"This is not the best area of the city for you to live in, Mrs. Stillwater. I know you would be welcome to stay at either our family town home or the Yardleys. Would you not consider doing that? It would ease my mind immensely."

"No, I cannot, Lord Dudley. I need to stay here until I find work. I hope that work will also provide lodging, so I don't expect to be here much longer."

"You have found employment?"

"Not yet, but I am sure I will find something soon."

"And if you don't?"

"Then I will reconsider what I am doing. But it is none of your concern, sir. Regardless of what you said to that man, I am not your responsibility."

"Being that you left the safety of Stillwater Estate because of me, ma'am, I beg to differ. But having seen what you face here, I am asking you to please return with me. We miss your company, especially the Kingsleys."

"Thank you for your offer, sir, but I am staying here. I thank you for your timely intervention as well but rest assured that I will be more aware of my surroundings from now on. If you will excuse me," she said, attempting to get up from her seat.

John wanted to gather her up and take her to the carriage. But he was a man of his word, and he had given his word to both the Kingsleys and himself that he would not act against her wishes. So, instead, he only assisted her up the steps and to the door. When she reached it, she said, "It was good to see you, Lord Dudley. Please take my greetings to the Kingsleys."

With that, she opened the door, entered the building, and closed the door behind her. John heard the click of a lock seconds later. *Well, at least they take safety precautions inside the building. But outside of it, these women seem to be on their own.* He shook his head, retreated down the steps, and returned to the spot where his driver was still standing over Mrs. Stillwater's assailant.

"What do you want to do with bloke, sir?" the driver asked.

"If we have some rope, let's truss him up and drop him off at the nearest police station. I don't want him anywhere near here."

"If you watch him, I'll go grab some rope from the boot of the carriage."

John nodded. "He's not going anywhere. Get the rope, and let's tie him up."

The driver complied and soon the assailant was tightly bound and lying on the floor of the carriage, with John's feet keeping him down. The driver had spotted a police station as they'd travelled to the YWCA, so he headed in that direction. When they got there, they pulled the man out of the carriage and walked him into the station, where the officer took one look at him and shook his head. "Michael in trouble again? When will he ever learn?"

John gave his statement, and before long, the officer took charge of the assailant, leaving John and his driver free to head back to the estate.

***

When the housemother and other women saw the bruises on Cassandra's arm, they immediately asked what had happened. She did her best to explain, but then the housemother spoke up. "There was a gentleman here earlier this afternoon asking questions as to your whereabouts. He said that he would leave a note for you, but he has not returned. Do you think he is the one who did this to you?"

After Cassandra asked her to describe the visitor's appearance, she was able to shake her head, recognizing Lord Dudley in her words.

"It was not him. In fact, it was he that rescued me from my assailant. I don't know what would have happened had he not been there."

"You know him?"

"Yes. He is the new manager of the estate I left. He was here to make sure I was well and needed nothing."

"That is what he said. I am glad he was there to save you today. Will he be back?"

"No. I assured him that, other than today's incident, I was fine and needed nothing from him. I don't expect to see him again."

"Well, but if he comes around again, I will be more courteous to him. I am afraid I was rather abrupt, being that I did not know of his connection to you."

"Thank you, ma'am. Now, if you will excuse me, I would like to lie down for an hour. I guess I am more shaken by this experience than I realised."

The housemother nodded. Then she asked one of the other women to assist Cassandra to her room and help her disrobe, so that she would be more comfortable during her rest. One lady stepped forward and did as the housemother had suggested. But once Cassandra had removed her outer clothing and put on her night robe, she left her alone to rest.

As soon as the door closed, and the room darkened, Cassandra started to shake. The memories of what had happened, and what could have happened had Lord Dudley not been there, suddenly overwhelmed her. Would she ever be able to walk alone on these streets again without fearing danger? Should she perhaps take Lord Dudley up on the offer and seek shelter at either his or the Yardleys' town house?

She had planned this move so carefully that she could not understand why God had allowed her to be attacked. Was she acting outside of His will for her? Perhaps she needed to pray some more and confirm that this is what He wanted for her. If not, she would need to revise her plan. So, for the next hour, while she rested, Cassandra prayed for God's wisdom to be revealed to her, and that her eyes, ears, and heart would be open to His guidance. Feeling much more at ease with this complete, she felt ready to face the world again.

That evening, after dinner, the housemother reviewed the rules of living in the boarding house once more, inspired by Cassandra's assault earlier that day. She asked the women to always walk in groups of two or three, and if that were not possible, to hire a hack to take them to or from their destination. She told them that the sponsors of the association had provided extra funds for that specific purpose, in order to keep the women safe from danger.

The women agreed to abide by the rules and to help keep each other safe. Then the housemother looked around and took a deep breath.

"I have a final announcement to make. In a month's time, I will leave here to live with my sister in Berkshire. The position of housemother will be available, should any of you wish to apply. I will be the one hiring the new housemother, so please direct your interest to me. That is all. Have a good evening."

A buzz started around the room. A new housemother? Would that be a good position? What would the salary be?

Cassandra was also thinking about the position. If she applied, and was successful, she could live and work here without having to venture out alone again. She wondered what qualifications the position required. Tomorrow, she would ask the housemother about those requirements. She could see herself in the position, but would the other women accept her when she had only recently come to live with them? That was all food for thought and for more prayer. Perhaps this was God's answer to her earlier prayers. She would have to ask Him again tonight.

Later, Cassandra did just that. She thanked God for revealing a position for her, in which she would be safe. She asked Him again to confirm whether this was in His will for her. If it was, would He place the same thoughts in the housemother's mind? That way, Cassandra would know that it came from Him, and not solely from her own desires. Having determined that, she closed her eyes and went to sleep.

**

Back at Stillwater Estate, her friends were not as comfortable with the idea of her continuing to live at the YWCA after what had happened that day. John had told the Kingsleys about the incident when he arrived back from the city. It shocked them to hear of the assault, but they were quick to praise John for coming to Mrs. Stillwater's rescue. What if John had not been there? What might have happened to her? They did not want to think about that. God had obviously placed John there today. But what about all the days to come? Who would be there if another attack occurred? They would have to pray continuously for her safety from now on. If only she had come home with Lord Dudley…

***

Meanwhile, in a country far to the south of England, Bethany was wondering if her matchmaking efforts had worked. In sending her letters to Cassandra with John, she'd had two thoughts in mind: to inform Cassandra of how wonderful life was for her, Sam, and their children at Yardley Downs; and to introduce Cassandra to John, hoping that they might find happiness together. Bethany had not told Sam of her second desire after their previous matchmaking attempts with Joe and Joann had almost ended in disaster. But now that the Winters were happily married and settled in Fremantle, Bethany had decided to try her luck at setting up her sister-in-law Cassandra, with Sam's cousin John. Cassandra deserved a good man, especially after living with Howard for all those years, and Bethany was convinced that John was just that man. So, she plotted. And she prayed.

Chapter 13

The next morning after breakfast, Cassandra asked the housemother if she had a moment to speak with her. She said that she did, and after inquiring after Cassandra's health, they went to the parlour. They found it empty, so they went in and sat down in a couple of chairs near the fireplace.

"Now, what can I do for you, Mrs. Stillwater?"

"Uh, I was wondering, after your announcement last evening, what you are looking for in a new housemother for the building."

"Why? Might you be interested?"

"I might, but I don't know if I have the skills needed for the position."

"I expect that you do, but yes, I will tell you what this position requires. First, you must be a dedicated Christian woman who upholds the rules of the association. You must not have any hidden vices such as drinking alcohol to excess or gambling. Furthermore, you must be a woman of excellent moral character, exhibiting many of the fruits of the Spirit, such as kindness, gentleness, and self-control, so that you can lead younger women to better themselves. You must be able to manage a budget and not overspend. To avoid a divided mind, you must stay single and not consider getting married. That is about it. Do you have questions?"

"Uh, you mentioned managing a budget. Is it like a household budget or something larger?"

"You could compare it to a large household budget. You mentioned on your arrival that you had come from managing an estate. If you could do that, you could easily look after our budget."

"The reason I came here was because the estate was faltering under my care, ma'am. I was looking for ways to fix the problems, but as nothing was working, I asked to be relieved of my position."

"I see. So, you believe that the problems on the estate were all your fault?"

"Yes, although the drought devastated our crops and hayfields, meaning we had to buy feed for our animals."

"And without the drought, would the estate have failed under your management?"

"I don't know. I don't believe so."

"That is enough for me. No forces such as a drought will affect the boarding house. Yes, it means the price for food rises, but the sponsors have never turned me down when I need more money."

"That is good to know. I don't think I could handle another budget affected by drought."

"I don't know that I could either, Mrs. Stillwater. Now, one more question: You are a widow, are you not?"

"I am. My husband died five years ago."

"Do you have children?"

"Yes, four boys."

"And what are they up to now? I presume they are living elsewhere, or you would not be here."

"Yes, they are all at school. I have sent notices to them with my present address, but the school term does not end for several weeks, so I have not yet seen them."

"What will happen to them when school breaks?"

"I don't know. I suppose they will go back to the estate. They have nowhere else to go. I don't suppose they can come here and stay with me."

"No, that would not be possible, even with young boys. You would have to visit with them outside of these walls."

"That is something I need to think about. Thank you for reminding me, ma'am."

"You are welcome. So, would you like to apply for the position?"

"I would."

"Excellent. I will keep you in mind. Consider this your formal interview."

"Thank you for speaking with me this morning. I appreciate your time."

"That is why I am here, Mrs. Stillwater, to be a mother to everyone who lives here, no matter who they are. Now, if you will excuse me, I need to discuss today's menu with the cook."

"I understand and thank you again for considering me for the position."

"You are welcome. I will let you know at the end of the month whether you are the successful candidate."

"I'll look forward to hearing from you. Have a good day, ma'am," said Cassandra, as the housemother rose and left the room.

***

Cassandra stayed sitting in the parlour for a while, just thinking over her conversation with the housemother. The woman had made it sound like she had a good chance of getting the position, although it had only been announced last evening, so perhaps other candidates would come forward as well. But the one thing she had not thought about was her boys and where they would stay during school breaks. They had always come home to the estate. They loved being there: riding, helping Mr. Wiley with the chores, and just being boys in the country. Now, what would they do? She was sure the Kingsleys would welcome them with open arms, but what about Lord Dudley? Would he also welcome them, or would they be rejected because she was no longer living there? If she heard the latter, her heart would break. She lived only for her sons. She had done so most of her married life and now as a widow as well. They were wonderful boys, and she was proud of them. But would they be proud of her, leaving the estate and coming to work in London? That was something she was not quite so sure of.

Knowing she had to find a place for them for the next school break, she determined to write to the Kingsleys. She was out of ink, and having no appointments that day, she decided to walk to the stationery shop. It was only a couple of blocks away. She tried to trust that she would not be in any danger as it was the middle of the morning, but it wasn't easy. Still, she would have to go out sometime, and this would be a test of her nerves. She would tell the housemother where she was going and when to expect her back, so that if anything happened, they would immediately come looking for her. With that decided, she went to the kitchen, where she found both the housemother and the cook talking about the day's menu. When Cassandra walked in, they both looked over at her.

"Excuse me for interrupting, but I wanted to let you know I am going to the local stationers to get some writing implements. I won't be long. Before yesterday, I would not have said anything, but I am not comfortable walking around without you knowing where I am. I hope you don't mind."

The housemother shook her head. "Of course not, Mrs. Stillwater. I'm glad you told me. Are you sure you are all right with being on your own?"

"Yes, I have to do this. And it is only mid-morning, so it should be safe. I'll let you know as soon as I am back home."

"Thank you. I'll count the minutes until you return."

"I won't be more fifteen or twenty minutes at the most. I'll see you soon," said Cassandra, before turning and heading back down the hallway.

Reaching her room, she gathered up her reticule and cloak before heading out. It was a beautiful morning, and she breathed deeply of the slightly salty air that always arrived with the incoming tide on the Thames. But there was no time to linger, so she walked swiftly towards the shop, looking around her at all times for signs of danger. Fortunately, there were none. She reached the shop, made her purchases, and returned to the boarding house without incident. Stepping inside, she breathed a sigh of relief. She had done it, and she could do it again when the need arose. Fear would not stop her.

Because of her promise to the housemother, she went to her office and let her know that she was back. The housemother smiled and nodded, before looking back down at her ledger. So, Cassandra left and went to the small writing desk in the parlour. She put her purchases down, opened the ink well, took out the sharpened quill, and started to write:

Dear Mr. and Mrs. Kingsley,

By now, you will have heard of my misadventure yesterday afternoon, which could have resulted in great harm except for the fortuitous presence of Lord Dudley. I believe he was there by God's design. I cannot think of another reason he would have been outside the boarding house. But praise God, except for a bit of bruising, I am unharmed. Please do not worry about me. I am well.

I am writing to you of another concern, one which is dear to my heart. In a few weeks' time, my sons will be released for their midterm school break. As you know, they normally come to the estate for their vacations. I pray you will continue to welcome them, even though I am no longer with you. There is nowhere else they can go, and I do not wish them to remain at their schools during the break. That would not be healthy for them.

Please talk to Lord Dudley about this situation, and if he has any concerns with this arrangement, let me know as soon as possible. Perhaps, if he is not agreeable, I can take the boys to the beach for their break, as I am still unemployed. I cannot have them here at the boarding house, for obvious reasons.

I think of you often and miss you greatly. Hoping you are doing well.

I look forward to hearing from you regarding my request.

Your loving friend,
Cassandra Stillwater

Cassandra folded the page of parchment, put it in the envelope, and then sealed it with a bit of wax that was on the desk. Then she walked to the front door and deposited it in the mail basket. There. That was done. Now, all she had to do was wait for a reply. Hopefully, it would be positive, although the idea of spending a couple of weeks at the beach with her sons was a delightful one. Perhaps she would look into that for their next break regardless of the answer she received for this one. Of course, if she was working by then, she might not be able to get the time off. But that was for the future. She remembered a Bible verse in which James reminds Christians of how to live: *Go to now, ye that say, today or tomorrow we will go into such a city and continue there a year, and buy and sell, and get gain. Whereas ye know not what shall be on the morrow. For what is your life? It is even a vapour, that appeareth for a little time, and then vanisheth away. For that ye ought to say, If the Lord will, we shall live, and do this, or that.*[4]

Yes. She would live for today and let God take care of the future. And so, for the rest of the day, that's what she did.

***

Unfortunately for Cassandra, her letter to the Kingsleys was misplaced in the mail and did not arrive until the same day that a carriage dropped off the boys at the front porch of the Stillwater Estate. Not wanting to wait for Kingsley to open the door, the boys grabbed their bags as Peter opened the door and called out to announce their arrival. "Kingsley, we're home!" Not getting a response from him, they headed towards the front parlour. The door was open, so they rushed inside, only to fall back when they saw a stranger seated at the desk.

"Who are you?" Peter asked.

"The better question, I believe, is who are *you*," said John, although seeing the boys lined up before him, he had a fair idea of their identities.

"We are Stillwaters," replied Peter. "This is our mother's house and that is our mother's desk. Why are you sitting there?"

"You ask a lot of questions, young man," said John. "But I will answer them for you. I am John Dudley, and I am the new estate manager. Your mother has removed herself to London. Did she not inform you of that fact?"

"Yes, but I did not believe the note she sent. Mother hates living in London. She would not willingly move back there again. Did you force her to leave?"

John raised a single eyebrow at this. "I did not. In fact, she left without my knowledge. I only found out later that day from the Kingsleys. Why would I make her go?"

"So, you could get the income for being the estate manager. It is a profitable position to have."

John laughed. What need did he have of this position? Obviously, the boys had no idea who he was. Choosing to say nothing about his peerage, John just shook his head. "Well, let's ring for Kingsley. He will verify my story. In the meantime, would you like to sit down?"

"No. We will stay standing, sir, until we talk to him."

"Fine. Oh, I hear his footsteps now. We will sort this out straightaway."

Kingsley strode hurriedly into the room. Not seeing the boys at first, he said, "You rang, sir? I'm sorry. I was in the kitchen having tea with Mrs.

Kingsley. We were reading a letter from Mrs. Stillwater. It says that the boys may arrive here for their school break."

He had hardly finished speaking when the boys all rushed over to hug him.

"Kingsley, we are here!" said Peter. "But why did you get a letter from Mother?"

"Boys! Oh, it is wonderful to see you! You have all grown taller in the past couple of months. This is Lord Dudley. He is a nephew of the Duke of Yardley, a cousin to your Uncle Samuel. He is the new estate manager."

"But why? And why is Mother in London?"

"She left the estate to find a position there, Calvin, and she has been there for the past month. She did not want to be the estate manager any longer, so the duke hired Lord Dudley for the job. Not having any more responsibility here, she left us to work in London. She mailed us a letter a couple of weeks ago, but it only arrived today. She asked Mrs. Kingsley and I to look after you for your break if Lord Dudley is agreeable. Are you, sir?" he asked, turning back to John.

"Of course they can stay, Kingsley. Where else would they go?"

"That is what Mrs. Stillwater wondered as well. Thank you, sir. Perhaps if she knows the boys are here, she will come back for a visit."

Listening to their conversation, the boys realised that what John had said was true. Their mother was no longer living here; she was in London.

John turned back to the boys. "I am sorry you did not find your mother here. I asked her to come back home a couple of weeks ago, but she refused. She is always welcome to live at Stillwater Estate; it is still her home."

"Maybe if she comes to visit us, she will stay," said Arthur. "I don't want her to be in London, mister. It is not a nice place to live."

"Only some parts aren't nice, Arthur," said Peter.

"Yes, like where we used to live," said Calvin. "That was terrible. We could not play out in the yard because of the people living around us."

"I am sure Mother is staying in a lovely part of the city, Calvin. Isn't she, Lord Dudley?"

John gulped. How was he to tell these boys that their mother had been assaulted walking home alone before the sun had even set? That would not paint a pleasing picture. Fortunately, Kingsley stepped in and saved him from having to speak.

"Your mother is staying at a safe home for single women. She is content with her new lodgings and looking for work nearby. Now, I'm sure she doesn't want you starting your break with sad faces. Why don't you go into the kitchen to see Mrs. Kingsley? I'll bet she can find some snacks for you. Are you hungry?"

"I'm always hungry, Mr. K," said Arthur. "Let's go see Mrs. K right now."

The other boys laughed at their little brother. It was true. He could eat all the time and never get full. Mother used to say he had a hollow leg, whatever that meant. But they were hungry too, so they agreed to accompany Kingsley to the kitchen.

As they left, Peter turned and looked at John one last time, with a look that seemed to suggest his dissatisfaction with the story he'd been given and his determination not to rest until he'd found out every detail. Maybe then he would understand his mother's continued absence from the estate. John hoped Peter really would come to understand it, so that he could perhaps help him to do the same.

***

While the boys were enjoying their snacks, back in London, Cassandra was wondering why she had not heard back from Kingsley. According to her calendar, today was the day that her sons would arrive at the estate. Had they already done so? If they had, what kind of reception did they receive from Lord Dudley? Would he let them stay or send them back to the city? She had all these questions and no answers. She finally decided that she would have to break down and visit the estate tomorrow to satisfy her curiosity and put her fears to bed. *Yes,* she thought, *that is what I must do.* Tomorrow, she would face Lord Dudley once again...

***

John had been correct. Peter was not accepting his explanation about why his mother had left the estate. She loved living out here and had said, on more than one occasion, that she hoped to live here for the rest of her life. She would never voluntarily go back to live in London. Peter knew that. No, something or someone had made her leave, and Peter had decided that this person's name was Lord Dudley. He was determined to keep the man firmly in his sights for the entire duration of his visit. And before he was forced to leave to go back to school, he would know the full truth of his mother's absence from Stillwater Estate.

Chapter 14

Cassandra's first thoughts the next morning were of her plans for the day. The first of these was how she would get out to the estate. It was not as easy as asking for a carriage to be readied for her. There was no one here like Kingsley to make such arrangements. But if she wanted to hire a hack for the day, how should she go about finding one? It seemed to her that the person most likely to have the answer to such questions would be the housemother. Cassandra was confident that someone would have previously asked her the same questions, and in any case, it would be useful information for her to have as well, assuming she were to become the next housemother.

She quickly dressed and headed down to the dining hall for breakfast, hoping to find the housemother there. She was in luck. The housemother was still finishing her meal when Cassandra arrived in the room.

"Good morning, ma'am. I see you are almost finished eating. Would you mind answering a question for me?"

"Certainly. I will if I can, Mrs. Stillwater. What is it?"

"I was hoping to make a trip out to my former home today, and I need to hire a hack. How would I go about doing that from here?"

"They congregate on the street where the stationers are located. You will need to walk over there to hire one. Do you wish anyone to accompany you?"

"No, it is only a couple of blocks. I plan to leave right after breakfast, so I will be fine without an escort. Thank you for the information."

"You are welcome. I don't know what their fee will be, especially if you ask them to wait, and then bring you back. But it will be quite costly."

"I'm sure I have enough money to pay their bill, but I will ask before I leave. Please continue with your meal. That was all I needed to know."

The housemother nodded and started eating again while Cassandra went to the sideboard and filled a plate for herself, before coming to the table and sitting across from the other woman. They exchanged pleasantries for a while until the housemother left to begin her duties for the day. Then Cassandra went to her room to get ready to leave for Stillwater Estate.

***

Cassandra estimated that she would need £two sterling for the day's trip. It was costly but not unmanageable. And if she could see her sons today, the price would be worth it. She put the needed monies in her reticule and walked down to the stationer's store, where a group of cabbies were waiting to pick up passengers, just as she'd been told to expect. The first driver she approached told her that none of the drivers here could take her all the way to her destination, but that he would take her to Charing's Cross, where she could hire a cab to take her the rest of the way.

So, she paid him one shilling and got into his cab. Soon, they were in the centre of London, where she transferred to another cab. The driver told her that it would be costly, but that he would wait for her out in the village near the estate, and then bring her back. Cassandra agreed with his price, and they headed out of the city.

Soon, they were on the road and passing familiar sights along the way. Within the hour, they arrived at the front gates of the Stillwater Estate. The driver dismounted, opened the gates, and walked the horses through, and then shut the gates behind them the carriage. Then they pulled up to the front porch. After the driver helped Cassandra out of the cab, she asked him to wait, so she could determine if she would need a ride back to the city, He agreed, and she hurried up to the door and opened it, shocking Kingsley with her presence.

"Mrs. Stillwater! Welcome home!"

"Greetings, Kingsley. I am only here for a visit. I will explain my presence in a few moments, but first I need to know if I can get one of the estate drivers to take me back to the city later today. If so, I will dismiss my cabbie, but if not, I shall let him know he needs to wait on me."

"Of course, we can provide transportation back to London, ma'am! You should not think that we would not do that for you."

"Thank you. As I am no longer living here, I was unsure. Would you mind taking this money and paying him for me?" she asked, reaching into her reticule and pulling out the needed cash.

"We will reimburse you for your costs, ma'am, but in order to speed the cabbie on his way, I will use your money now and pay you back later from the household funds. All right?"

"That is fine. I will wait until you get back inside, and then explain why I am here this morning."

"Good, ma'am," said Kingsley. "I will only be a minute." Then he hurried outside. Before long, he was back in the foyer. "Now, please come in and sit down. Would you like a cup of tea?"

"I would love one. Thank you. May I come to the kitchen with you and greet your wife?"

"She will be overjoyed to see you again, Mrs. Stillwater. So, please do."

Cassandra followed Kingsley into the kitchen, and his wife's reaction was as they'd expected. She ran over and hugged Cassandra for a long time, before letting go and saying, "Oh, Mrs. Stillwater, it is so good to see you back. Lord Dudley will be pleased to have your company again."

Cassandra held up a hand. "I am only here for a visit; I have not returned to stay."

"Oh, I was hoping you had come home for good."

"No, I'm sorry if I disappointed you. I wanted to see if my sons had arrived for their school break. They should have come yesterday, I believe."

"Yes, they are here," said Kingsley. "They are out in the barn with Lord Dudley and Mr. Wiley. Would you like me to bring them back into the house?"

"No. If after tea they have not come in, I will surprise them in the barn. Are they well?"

"They appear well, ma'am, and Master Arthur's appetite is as voracious as it has always been."

"Oh, dear." Cassandra laughed. "I hope they don't eat through all your supplies while they are here."

"I'm sure they won't, Mrs. Stillwater," said Mrs. Kingsley. "But if they do, we will simply have to buy more food earlier than expected."

"Do you have the funds to do so?"

"Yes, Lord Dudley received money from the Duke of Yardley's bank, so we do not have any worries about money at the present time."

"That's good. I would hate to think that you were not eating well."

"We are doing well. But what about you? How are you faring?"

"I am well. The food at the boarding house is plain but sufficient for my needs. I miss your cooking though, Mrs. Kingsley."

"Well, I miss cooking for you, ma'am. It was always a pleasure to serve you."

"Thank you. Now, can I be presumptuous and ask for a cup of tea? My throat is dry from my travels this morning."

"Of course, you can have tea, ma'am. And perhaps a fresh scone?"

"How can I resist? I may even have two scones with my tea to make up for my lack of them in recent weeks."

"I will send some back with you. They won't be as good as when they are fresh, but they will be quite edible for the next couple of days. Now, I'll get the water boiling for tea, and we can talk about what's been happening in your life and ours since the day you left us."

Cassandra agreed and sat down at the table. Kingsley sat across from her while his wife bustled around getting tea for everyone. Just as they were about to eat, the back door opened, and a young boy's voice said, "Mrs. Kingsley, is it time for morning tea? I'm starving."

Mrs. Kingsley was about to reply to Arthur's question when she saw Cassandra put a finger to her lips. She stayed silent while Cassandra pushed back from the table and answered: "Yes, dear, we've just sat down. Would you call your brothers and Lord Dudley in to join us?"

As soon as he heard his mother's voice, Arthur ran up the stairs into the kitchen towards her, even as she got to her feet and opened her arms in anticipation of his hug.

"Mama, you're here!" He wrapped his arms around her and held on tight.

Cassandra both laughed and cried as she held her youngest son close to her body. "Yes, I came for a visit. Now, let me look at you."

Arthur dropped his arms and took a couple of steps away from her. Looking him up and down, she smiled. "I believe you have grown at least an inch taller since I last saw you. Soon you will be as tall as your brothers."

Arthur beamed at these words, but it only lasted a moment, interrupted by another voice from the kitchen doorway. "He will not, Mama. We have all grown as well."

Cassandra whirled around to see her three other sons crowded into the doorway. She reached out her arms, and they rushed towards her, quickly enveloping her.

"Peter, Wendell, Calvin ... my darling boys. I have missed you terribly."

"We have missed you as well, Mother," said Peter, the self-designated spokesman for the group. "Have you come back to stay at the estate?"

"No, I am just here for the day. Later, we can talk about my new life in the city. But right now, your brother is hungry, as he always is. So, why don't you all wash up before joining the Kingsleys and me for tea?"

The boys nodded and headed to their rooms to do as Cassandra suggested. Then she heard another voice coming from the back door as she was about to sit down again. "Does that invitation include me as well, Mrs. Stillwater? I would like to have tea and hear your story too."

Cassandra turned and saw John lounging in the doorway, wearing a huge smile upon his face. "You are the estate manager now, Lord Dudley, so you can come and go as you please. I have no say over you."

John straightened up and walked over to stand about two feet away from her. Looking down into her upturned face, he said, "Then I will use my station to accept your invitation, ma'am. Welcome home."

"Goodness," said Cassandra, "why does everyone assume I have returned to stay? I am only here to visit, and then I will return to London. Perhaps I should have sent a message informing you of my intentions before I arrived."

"If that message came as late as the letter about the boys' school break, ma'am," said Kingsley, "then you may have arrived before we received it. We are glad to see you, even if it is only for a day."

"Thank you, Kingsley. Now, I hear my sons running down the hallway, so why don't we find chairs for everyone and have a lovely time with each other? All right?"

The others nodded, and Kingsley and John went into the dining room to bring more chairs, while Mrs. Kingsley and Cassandra put out more teacups and food on the table. When the boys arrived seconds later, everyone found a place at the table and started talking at once, until John put up his hand. "This is a special occasion for all of us, so before we eat, I think it is appropriate to thank God for bringing us all together today. Do you all agree?"

In complete accord, everyone closed their eyes and bowed their heads, while John thanked God for the food and the company around the table. A chorus of amens followed his, and then the boys all started questioning their mother again about her absence from the estate. Cassandra did not know who to answer first, so she said, "Boys, one at a time, please, starting with Peter."

Not wanting to discuss his concerns about Lord Dudley in front of everyone, Peter said, "I would like to speak with you privately, Mother, so why don't you answer my brothers' questions now? We can talk later."

Seeing the seriousness in his eyes, Cassandra nodded and turned to Wendell. "I guess it is your turn, Wendell. Do you want to ask me anything?"

Following his brother's lead, Wendell said no, and passed to Calvin, who then passed to Arthur. Not knowing what was going on, Arthur said, "Did Lord Dudley make you leave, Mama? I thought you were going to live here for the rest of your life. Wasn't that why Aunt Bethany let you come out here?"

"No, Arthur," said Cassandra. "Lord Dudley did not force me to leave. It was my decision. Yes, I did like it here, but I also like where I live now. We could not have two estate managers at Stillwater, so I left. It was not his fault. In fact, he did not know I was planning on leaving. He only found out after I was gone. Isn't that true, Lord Dudley?"

"It is, and I was sad to find out your mother had left without first talking to me, boys. I even went into London to persuade her to come back home, but she refused my offer. She knows she can come back here to live any time she wants to. Don't you, Mrs. Stillwater?"

"I do, but right now, that is not in my plans. So, in the future, we will have to make plans to meet in the city, boys, or perhaps take a holiday somewhere. Would you like that?"

"Yes!" shouted the boys in unison, leaving no doubt in the listeners' minds as to their opinions of this idea.

"Then that is what we will do, as long as I can get the time off from my employment," she said. "We can all look forward to spending two weeks together when you have your next break."

"Can I come too, Mrs. Stillwater?" asked John with a glimmer of mischief in his eyes.

"No, Lord Dudley, this is one time when your role as estate manager will not work to persuade me to include you in our plans. This is only for my sons and me, no one else."

The boys laughed at John's frown. Then he nodded. "So be it, ma'am. I will have to content myself with only the company of the Kingsleys and Mr. Wiley while you and the boys are away frolicking on holiday. But I won't be happy about it."

Cassandra laughed at the downtrodden look on his face. "I am used to those kinds of faces, Lord Dudley. You cannot persuade me to change my mind with that look. It will not work."

John laughed, and then changed the subject to what he and Cassandra's sons had been doing that morning before she'd arrived. As soon as he started telling stories about the boys' antics, they began chiming in and telling their own stories. Before long, teatime was over. Kingsley went back to his station in the foyer, John and the boys headed back out to the barn, and Mrs. Kingsley puttered around the kitchen, clearing the items from their tea. Cassandra was the only one left with nothing to do. Mrs. Kingsley gently rebuffed Cassandra's offer to assist her.

"It would not be proper, ma'am. You may sit here and visit with me while I work, or perhaps you would like to spend more time with your sons in the barn? Your time is short, so why don't you do that?"

"If you do not need me, then perhaps I will do as you suggest. I want to see as much of the boys as I can today, and I am sure Lord Dudley will not mind my presence. Thank you for the delicious tea and scones. I look forward to having another wonderful meal at noon with all of you. But until then..."

Mrs. Kingsley waved her off and said that she would see her at noon. Cassandra headed out of the kitchen and across the yard towards the barn, where she could hear the eager voices of her sons. But before she got there, Peter stepped out from behind a tree, making her jump. "Mother ... I have been watching for you. May we talk now?"

"Peter, you startled me. I thought everyone was in the barn. Why aren't you with your brothers? Is something wrong?"

"I am sorry to have frightened you, Mother. I did not know how else to speak to you in private. Are you all right?"

"Yes, of course, son. I was just surprised, that's all. Certainly, we can talk. Where you like to go?"

"Let's walk down to the gate. There is no one there, so I can tell you my suspicions about Lord Dudley, and find out why you really left. I don't believe you told us everything in the kitchen, and I need to know exactly what is happening."

Cassandra agreed to walk with him. As they walked, she told him about how the estate had been faring under her management and that she had asked the Duke of Yardley to find a replacement for her. She also mentioned her previous time with John, how they had not got on well, and that having later found out that John was to be the new manager had been the impetus for her moving out of the estate and back to London. She skipped some details of what had previously occurred with John, as she did not want Peter spreading stories about him.

"Does that answer your questions, Peter?" she asked, hoping that she had given him enough information to satisfy his curiosity.

"Somewhat, Mother. I think you are still keeping some information from me, but I know enough now to answer the questions my brothers will ask me."

"Thank you, Peter. Yes, there are things you do not need to know, as Lord Dudley and I have resolved them. Please do not blame him for my leaving. It was not his fault."

"I'll try not to, Mother. But I still dislike the idea of you living in the city, especially near the docks. Can you not find anywhere else to live that would be safer for you?"

"I did not say anything earlier because it is not a certainty, but I may become the housemother of the boarding house, Peter. With that job, I can live and work in the same place, so my safety will not be an issue. I will send word to you once I know if I have been successful in procuring that position."

"If that is what you want, Mother, then I am happy for you. But I do not think Aunt Bethany will be happy to hear you have left the estate."

"No, I don't suppose she will be, but what's done is done, and we must carry on. She was very kind to provide us a home for the past five years, but soon you and your brothers will have lives of your own, and I will be alone at Stillwater. As such, I think this is best for all of us. There is no going back to the way things were. We can only move forward."

Peter nodded, then took his mother's arm, and they strolled back towards the manor. On the way, he filled her in on all his studies and activities at school, as well as his hopes and dreams for the future.

***

John noted that Peter had not come into the barn with his brothers. Being that he was almost a man, though, and knew the estate well, John did not worry about him. His only concern was Peter's lingering doubts about John's place at the estate. Would Peter ever forgive him for taking over Cassandra's role? Yet, truly, what did it matter? He would seldom see the boys. Cassandra planned to take them away on their next break, and if that went well, she would continue doing so for every school holiday. Then John's time at the estate would be over, and he would head back to Australia, perhaps never to see any of them again. No, let Peter have his concerns; John's were simply managing the estate well and leaving it in good shape for the next manager, whomever that might be. That is where he would focus his thoughts and energy, not on a boy worried about his mother's welfare.

***

Later that afternoon, after a satisfying lunch and a motherly chat with each of her sons, Cassandra decided that it was time for her to head back to London. She asked Kingsley to have a carriage brought round for her, hoping that this would minimise the fuss over her departure. But as soon as the boys saw the horses being tethered to the carriage, they knew Cassandra was preparing to leave. Along with John, they left the barns and headed up to the manor to say their goodbyes. Seeing them standing beside the carriage when she left the house, Cassandra almost burst into tears. This was even harder than when she'd have to send them off to school at the end of one of their breaks.

She straightened her shoulders and gulped back the tears before walking out to where they were standing. The boys frowned as she approached, and seeing this, she shook her head. "Now, none of that, boys. You knew I was only here for a few hours. Be thankful for the time we had together, and do not look like that. We will see each other again soon, and then, perhaps, we can spend two wonderful weeks together. So, give me a hug and a smile, something positive by which to remember this day. All right?"

The boys did as Cassandra asked, one by one, although she could tell their smiles were forced and insincere. The hugs were tight and lingering on both sides.

Finally, she stepped away from Arthur and turned to John. "Thank you for looking after my sons, Lord Dudley. I pray they will not cause you any problems while they are here."

"I'm sure they won't, Mrs. Stillwater," he said, taking her hand and pressing it gently before releasing it. "It was wonderful to see you today. Have a pleasant trip back to London and please come back again for another visit soon."

"We shall see, Lord Dudley. My need to come here today was to visit with my sons. Without them here, I see no reason to return."

"I wanted you to know that you are welcome here any time and if you choose to return—"

"I know," interrupted Cassandra. "But my plans do not include such an occurrence. Now, it is time for me to leave, so I can get back in time for dinner at the boarding house. Boys, be good for Lord Dudley and the Kingsleys. I love you all." Then she turned, and with John's assistance, climbed up into the carriage. Then John stowed the steps inside it and closed the door. Standing back then, he signalled the driver to proceed. With a nod from the man, and a gentle flick of the reins, the horses began walking down the lane.

Cassandra peered out the window until she could no longer see her sons, and then settled back in her seat. Knowing that the driver would neither see nor hear her crying, she her tears flow, her shoulders shaking with sorrow.

Chapter 15

It was a sombre group that headed back to the barn after Cassandra's carriage had left the estate. The boys kicked stones as they walked, looking down at the ground. Her departure had saddened John as well, but he was wondering what he could do to cheer up the boys. He suggested several activities, but all of them were met with negative reactions. So, in the end, John fell silent and let the boys deal with their emotions in their own way. When they got to the barn, John left them to their own devices, and seeing Wiley working in a distant corner, he headed off to converse with him. Once he was out of earshot, the boys began to talk.

"Why didn't she stay?" asked Arthur.

"She couldn't," replied Peter.

"Why not?"

"Because of Lord Dudley."

Calvin frowned. "What does Lord Dudley have to do with Mother leaving again, Peter?"

"Almost everything, I think."

"Then we need to get rid of Lord Dudley," Wendell said. "But how can we do that?"

"Kill him?" Arthur asked.

"No, of course not, Arthur. We only need to get him to leave the estate. Then Mother will come back, and everything will be as it was before he showed up."

"I don't know how we can do that, Wendell," Peter said. "After all, the duke appointed him as the new manager, and one does not go against a duke's wishes."

"I suppose not. But what if Lord Dudley decided he did not want to stay here any longer? Then the duke couldn't keep him against his will, could he?"

"I guess not. But Lord Dudley seems content at the estate. What would make him want to leave?"

"I don't know," replied Wendell, "but we have almost two weeks to come up with something. Surely, we can find a way. We only have to think..."

The other boys agreed with him, and so they spent the rest of the afternoon plotting to get rid of John without murdering him; their mother would never approve of that plan.

***

Cassandra arrived back at the boarding house just in time for dinner. She quickly shed her outer garments and rinsed her hands before heading to the dining hall. The other women acknowledged her presence with smiles before the housemother said grace, and then they all started eating. At the end of the meal, before the women started getting up to leave, the housemother stood up.

"I have an announcement. As you know, I will leave within the next week to live with my sister, and I needed to choose a new housemother to replace me. Only one person came forward to apply for the position, so Mrs. Cassandra Stillwater will be your new housemother. Congratulations, Mrs. Stillwater. I am sure you will do a fine job."

The announcement startled Cassandra. She'd known that she was being considered for the position but hadn't known that she had been the only candidate. Was she the best person for the job, or had she only been chosen because she was the only applicant? She hoped it was the former and not the latter.

Regardless, she now had work in London—work that did not require her to leave the premises, except on rare occasions. She was in a safe position and could manage her hours to accommodate her own needs and those of her sons. So, why was she not feeling thrilled at this announcement? She did not know. Perhaps it was because she'd had such a pleasant day out at the estate, enjoying both her sons and the fresh air of the country. She sighed softly. Regardless of her feelings, she knew that this was where she would be. So, she smiled and accepted the congratulations of the other women, before heading back to her room to sort through the day.

***

Unaware of Cassandra's new position, John was wondering how he could lure her back to the estate. She obviously missed living here. Perhaps only her pride was preventing her from saying so. But she needed a purpose to return. It could not be for her sons' sake, as they would soon be back at school. No, it had to be something that fulfilled her dreams and wishes. But what could that be?

John knew that he could not confide to her his plans to move permanently to Australia once his one-year term as estate manager was done, to entice her to resume her former responsibilities once he had left. No, it was her choice to no longer manage the estate that had brought him here. Regardless of his future intentions, he had seen no signs that she'd regretted her decision to give away the responsibilities of the position. So, what else could there be for her here?

Mrs. Kingsley handled both the housekeeping and cooking duties for the manor, and she was not yet of an age when she would easily give those up. Wiley took care of all the outdoor duties, and somehow, John could not see Cassandra out in the barn, mucking out the stalls alongside him, even though the notion did paint a rather humorous picture in his mind. No, he had to come up with something that suited both her nature and her abilities. He would have to ponder this more thoroughly and perhaps pick her sons' minds as to what they thought she excelled at most naturally.

Yes, that was a good idea. He would speak to the boys and find out their mother's best qualities, then design a position here just for her. With that in mind, John went to find the boys and discover more about Mrs. Cassandra Stillwater.

***

The boys loved to talk about their mother and extoll her best qualities. She was loving, considerate of their feelings, not overbearing, and always listened to them. When they had been younger, she'd been the only parent who'd spent time with them; they had seldom seen their father, let alone conversed with him. They knew that Cassandra had always put their needs ahead of her own, especially back when they'd had little money. Some days, their breakfast and dinner plates would be loaded with food whereas hers would be practically empty. On those days, she had always made excuses like she was trying to lose a bit of weight, or that she had eaten too much at lunch and was not hungry for dinner. But even as young as they had been when they were living in London, the older boys had known that it was because their father had taken money out of the household budget again for his own needs, rather than leaving it for Cassandra to feed the family.

Once they'd moved out to the country, and their father was no longer around, things had been much better, and Cassandra had eaten as heartily as they had at mealtimes. They knew that she still spent little on herself because of her chosen style of dress, but they were glad to see that she was well-fed and healthy. Now, though, with her living on her own in the city, the boys worried about both things, as did John.

Though the boys shared valuable information about their mother, John still had no idea as to what role Cassandra could assume should she return to the estate. Perhaps he should speak with the Kingsleys. They might shed more light on the subject and help him come up with a solution. After all, they were as concerned about Cassandra's welfare as he was. Tomorrow, he would sit down with them. *Mayhap, the three of us can find a role that would bring Cassandra back home.* Having settled that, John spent the rest of the evening relaxing in the front parlour with Cassandra's sons.

***

Peter was also worried about what Cassandra had told him, but even more so about what she had not said. He'd listened to John and watched him discreetly that evening, while the younger boys had expounded their mother's virtues, choosing not to enter the conversation very often. He'd just sat back in his chair, listening to John's questions and his brothers' answers. Infrequently, he would answer a question, when it was something that his younger siblings had little knowledge about. But mostly, he was silent and observant. He did not know why John was asking them these questions; he had not given them a reason other than he would like to know more about Cassandra, and who better to tell him than her sons.

Is Lord Dudley planning to use this information against Mother to keep her from ever coming back to the country? Or is he genuinely interested in learning more about her?

Perhaps he was even thinking about courting her. They were of a similar age, so that would not be out of the question, unless Lord Dudley required a blood heir of his own. Peter was certain his mother was past childbearing age, although he did not know much about such things. While his mother was not old, Peter knew for a fact that she was also not a young woman anymore. If indeed, Lord Dudley, was thinking of courtship, and eventual marriage, how did he feel about that? Peter wanted his mother to smile again, but he was not sure that another marriage, especially to someone like Lord Dudley, would serve that purpose. For the rest of his school break, he would need to focus on learning more about this man, just in case he was looking to become their stepfather. Peter narrowed his eyes as he stared at John. Yes, he would watch him closely until the day he left to go back to school.

***

John noted Peter's steady gaze upon him throughout the evening. He also noticed that the young man had said very little, leaving it up to his brothers to talk about their mother. John wondered about Peter's behaviour but did not want to say anything about it. Perhaps he was simply angry about his mother having left after such a short visit and was still blaming John for her departure. There was nothing John could do about that, and he opted not to challenge Peter on his thinking, whatever it might be. They still had a great deal of time to spend together before the boys went back to school, and John wanted it to be a pleasant time for them, not one fraught with discord. So, he would continue to be cordial to Peter, and to his brothers, and hope that this would be enough to bring about an accord between them. And if not ... well, at least he would have tried, and that was all he could do. The rest would be up to Peter.

***

While John and Peter were taking each other's measure, Cassandra was contemplating her upcoming role as housemother. She knew it differed significantly from being a mother to four sons. That role had come easily to her as her love for her boys had superseded everything else—except, of course, her love of God. But being a housemother to young women? That was new. What did she know about caring for young women? Perhaps it would only be a matter of looking after their basic needs of food and shelter, and nothing else. She would have to speak with the housemother about these issues in the next few days before she left the premises. After that, Cassandra would have no one to call upon for advice, and that caused her a great deal of concern.

Would she fail at this, like she had at estate managing? What would she do then, and where would she go? Her options were becoming increasingly limited. Cassandra shook herself to clear her head of the negative thoughts. No, she would succeed at this. There was no reason she could not do this work. She only had to convince herself of that fact. Her prayer was that God would guide her as she took on these responsibilities. She knew that she would need to rely a great deal on Him as she adjusted to this role. So, before she went to sleep that night, she knelt at the side of her bed and asked for His direction and help as she took on these different duties. Leaving it with Him then, Cassandra climbed into bed and went to sleep.

***

The next morning, with neither knowing the other's thoughts, both John and Cassandra got up with purposeful determination: John to bring Cassandra back to the estate; and Cassandra to learn how to live without it. The only question was which of them would be successful in bringing their intentions to fruition.

And when the boys arose that same morning, they had their own goal to pursue, ridding the estate of Lord Dudley. If he wasn't here, then their mother would have to come back to look after things again. But what could they do to make him leave?

After breakfast, each of them began planning for the future.

Chapter 16

Cassandra met with the housemother to discuss her duties and her concerns, the latter of which the housemother quickly dismissed. John sat down with the Kingsleys, and the boys went out to the barn to do their chores while also speaking with Mr. Wiley. They thought he might have some ideas of what they could do to send Lord Dudley on his way. After all, he was a friend of their mother's, and they were sure that he would also want her to come back and resume her duties as estate manager. But they knew they would have to be careful in how they approached the subject and watch their words in his presence. Mr. Wiley was friendly with Lord Dudley, and they did not want him to get wind of their plans. It was going to be a challenge, but they were more than up for it.

***

Once inside the barn, the boys noticed that Mr. Wiley was already there, giving directions to two stable hands. As the eldest, Peter was chosen to approach the steward. They did not want Mr. Wiley to become suspicious if they started questioning him as a group. Seeing that Lord Dudley was nowhere in the barn, Peter walked over to the steward. "Morning, Mr. Wiley."

The steward looked up and smiled. "Oh! Morning, Master Peter! It's a fine morning, is it not?"

"It is indeed. A perfect day to be out in the fresh air."

"Yes, you will be missing that when you return to school. What were you and your brothers planning to do today?"

"After we help you with the chores, we were hoping to go out riding for a bit."

"That sounds like a grand idea. I have little for you to do this morning. The hands are going to muck out the stalls, so if you want to take the horses out for some exercise, that would help them out as well."

"Thank you, sir. Uh... I had one other thing I needed to ask you before we leave to do that."

"Oh, what is that?"

"How is Lord Dudley working out as the new manager? Is he as good as Mother at doing the job?"

"He is a fine manager, Peter. One of the best. Why do you ask?"

"No particular reason. I wanted to make sure that you enjoyed working with him, and that he was not causing you any problems. Being that I am the oldest member of Aunt Bethany's family still at the estate, I feel I have a responsibility to make sure everything is running smoothly."

"Well, since Lord Dudley arrived, and we got some extra money from the Duke of Yardley, things are good, Master Peter. You have nothing to worry about at the present time. Now, when Lord Dudley leaves—"

"Oh! Is he leaving soon?"

"No," he replied, frowning slightly. "At least, not to my knowledge. But he has always made it clear that he does not plan to stay here permanently."

"I was not aware of that, Mr. Wiley. I thought he was here to stay."

"No." He shook his head. "He has informed me he was giving the duke a year to find a permanent estate manager, but that he would not be staying any longer than that."

Peter pondered the steward's words. Perhaps there was a way he and his brothers could shorten Lord Dudley's time at the estate without causing him harm. Then his mother would come back, and things would be just as they had been in the past. But what reason could they find for his leaving and not returning? That was the dilemma. He would have to talk to his brothers and find out if they had any ideas. *And what better time to do so than on a private ride in the meadows?*

Peter thanked the steward for his time and hurried back to where his brothers were waiting for him. They had horses to saddle, this day, and a plan to contrive. There was no time to waste.

***

John, too, was trying to come up with a plan to get Cassandra back to the estate. He and the Kingsleys were sitting at the kitchen table, putting a list of ideas forward before quickly dismissing each one. They were no nearer a solution than they had been thirty minutes ago.

"Why is this so difficult?" said John. "There must be something here that would entice Mrs. Stillwater to return?"

"Perhaps... No, that would not work," said Kingsley, not bothering to even voice his idea.

"Maybe if I gave her the housekeeping responsibilities and only kept the meal preparations for myself. Would that be enough, do you think, Lord Dudley?" asked Mrs. Kingsley.

"Would she be satisfied with that?"

"No ... probably not. I easily manage the two roles, especially now that the boys are away at school."

"Then she will see right through our plans as a weak excuse to have her return."

"I suppose so, but I cannot think of anything else to lure her back, sir."

"Neither can I," said Kingsley.

"Nor I," said John, sighing. "It appears that we are at a loss for feasible solutions, and unless we find a suitable one, Mrs. Stillwater may never return to her rightful place at the estate."

The three of them looked at each other sorrowfully as they pondered that thought, which they did not want to even consider. Perhaps it was in God's plans for her, and who were they to go against His sovereign will? They could only petition Him with their concerns and leave it in His hands.

Having come to that conclusion, the trio left the table to go their separate ways with a common prayer in their hearts: to bring Cassandra back home where she belonged.

***

Knowing nothing of their prayers, Cassandra was intent on learning all that the housemother had to teach her. Unfortunately, her mind kept drifting back to the previous day and the enjoyable time she'd had at the estate. Even Lord Dudley's presence had not bothered her to any degree. And seeing how much her sons were enjoying being back in the country made her realise how good it had been for them to spend the last five years living there. She hoped Lord Dudley would not prevent them from coming back again. If he did, she did not know if even vacations at the seashore with her would make up for that loss. And would she even be able to get away from her new responsibilities frequently enough? She had not realised how extensive a role she had taken on, but from the sounds of everything the housemother was telling her, it would keep her very busy, indeed.

"Do you have questions, Mrs. Stillwater?"

Cassandra shook her head to clear it, hoping she had not missed anything important while she'd been musing about the estate. "No, I don't think so, ma'am."

"Well then, as of tomorrow, I will let you assume the responsibility of housemother. I will be here for a few more days to help guide you if you need help. Don't hesitate to call on me if you do."

"Thank you, ma'am. I am glad you are not leaving just yet. I hope I am up to the job."

"I am sure you are. But it can be overwhelming at first. I certainly found it that way when I first arrived, but then things started falling into place. It will be the same for you."

"I wish I had your confidence, but I will take your words to heart. Thank you again for this opportunity."

"You are welcome. Now, if there is nothing else, I have a few things I need to do today. Please excuse me and enjoy your last day of freedom."

"I will. I look forward to starting my new work tomorrow. Morning, ma'am." With that, Cassandra turned and headed back to her room to contemplate the immensity of what she had signed on to do.

***

But even as Cassandra deliberated, John and the Kingsleys prayed, and the boys plotted, there was a new and unforeseen factor about to come into play: Lord and Lady Yardley, who with their young children had left Australian shores several months earlier on their way back to Britain for a long-awaited visit.

Chapter 17

Bethany's last childbirth had gone smoothly and she had recovered quickly. She was now the mother of three beautiful children and could not be happier with her life. David, her oldest, was five years old and full of energy. On the days when he could not get outside to play, it was a challenge to keep him busy and entertained. And when he didn't find such entertainment, he would start pestering his sister, Cecilia, who was three and a half. She was now at an age where she hated her brother stealing her toys and was quick to let the entire household know how she felt. But when he was not around, she had a sweet temperament that made her a joy to live with.

And now, there was the new baby, Douglas. At three months of age, he only cried when he needed food or a nappy change. Other than that, he was the most contented of the children. Bethany felt blessed to have such a wonderful family and was not averse to the idea of having more children, though not right away. First, she wanted to go back to England to see her friends and family; that was her priority.

Fortunately, her husband, Sam, was of the same mind, and so they had packed up their little ones, and after a month's stay in Fremantle to visit with their friends, Nick and Sally Tremblant, and Joe and Joann Winter, they had sailed for England. Sam had needed to keep a tight leash on David and Cecelia to keep them from climbing on the rigging or falling overboard when they climbed up on the railing to see the sights as they sailed past. Bethany kept busy looking after Douglas. The division of labour between Sam and Bethany worked well, and they were enjoying the voyage.

Until the day the ship turned to the west where the Indian Ocean met the Atlantic. Then the waves grew rougher, and the older children had needed to be confined to their cabin in order to keep them safe. This pleased neither David nor Cecelia, and they were quick to let their parents know of their displeasure. Fortunately, they did not run into any great storms in the passage. And once they reached the west coast of Africa, the waters calmed, and so did Bethany's nerves, as they were able to let the children out on deck to play under Sam's watchful eye.

From that point on, they usually sailed close to shore, so Sam entertained the children with discussions of the birds and animals they saw that were native to those lands. Generally, by night-time, David and Cecelia were worn out from all their adventures and slept soundly through the night, only to begin their quests all over again the next morning. Fortunately, they were both good sailors, so there was seldom a time when Bethany had to nurse them through bouts of seasickness. Often, when the ship put into port to resupply, Sam would take the children onshore with him to experience the sights, sounds, and fragrances of these exotic lands. This allowed Bethany a much-needed respite, in which she could relax and enjoy a bit of time for herself and Douglas. When Sam and the children returned, she was always quick to allow Sam to have his own time as well, while she listened to the stories of the children's explorations.

And so, the journey went on, day after day, week after week, month after month, until one day, they sailed past the English Channel on route to their last port: Portsmouth, England. Their journey was almost over.

Bethany and Sam had chosen not to send word ahead to their family that they were on route to see them. And as such, there was no carriage awaiting their arrival in Portsmouth. Sam set about hiring a large carriage to transport them to London, as well as arranging for their mound of luggage to be sent to his townhouse in the city. Unless one of his younger brothers had taken up residence there while they were in Australia, that was where they intended to stay while visiting England. If one of them had, then there would be plenty of room for them to stay at the duke's townhouse, which they knew the duke and duchess would prefer, though Sam and Bethany would rather have a space of their own for their lengthy visit. With three children underfoot, it was more of a necessity for their family than a wish.

The next day, having settled the requirements for transportation of their trunks, the family set off on the long day's journey to London. They planned several stops along the way to allow David and Cecelia the opportunity to run about and wear off excess energy, so it would take them the entire day to reach the city. Such stops were necessary though, as without them, they would have to contend with two fractious children, and the thought of that was not something they wished to bear.

Finally, after a long bumpy ride, the lights of London appeared in the distance. By this point, the children were worn out and half asleep, so when they reached the station, Sam quickly hired a hack to take them to his townhouse. Soon, they were at the doorstep, and the lights in the front windows welcomed them home. Sam ran up and found out that there were enough staff in-house to meet their needs for the night. Then he and a footman carried David and Cecelia into the house and straight up to the nursery, where the housekeeper and a maid had hurriedly made beds for the children. Once they'd gotten them settled, and brought in what little luggage they had brought with them in the carriage, Sam and Bethany went into the front parlour and collapsed on the settee. Then they just looked at each other and shared a smile. They had endured the journey. They were home.

***

David and Cecelia were up early the next morning, and finding themselves in strange surroundings, immediately sought out the comfort of their parents. The maid, who had been watching over the children for the night, apologised to their parents for waking them up but was forgiven as Sam and Bethany welcomed their offspring into their room. His siblings' arrival had also awakened Douglas, who added his voice to the fray. So, while Bethany fed him and entertained the older children, Sam dressed for the day. Then he took the children back to the nursery and helped them dress before heading down to the breakfast room with them. By this time, Bethany had finished feeding Douglas and dressed herself. She took him to the nursery and settled him down, with a maid watching over him, before going down to share breakfast with the rest of the family.

Still in awe of everything around him, David smiled at Bethany when she arrived, "Mama, did you make all this food for breakfast?"

Bethany laughed when she saw the requisite full English breakfast on the sideboard. "No, darling, I was asleep until you and CeCe woke me up. The cook made breakfast for us all."

"The cook?" asked David with a frown.

"Yes, in England, we will have a cook to make all our meals. It is the way they do things here."

"But what if I don't like the food? Will you cook for me then, Mama?"

"I am sure you will like the meals. But if there is something you don't like, perhaps I will cook for you, but only then. All right?"

"I suppose so."

Bethany could tell that her answer did not satisfy him, so she took the two children over to the sideboard and helped them pick out things they were familiar with. This was not the time to try and introduce new foods. Once they had their plates full, the footman filled a plate for her and set it at one side of the table. Sam sat at the head of the table, with David to his left and Cecelia to his left. This way, each child had a parent to attend to their needs. Once Sam had a plateful of food in front of him, he asked the blessing, and then they started eating.

Between mouthfuls of food, the children peppered them with questions, most of which Sam and Bethany put off until they'd finished eating, fearing that it would be time for the noon meal before they'd even left the breakfast table otherwise. So, they encouraged the children to eat, and not talk, and by doing so, it only took an hour to finish their meal. Then they went to the front parlour to discuss plans for the day.

"I think the first stop of the day has to be your parents' townhouse, Sam," said Bethany. "They will be hurt should they somehow discover we are in town and have not gone directly to see them."

"I agree, Beth. And as we don't want to send a note ahead, and ruin the surprise, we will get everyone ready and head over as soon as possible."

"That's fine with me. As we don't have our trunks yet, we can just help David and Cecelia freshen up a bit, pack a few things for Douglas in a small portmanteau, and leave within a few minutes." Turning to the children, she said, "Would you like to visit your grandparents this morning?"

David smiled. "Grandmother and Grandfather are here?"

"Close by, son," Sam said, smiling back at him.

"Yes, please," said Cecelia.

"Well," Sam said. "Now, you need to go back upstairs to the nursery with your mama to wash your hands and comb your hair. I'll arrange for transportation, Beth."

Bethany smiled in agreement before herding the children upstairs. Sam spoke with the butler, who said that he would send a footman to the nearest livery to fetch a landau and a team of horses. And with those plans in place, Sam headed upstairs to make himself presentable for his parents.

***

Soon the landau with two shiny black horses arrived in front of the townhouse. Bethany got in first. Then Sam handed her the baby, after which he and the children climbed in and situated themselves on the seats, with Cecelia beside Bethany, and David alongside Sam. Once they were seated, Sam directed the driver, and they set off to see the duke and duchess.

Only minutes later, they arrived at the impressive portico of the ducal townhouse. Sam jumped down, and then assisted the children and Bethany out of the carriage. He then paid the driver and told him he did not need to wait, as Sam was sure that his father would provide them with a carriage for the ride home. The driver tipped his hat before leaving the family standing outside the property's picket fence. Sam opened the gate, then ushered his family up to the door and knocked.

Seconds later, Parker, the family butler, opened the door. At first, he wore a serious look, but it immediately turned into a smile once he recognized who was standing on the step.

"Lord Yardley? Lady Yardley? Are my old eyes deceiving me?"

Sam laughed. "No, Parker, it is me and my family, home for a visit."

"Your family?" he said, looking down at David and Cecelia, and then at Douglas in Bethany's arms.

"Yes. You remember my wife from our previous visit, I am sure, but we are now a family of five. David is our oldest child. Cecelia is next, and then Douglas, who is resting in his mother's arms. Quite different from when Bethany and I left for Australia, isn't it?"

"Indeed, it is, sir. But please, come in," he said, ushering them through the door and into the foyer.

Sam stood back as Bethany and the children preceded him into the open space. David and Cecelia's eyes widened with wonder as they took in the high ceiling and grandeur of the room. "Papa," said Cecelia, pulling on his arm, "is this where the princes and princesses live?"

Sam laughed. "No. They live in a palace. This is where your grandparents live. Would you like to meet them?"

Cecelia nodded her head vigorously, as did David, though both of them seemed nearly struck silent by the beauty of the foyer.

"Then we shall." Turning back to Parker, Sam said, "Where would we find my parents, Parker?"

"I believe they are in the morning parlour, Lord Yardley. They just arrived back from the country yesterday. It is fortunate they are here to greet you. Shall I announce you?"

"No, I would like to surprise them. We will announce ourselves, thank you."

"Well, sir. And may I say again how pleased I am to see you."

"Thank you, Parker. It good to be home again. Now, children," he said, turning back to his family, "follow your mother. She knows the way to the parlour."

Bethany nodded and turned towards the hall that led to the morning parlour. David and Cecelia followed her silently while Sam brought up the rear. When they approached the open door and heard Sam's parents' voices beyond it, Bethany smiled and stepped back as Sam moved into the doorway and took a purposefully casual step inside the room. "Good morning, Mother and Father. How are you today?"

After a single instant of shocked silence, a female scream of joy pierced the air, followed by words of amazed disbelief. "Sam!? Are my ears and eyes deceiving me, or it is really you?"

Sam laughed. "No, Mother, your senses are not lying to you. I am home for a visit." He moved farther into the room, while Bethany and the children continued to wait in the hall.

"It is wonderful to see you, my son," said a deep male voice then. "Did you just arrive?"

"No, we arrived last evening and spent the night at my townhouse. I was glad to see it was unoccupied, so we did not have to disturb you until this morning."

The duchess frowned dismissively. "Disturb us? Nonsense, but you—Wait, you said, 'we.' Is Bethany with you? And if so, where?"

"She is waiting in the hall with the children, Mother."

"In the hall? Samuel Edward Yardley, you bring them in this moment! If you don't, why... I don't know what I will do to you exactly, but I will punish you! See if I don't."

Taking this empty threat as her cue, Bethany herded the children into the parlour then to meet their grandparents. "Good morning, Mother and Father," she said. "I am so happy to see you again."

"Bethany, my dear!" said the duchess, rushing over to envelop her in her arms. "I can't believe it! You are here!"

"Yes, Mother, we are." Bethany returned the hug as best she could with Douglas between them.

"It is so good to see you," said the duchess unnecessarily, "and to finally meet my grandchildren. Please, introduce me at once."

Bethany smiled and did as the duchess had demanded. "Certainly, Your Grace. This is David Edward Yardley, our eldest. He is five years old. Then comes Cecelia Anne Yardley. She is three. And finally, the baby in my arms is Douglas Samuel Yardley. He is almost a year old now. Children, this is your grandmother, the Duchess of Yardley, and the man standing behind her is your grandfather, the Duke of Yardley."

David tugged on Bethany's sleeve, and she stooped to look into his eyes. He turned his head quickly and whispered something in her ear that made her laugh and shake her head. "I don't know that, David. Adults don't talk about those things. It is not polite to ask."

"What did he want to know?" asked the duchess.

"Can I tell her?" Bethany said to David.

He nodded, so she said, "Since I told you David's age, he wanted to know why I did not tell him yours as well."

The adults chuckled before the duchess turned to David with a nod. "That is a good question, David. I don't know why we don't talk about our age when we get older. Perhaps it is because we don't want to think about it. But these grey and white hairs on your grandparents' heads come with age, so I guess you could say that we are old, at least from your perspective. Does that answer your question?"

"I guess so. Mama and Papa are old, and if you are Papa's mama, then you must be very old."

"You are correct, David, but let's only talk about it when we are alone and not in company. All right?"

David nodded.

"Excellent. Now, I am not too old to ask for a hug. May I have one?"

David nodded again, and his grandmother crouched down and opened her arms. He moved into them, and she squeezed him tightly before releasing him. Then she turned and said to Cecelia, "May I also have a hug from my beautiful granddaughter?"

Cecelia, a little shy, moved forward only after a gentle nudge from her mother. When she was in her grandmother's arms though, she lifted her own and gave the duchess a little squeeze around her neck, which brought tears to the woman's eyes. The duchess released her then, and Cecelia stepped back to the comfort of her mother's side. Then she too pulled down her mother's sleeve to whisper something in her ear.

"Why don't you tell your grandmother that, CeCe? I am sure she would love to hear it."

Cecelia swallowed nervously. Then in a small voice, she said, "I like your smell, Grandmother. It reminds me of flowers from home."

At these words, the duchess reached out again for another hug, even as tears of joy started pouring down her face. Cecelia moved back into her arms, and they hugged each other closely for a long moment before the duchess released her once more. This time, Cecelia stayed by her side with a big smile on her face, and when she noticed the duchess struggling a bit to get up from her crouching position, she reached out a hand to help her.

"Thank you, my dear," said the duchess, once she was upright again. "Your help was exactly what I needed. You are sweet to help an old lady like that."

Cecelia's smile grew even bigger at her grandmother's praise. When the duchess moved over to Bethany to view the baby, Cecelia stayed glued to her side.

"And now to hold the youngest member of our family, named after his grandfather," said the duchess, reaching out to take Douglas from Bethany's arms. "You said he is eleven months old?"

"Yes."

"He is a large baby for his age."

Bethany laughed. "Yes, I tend to have large babies. I wonder why that is?" she said, looking over at her husband and father-in-law, both of whom were rather tall.

"The curse of marrying a Yardley, my dear. All of my sons were big babies, as were your sister-in-law Hannah's. I shall likely have to warn prospective brides of my remaining sons of that fact before they marry. They may want to think twice about marrying either of them once they know that truth."

"I doubt it will make any difference, Mother," said Bethany. "I know it would not have changed my mind about marrying Sam."

"No, I suppose it would not, Bethany. These Yardley men have a way of worming their way into our hearts, and once they get in there, they never leave." The duchess cast a loving glance over to her husband.

"As do their wives," the duke responded before moving forward and joining the women. "Now, I believe it is my turn to greet my grandchildren." Doing as his wife had done only moments before, the duke crouched down and put out his hand to David. "Young man, I am your grandfather. I am pleased to meet you after all this time."

David walked over, grasped his hand, and shook it. "I am pleased to meet you too, Grandfather."

The duke laughed at his formality before pulling him in for a quick hug. When he released him, he turned to Cecelia and extended both his arms to her. She ran over and hugged him tight. Then with her in his arms, the duke stood up. "You have your mother's beautiful eyes and hair. Did you know that?"

She nodded but remained silent.

"It's a good thing you look like her and not your father. We would not want that now, would we?"

Cecelia giggled and shook her head.

Sam harrumphed from behind his father.

"I am so glad to have a beautiful granddaughter," the duke said. "Until now, all I have had is grandsons. You are my only granddaughter, so I will attempt to spoil you rotten. Is that all right with you?"

A tiny yes emerged, though it was loud enough for everyone to hear.

"Not too much, Father," said Sam, coming over to stand beside the duke. "Otherwise, we will have a terrible time dealing with her after we go back home."

The duke shook his head. "It is my prerogative as a grandfather, Sam, so you will have to deal with the consequences. I intend to spoil all of your children to the nth degree while you are here, and that is not only the word of your father but of the Duke of Yardley as well."

On hearing this, Sam turned to Bethany and sighed dramatically. "Dearest, I think our visit is over. I cannot bear the thought of raising children whose grandparents have thoroughly spoiled them. We need to leave now, pack our bags, and head back to Australia."

Bethany kept a straight face as she nodded and reached out to take Douglas from his grandmother. But David ruined the show. "No! I don't want to go back home! I like it here. I want to stay with my grandparents and be spoiled."

His words broke the ice, and the adults laughed as Bethany reassured him that his father was only teasing, and that they would stay for a long, long time. Then the duchess changed the subject and asked if anyone was hungry.

"We finished breakfast before we came, Mother," said Bethany, "but I think know of a couple of children who can always eat, day or night. Don't you?"

The duke and duchess nodded their heads in unison, and then the duchess walked over and pulled the cord to summon Parker. When he arrived, she asked for a fresh tea tray and lots of treats for the children. He agreed to pass on her request to the cook, and then left to do the duchess's bidding.

Soon, the tea tray arrived, and they settled everyone with a cup of tea—even the children, who truly only had milk with a few drops of tea mixed in. Then Bethany asked a question dear to her heart:

"Have you seen Cassandra of late? How is she doing?"

***

Silence pervaded the room.

Chapter 18

Finally, the duke shook his head. "No, Bethany, we have not seen her in a while. I believe the last time I saw her was when we repaired to the country, was it not, Margaret?"

"Yes, I think you are right. We stopped in on the way to the country house, and then you made another visit to her a few weeks later. That was the last time we had contact with her."

"Was she well when you saw her, Father?" asked Sam.

"Yes. She was tired but had no other complaints."

"Has any of the family seen her since your last visit?" asked Bethany.

"John has seen her a few times, I believe."

"John has?"

"Yes, he has had time to spare since coming home, so he has visited the estate on a couple of occasions."

"Douglas," said the duchess, "Bethany and Sam need to know the truth about Cassandra. There is no point in concealing it."

"What truth?" asked Bethany.

"Cassandra is no longer living at Stillwater Estate. John is the new estate manager, and Cassandra is living in London."

"What?"

"Yes, I am sorry to have to give you this news, Bethany, but you would have learned it soon. Cassandra asked me to find her a replacement as the estate manager. She was quite adamant about it. So, I asked John to step in and handle things for you. He said he would do it for a year, after which he intends to carry on with his own life plans."

"I still don't understand why Cassandra would leave the country. She loved it there, as did the boys. Even if she did not want the responsibility of managing the estate, why didn't she stay? I only gave her the role so she would have something to do with her time, not because I expected her to work for her living."

"I don't know, Bethany, but I suspect it had something to do with John taking over. From what he tells me; she did not take well to his coming. Perhaps if another manager were in place, she would return, but that is only speculation on my part."

"Are the boys still going out for their school breaks?"

"Yes, I believe they were there for the last one. They relish getting out of the city."

"Do you know where Cassandra is living?"

"From John's last report, I understand that she is at the Young Women's Christian Association boarding house near the river."

"Is she working there or boarding at the house?"

"Again, I don't know, Bethany. I am sorry to lack the information you seek."

"It is all right, Father," she said, before turning to Sam. "Sam, I need to go to the YWCA as soon as possible. My heart will not be at rest until I have seen and talked to Cassandra. I must find out why she left the country."

"I understand, love, and will arrange for you to do so within the next few days. As I understand the boarding house is near the docks, and I am not comfortable with you hiring a hack to travel to that part of town, I will need to secure a carriage and driver, etc., before I let you go."

"Yes, I would prefer that as well, Sam, so I agree to wait until we make those preparations. But please do it as soon as possible. I am fearful for Cassandra's welfare."

"It was in my plans to speak to Father today about the use of one of his carriages and drivers, Beth. Do you agree with that, Father?"

"Of course, Sam. I would not have it any other way. After tea, you and I can go out to the stables and select a carriage and team of horses. I also have someone who is presently not driving for me; he should be an excellent fit for you and your family."

"Thank you. That is one less staff member we need to hire. So, now that we have a plan, Beth, we can decide the best time for you to see Cassandra within the next few days. Would you like me to accompany you?"

"No. I think it is best if I go alone, Sam. She will open up more fully to me if it is only the two of us in the room."

"Very well. With everything so new for the children, they might not appreciate being left only with the servants in any case."

"You can always bring them here, Sam," said his mother. "We will be happy to have them anytime you and Bethany need to go somewhere."

"Thank you, Mother. I know we can count on you. But we do not aspire to be a burden either, do we, Beth?"

"No, we don't. I echo Sam's thanks, Mother. Perhaps, later in our time here, we will take you up on the offer, but not just yet. As Sam said, the children need at least one of us with them at all times right now."

"Well, but don't be strangers. I want to spend as much time as I can with you and Sam, and my darling grandchildren, while you are in London."

Bethany laughed. "You will see us so often that you will tire of us." She then looked down at her two oldest children and saw their eyelids beginning to droop. "Sam, I think we need to leave soon so the children can have a rest. Can you and your father find a carriage and team soon to take us home?"

"We can, love," said Sam, also looking down at his drowsy offspring. "Perhaps we will take one of the readied coaches, and then I will come back with the driver to arrange for our own team. Would that be acceptable, Father?"

"Of course, Sam. Let's do that now, while the ladies get the children ready to depart," said the duke, standing up and walking with Sam to the door. "Margaret, we will meet you and Bethany at the front gate in a few moments. All right?"

The duchess nodded, and the men left the room. Bethany gave the duchess her sleeping baby, and then turned her attention to her older children. Tugging gently on their hands, she said, "Get up now, David and Cecelia. We are going home, and you can rest there in your beds. It has been a long morning for you both."

The children struggled to their feet and held Bethany's hands as she led them down the hallway. In the foyer, Parker helped her put cloaks on Cecelia and David before opening the door. As soon as the carriage came around, the women and children walked out to the gate.

"It is so silly," said the duchess, wiping away tears after handing Douglas back to Bethany. "I feel like I am saying goodbye again when you have only arrived home."

"I know, Mother," said Bethany, giving her a one-armed hug. "But thankfully, this will only be one of many visits to come. We plan to stay for almost the next year, so we will have plenty of time to be together. But for right now..."

"I understand. I, too, once had little ones who needed rest, Bethany. You are a mother to my grandchildren. I am so glad you and Sam fell in love and got married, so I can have these precious times with you. You go home and get some sleep as well. I will see you soon."

Bethany nodded and climbed into the carriage with Sam's assistance. Once they were all in and seated, the duke gave the driver a signal to proceed, and they left for their own home, only a short distance away.

Waving to the duke and duchess still standing by the gate, Bethany thought about how blessed she was to be in Sam's family. There were no two people on earth who were more giving than her in-laws, except perhaps her husband. She looked over and smiled at the man, wondering again how she was in such a fortunate position, instead of a marriage like Cassandra's had been. Thinking of her sister-in-law, her smile faded, and she saddened. *Oh, Cassandra, what has happened to you...*

***

While Bethany was pondering Cassandra's situation, Cassandra, too, was wondering about it and what she had gotten herself into when she'd taken this position. It was not the counting and ordering of supplies that were the problem; it was the other women living in the boarding house with her. Several of them were completely petty-minded. They came to her at all hours of the day and night, complaining about their rooms, their food, and the other women annoying them. If there was a grievance to be made, they made it. That was one aspect of the job the former housemother had not told her about.

Having never lived in a situation like this prior to coming to the boarding house, plus having spent most of her time in her room except for meals, Cassandra had been unaware of what was going on around her. To be fair, not all the women acted in such a manner, only a select group. But that was enough. Some complaints were reasonable, and she dealt with them, but others were uncalled-for. Some women wanted more meat on their plate at dinner-time, whereas others wanted it to be full of vegetables. Both complaints involved increasing the food budget, which Cassandra could not do unless the lodging prices also increased. And she knew what a response she would get from that.

There were the light sleepers who grumbled about the women who snored so loudly that they could hear them through the thin walls separating the rooms. The accusers wanted all the snorers to be segregated in one area of the house, so the non-snorers could get more sleep. Cassandra resisted that request, saying that she was not about to switch everyone around just to please a few. This resistance to action did not increase her favour with the complainants, and they kept coming with other petty requests. Some women were using the washroom over their allotted time, and others had to hurry with their toilette each morning in order to get to work on time. There were even issues about lost hairpins and accessories that were sure to have been stolen, although they always showed up eventually in the complainant's room. And so it went ... on, and on, and on, hour after hour, day after day.

On one such day, a carriage pulled up in front of the boarding house and a woman dressed in nice though simple clothes climbed down and eyed the building's drab, brown siding. Shaking her head a bit, Bethany headed up the cobblestone walk and climbed the wooden steps. No one was outside, so she lifted the iron knocker and let it clang three times before stepping back. Soon, she heard chains being released, and then the door opened to reveal Cassandra's profile, speaking a greeting even as she turned to see who was at the door. "Yes, can I..." Her eye widened in amazement then. "Bethany?"

"Yes."

"Bethany Yardley! You are here? In person?"

"Yes."

"I don't believe it. But how? Where?" Cassandra was at a loss for words.

Bethany laughed. "I will answer those questions if you have a few minutes. Do you?"

"Yes, of course. Please come in," she said, flinging the door wide and pulling Bethany inside by both arms. When Bethany was in the foyer, Cassandra still did not release her, sobbing her name over and over again. Bethany was in no better shape as she kept hugging her sister-in-law and refusing to let her go.

Finally, the two broke apart just enough to look into each other's faces before pulling together in another fierce hug. At last, satisfied with each other's presence, they released their grasps and stood back to survey one another.

Cassandra was the first to speak coherently. "Oh, Bethany, you don't know how good it is to see you. I have missed you so much. I did not know when we would be together again. You look good. Are you well?"

"Yes, but I wish I could say the same for you, my sister. What is going on?"

"Obviously, you know some of my story or you would not have found me, but I do not know where to start, Bethany. My life has turned upside down since last I saw you, and this is where I have landed."

"I know a bit from speaking with the duke a few days ago, Cassandra, but even that could not prepare me to see you as you are. Are you ill?"

"No. I am physically well but so tired, Bethany. My sleep never refreshes me."

"Can you come with me to a tearoom and tell me what is happening?"

"I suppose I could. There is nothing urgent for me to do at the moment. Please let me inform the cook, and then freshen up a bit. I won't be long."

Bethany agreed to wait, and it was not long before Cassandra was back with her. She had fixed her hair, taken off her apron, and pulled a shawl around her shoulders. Carrying a reticule in her right hand, she opened the door with her left before waving Bethany to precede her outside. When they were both on the porch, she turned and locked the door behind her, which worried Bethany even more than the look of the building.

"Do you have to keep the door locked at all times, Cassandra?"

"We do. With this building being as close as it is to the docks, we have some rather unsavoury characters wandering around. As such, we have to protect everyone inside the building."

"What about outside? Do you have guards patrolling the street?"

"No. The budget does not allow for such extravagance. The bobbies try to make frequent patrols, but even that is not done routinely."

"Have there been any incidents while you have been here?"

"Yes. A man tried to force me into the bushes one afternoon when I was returning to the house. Fortunately, or by God's grace, Lord Dudley was here and rescued me. If he had not been, I do not know what would have happened to me."

"How terrible for you! Were you hurt?"

"Only bruises, thankfully."

"And yet you are still here. Why?"

"Here is not the place to tell you, Bethany. Let us wait until we get our tea."

"Well. I don't know this area. Is there a tearoom close by?"

"Yes, there is one near White's Jewellers. I'll give the driver directions if you like."

"Please do."

Cassandra spoke to the driver, who told her that he was familiar with that area of the city. He then climbed up onto his seat, clicked the reins, and they were off.

***

Arriving at the tearoom, Cassandra pointed out a waiting area down the street for carriages. Bethany and Cassandra agreed that they would meet him there after they had finished their tea. The driver nodded and headed in that direction.

The tearoom was relatively empty, but Bethany requested a quiet table, set off from the others, so that she and Cassandra could speak freely without being overheard. Soon, they were seated at a lovely table overlooking a pond where geese and swans swam side by side. But the view did not interest Bethany. She was more intent on what Cassandra had to say. Their tea things arrived, and then Bethany looked at Cassandra.

"All right. We are private now. No one can hear our conversation, so tell me why you are living in a boarding house near the docks instead of at the estate."

Cassandra looked at Bethany, but before she could speak, she broke down crying. "I'm so ashamed, Bethany. I don't know what to tell you other than I'm a complete failure."

Bethany was uncertain what she had expected to hear from Cassandra, but it had definitely not been those words. *Cassandra? A failure? The same woman who raised four fine sons in a household ruled by a tyrannical husband? Of what could she possibly be ashamed?* Bethany wanted to probe but thought it best that Cassandra tell her in her own way. So, she waited.

Finally, Cassandra got her crying under control and could speak again. "I'm sorry you had to see that, Bethany. I'm not usually a crier, but lately ... well, everything is getting on top of me. I must be going through the change of life. I've heard that it affects some women's emotions. So, perhaps that is what's happening to me."

"How old are you now, Cassandra?"

"Thirty-four."

"Then unless you are going through the change early, that is not what is happening. There must be something else causing you distress."

"Well, yes, I guess there is. I took the job of housemother at the boarding house to earn a living, thinking that it would be easy. But I am finding it not at all what I expected. The household accounting and taking care of ordering supplies, and whatnot, is fine, but the women themselves are the problem. Some of them are so demanding and rude, not only to me but to other women as well. A few of them wanted me to change the rooms around so they did not have to listen to women snoring in the next room. Can you imagine that? When I refused, they became angry and even harder to deal with. If the original housemother was still in London, I'd head to her home and hand over the keys to her without a second glance. But she has moved to Surrey to live with her sister, so I can't do that. I'm stuck and don't know where to turn."

"It does sound rather awful, Cassandra. Were there no other options for work available to you when you came to the city?"

"Not really. I applied for a couple of housekeeper positions, but they turned me away because of my age. Did you know there was a minimum age you had to be for that job?"

"I suspect there was more to it than that, Cassandra. If the lady of the house was interviewing you, she might have been worried you were too pretty, and that was the reason she did not hire you, not because of your age."

"You are too kind, Bethany. Any looks that I may have had in my younger years have all faded away."

"You do not see yourself as I see you, Cassandra Stillwater. I see beautiful brown eyes, in a face framed by luxurious locks of chestnut hair. Your figure is still good, even after birthing four sons. And now I know what a challenge it is to lose that extra weight after childbirth. In fact, right now, you are too thin, but that is because of your present situation, isn't it?"

"Yes, I don't eat much. I have little appetite after listening to complaining women all day."

"So, the first thing we need to do is get you away from the boarding house. I am sure they can manage on their own for a while until they hire a new housemother. You don't have to stay and ruin your health because of it."

"But where would I go, Bethany? I can't go back to the estate. There is nothing for me there."

"When I asked you if you would like to move out to the country and raise your sons at the estate, did I ever say you had to take on the role of estate manager? I only suggested it because I thought you would want something to help occupy your time, especially after the boys left to go to school. It was never meant it to be a burden for you, Cassandra."

"I know, and I thought I could handle it. And I was until..."

"Until what?"

"Until the drought hit... Over the past couple of years, both the grain and feed crops have failed, and we had to buy feed for the animals, and the money was running out, and—"

"Stop right there, my sister. Why did you not write and tell me how things were? Did you try to handle everything on your own?"

"Yes. I did not want you to be ashamed that you had appointed me as the estate manager. But I could not find a way for the estate to survive. I was going to sell some of my jewellery to tide us over for a year, but God was working against me. Each time I came into town, the shop was closed, so I could not sell them. I did not want to tell the duke how I had failed you, but eventually, I knew I had to confess and have him appoint someone else in my place. When I found out Lord Dudley was going to take over from me, I had to leave the estate. We could not both live there amicably. So, once he arrived, I left and came to London to look for employment. And now you know how that turned out. I have failed again. That is the pattern of my life."

"You are not a failure, Cassandra! If I had known about the drought and the effect it was having on the estate, I would have had the duke, or Mr. Brown, promptly help you. You should not have had to bear that burden by yourself. I am sorry you felt you had failed me. You did not and have not done so. But perhaps you needed some time back in the city to see that your life is still at the estate. I am sure the Kingsleys miss you dreadfully, and perhaps Lord Dudley does as well."

"I miss the Kingsleys too, Bethany. They have been wonderful to me and the boys. Lord Dudley, perhaps, not as much."

"Why not? I quite enjoyed his company while he lived with us in Australia. David adored him. He is good with the children and will make a wonderful father someday."

"Exactly. He needs to be around young women, one of whom he can one day wed and have a family with. I have had my marriage and my children; the former I do not want to repeat, and I am too old to have any further children. So, if you are plotting what I see in your eyes, Bethany Yardley, you can forget that notion. There is no future for Lord Dudley and me. Please put that out of your mind."

"All right. But some day you have to tell me why you dislike him so. I cannot fathom it. But regardless of his presence at the estate, won't you please reconsider and return? I hate seeing you in this situation, Cassandra."

"For your sake, and only that, dear sister, I will consider it. But now, I need to get back to the boarding house and my duties there. I am still the housemother and cannot neglect my responsibilities."

"Well. But only if you assure me this is temporary. Otherwise, I will be on your doorstep daily. I will be a worse nuisance to you than any of the young women under your roof."

"That I do not need, Bethany Yardley, so I will think about what we have talked about today. I am so glad to have you home again. It is the brightest spot in my life, other than my sons, of course. Please tell me you are here for a long time."

"We are, and we will have plenty of time to spend together in the future. Now, let us find my carriage and take you home, my friend."

After paying the bill, the two ladies got up, and headed back to the carriage arm-in-arm. On the way, Bethany regaled Cassandra with hilarious tales of her children's antics over the past few days, which had her laughing all the way back to the YWCA. When they reached the boarding house, they exchanged a hug inside the carriage, and then Bethany watched as Cassandra hurried up the path to the front door. After unlocking it, she turned back and waved before disappearing inside. Then Bethany's carriage departed for the comfort of her own home and family.

***

Cassandra leaned against the door after she locked it. The joy of seeing Bethany and catching up with her after all these years apart was indescribable. She could not wait to see Sam again and meet the children. Even the stories about them had filled her with delight. Bethany had found such happiness with Sam after the cruel events that Cassandra and her late husband, Howard, had enacted upon her. To this day, Cassandra could hardly believe that she had gone along with Howard's scheme of falsely accusing Bethany of stealing her jewellery and sending her down to a penal colony in Australia. Fortunately, Bethany's future husband had been there for her all that time, and God had protected her from harm, even thwarting an assassin's attempt upon her life.

God had worked on Cassandra's conscience as well during that time, finally giving her the courage to confess her sin of perjury to a judge, which had led to Bethany's sentence being overturned. Cassandra had been afraid that Bethany would never forgive her or talk to her again upon her return to England. But instead, Bethany had readily forgiven her, knowing that Cassandra had only done it to protect her sons from their father. She had even provided a home for them, far away from their past life in London.

Cassandra had been astounded at Bethany's generosity and had vowed never to hurt her again, which had never happened until the drought had hit and the crops had failed. But even now, after hearing about her failure as the estate manager, Bethany still loved her and wanted the best for her. The question was whether or not she could forget about the past and return to

Stillwater Estate just to live, without managing its affairs? That was something she would have to pray on ... starting tonight at bedtime. But until then, she had a duty to uphold. She was still the housemother, and until the day she left the position, she needed to give her best to her work. So, she straightened her shoulders and headed for the kitchen to see what the cook was preparing for dinner.

Chapter 19

All the way home, Bethany chastised herself for inadvertently making Cassandra believe that the only way she could live at the estate was if she were the manager. She had never meant for Cassandra to think about it in that way. And certainly not to then think herself a failure because she'd had trouble keeping the estate afloat during the drought. *Poor Cassandra. If only she had reached out to the family for support, but then, she has never been one to trouble others with her burdens.*

Bethany knew that from their own experiences. She had seen how Howard, her stepbrother, had treated his wife and sons, depriving them of the necessities of life so he could spend his salary on gambling and other vices. She had tried to compensate for his deficiencies by bringing gifts to Cassandra and her nephews every chance she could. Cassandra had never complained about how Howard treated her but was always grateful for the extra supplies of food and clothing that Bethany brought for the boys, though she would seldom accept anything for herself. That was how Bethany had learned about Cassandra's independent spirit, and why learning the facts about the past couple of years did not surprise her. It hurt, but it was no surprise.

Now she had to find a way to get around Cassandra's independent attitude. And the first step would be helping her to find a way out of this latest role she had taken on.

***

Later that evening, after the children had gone to bed and Bethany and Sam were relaxing with a cup of tea in the front parlour, she told him what Cassandra had said during their teatime. It also saddened Sam that Cassandra had thought herself a failure over the past couple of years. Sam agreed with Bethany that no one could have predicted the drought or the impact it would have on Stillwater. He was sure it was affecting all the estates in that area, including his own family estate and his uncle's. After Sam talked to his father, they would plan a visit to Stillwater to see for themselves what was going on. Having made that decision, they relaxed in the child-free environment to enjoy the peace.

***

The following day, Sam left to visit his father, and Bethany took the children to Gunter's—one of her favourite places in London—for ices. Such places were unknown in the colony, so the children were unaware of what a treat they had ahead of them. Their grandmother joined them, as did their Aunt Hannah and all their London cousins. It was a fun and noisy group that occupied the table in the famous restaurant, as Hannah's sons sampled each other's treats, even while offering a taste of their ices to their Australian cousins. The women sat nearby but far enough away that they could visit without being disturbed.

"Sam said you visited Cassandra yesterday, Bethany," said the duchess. "How did you find her?"

"Unfortunately, not very well, Mother. Her physical appearance quite shocked me."

"Oh, I am sorry to hear that. Has she been ill?"

"No, not physically, although she confessed to being tired. Her new position is causing her a great deal of stress."

"What position does she hold, Bethany?" asked Hannah.

"She is the new housemother for the Young Women's Christian Association boarding house."

"So, she works and resides there?" asked the duchess.

"Yes."

"What does her role entail?"

"She orders supplies for the house and cares for the physical and mental wellbeing of the residents."

"That is a lot of responsibility for one person," said Hannah. "Is she having to cook for the young women as well?"

"No, thankfully, there is a full-time cook. Cassandra only consults with her regarding menus, supplies, etc."

"What is causing most of her stress?"

"The women, themselves. Apparently, there are a group of women among them who never quit complaining about anything and everything. Cassandra is quite tired of their continual, petty grievances, most of which she can do nothing to solve."

"Oh, the poor dear," said the duchess. "I can see why she would be tired, Bethany. Physical labour can be exhausting, but we can generally refresh ourselves with a night's sleep. But that kind of stress is not easily put aside by sleep. Is she hoping to find another position?"

"No. She said she applied for other jobs when she first came to the city but could not secure a position. She thought she was too old for most of the work she looked at, but I suspect it was her attractiveness that made the ladies of the households wary of hiring her."

"I agree, Bethany. Cassandra is not old. Now, if I were to be looking for a position..." The duchess patted her neatly styled grey hair.

Bethany and Hannah laughed with her at the unlikely thought of the duchess applying for work.

Sobering finally, Hannah spoke again. "So, if she has no other prospects for employment, and she is unhappy with her present position, what can she do?"

"I only hope that I can persuade her to return to the estate, not as the manager but simply to live there and enjoy life. I asked her to think and pray about it, so we will have to see what transpires after she does that. No other ideas have come to me."

"She is always welcome to come and live with us, Bethany," said the duchess. "If she decides not to go back to Stillwater, please make sure that she knows she could have a home with us."

"Thank you, Mother. I will let her know." Then turning towards the children's table, she said, "I see the children have finished their treats, so perhaps it is time to take them home. I do hope this will not spoil their dinners, but I wanted David and Cecelia to experience this right away. Thank you for coming, and for bringing your sons along, Hannah. It is wonderful for my children to get to know their cousins."

"And mine as well, Bethany. Rupert often speaks of the fun he had growing up alongside his cousins. It is too bad you live so far away, and the children will only see each other occasionally. Any chance you will move back to England?"

"No chance at all, Hannah. Our home is in Australia. We love it there. But we will try to come back as often as we can to visit our family and friends here in Britain. And perhaps you and Rupert will travel down to see us someday. We would welcome you with open arms."

"I am sure you would, but I doubt my husband would agree to such a journey. He is not much of a traveller. No, the most you can expect is for one or two of our sons to make the voyage, though not for a while."

"Then we will make the most of our time in Britain and store up lots of memories, not only for ourselves but for our children as well. Perhaps we could even get some of those new daguerreotypes done of the families so we can take your dear faces back home with us."

"That sounds like a wonderful idea, Bethany," said the duchess. "We will have to look into it before you leave. But as you know, I tear up at even the thought of you leaving again, so for now, we will not discuss it. It is time for you and Hannah to get your broods home, and for me to find out what Sam and Douglas discussed today. We will have to do this again soon." Then she stood up, signalling to the group that the afternoon festivities were at an end. Bethany and Hannah collected their children and herded them off to their respective carriages, while the duchess went to her landau. With waves of farewell, they all set off then in their different directions.

***

While the Yardley families were still heading home, Cassandra was about to receive an unexpected guest. When Cassandra heard the knock on the front door, she thought it was Bethany returning for her answer. But when she opened it, she was surprised to see the former housemother standing there.

"Ma'am!" Cassandra said. "What a pleasant surprise! Did you forget something when you left?"

"No. But I have had a change in fortunes, which has changed my long-term plans. May I come in?"

"Of course," said Cassandra, standing to the side. "Forgive my rudeness. I was so surprised to see you that I forgot my manners."

"I understand," she said. "Uh… Do you have time to talk?"

Cassandra nodded. "I have no pressing issues. Would you like to visit in the parlour?"

"That would be lovely."

"Then, please, after you," said Cassandra, still mystified as to why she was here. Once seated in the front parlour, Cassandra asked if her guest would like some tea.

"Perhaps later, Mrs. Stillwater. I want to speak with you."

"Of course. Please proceed."

"First, I need to ask how are you doing. You appear pale."

"I have to admit that the role is a bit more demanding than I had expected, but perhaps it will get easier as time goes on."

"Are you enjoying your new position?"

Cassandra thought for a moment. Could she be honest in her reply? And if she was, what would the former housemother think of her?

Seeing her groping for an answer, her guest said, "You can speak openly with me, Mrs. Stillwater. You need not worry about offending me."

Cassandra took a deep breath. "Well … I was not expecting to mediate quarrels between the young women or deal with their petty complaints, ma'am. The work of keeping the house supplied with goods and working out menus with the cook is fine, but my temper often frays when I receive yet another criticism from a resident. How did you ever stay calm in such circumstances?"

"Years of practice, I suppose. And I agree. That is one of the hardest parts of this position. I obviously did not prepare you for it sufficiently."

"I don't remember us having such a discussion at all, ma'am. If we had, I might not have taken the job."

"Are you unhappy in your new role?

"To be honest, yes. I would prefer to be a resident again and able to closet myself in my room when disagreements arise."

"Then perhaps God has led me here at an opportune time, Mrs. Stillwater. But let me explain. You recall that I left here to live with my sister in Surrey, do you not?"

"Yes."

"Well, that dream fell apart a couple of weeks ago. After being together only a week, my sister unexpectedly passed away."

"Oh! I am so sorry to hear that, ma'am... My condolences to you."

"Thank you. Having only lived in Surrey for that week, and having no other family or friends there, I was left feeling quite alone. I am used to having women around me. So, I have decided to move back to London. I do not need to work, but I want to have something to occupy my time. I had not come here with the intention of taking your job away from you but listening to you has given me an idea. Would you like me to resume my former position, so that you could simply be a resident again, or even go elsewhere if that is what pleases you?"

Cassandra did not have to think twice. God had answered her prayer. Without hesitation, she said, "Yes! When can you return?"

The woman laughed. "I need some time to close up my sister's house and arrange for the sale of furniture and so on. That should not take long. Shall we say a week from now? Would that suit you?"

"Very much so. You are an answer to prayer, ma'am. Do you wish to keep these changes a secret for now or can I inform the women tonight?"

"Whatever you prefer, Mrs. Stillwater. You are still in charge until next week."

"I am glad it is one of the last decisions I will have to make. I am overjoyed that you are returning, and I know the other women will be as well."

"That is all I needed to know. I am glad this works for us both. Now, I think I will take you up on that cup of tea."

"Why don't we head into the kitchen and share it with the cook, along with your news? I know that she will be just as glad to have you return as I am."

She nodded, and then together, the women headed to the kitchen to spread the news.

***

As soon as Bethany arrived back at the townhouse, she sent the children upstairs for a nap. The butler informed her that Lord Yardley had not yet returned from his visit with the duke, so Bethany decided to lie down with Douglas for a quick nap as well. He was teething again, and that often kept him up at night, along with his parents. Bethany knew that she could have had a maid tend to him, but she also knew that he needed the comfort of either her or Sam to cope with the pain. Thus, the two of them were taking turns caring for him. It would not be long until the teeth came through, and he would start sleeping through the night again.

Although Bethany longed for those nights, she also knew that it would be one more sign that her baby was growing up quickly. It wouldn't be long before he would no longer want such night-time cuddles with his mother. So, she was glad to have this special time with her son.

And cuddling him close to her body, she drifted into a light sleep. It seemed only moments, however, before she heard Sam calling her name. "Bethany? Beth, are you awake?" he asked, slipping down beside her and giving her a light kiss on her brow.

"I am now," she said. "When did you get home?"

"A few minutes ago. Molly told me you had come upstairs for a rest. Are you all right, love?"

"Yes, I'm fine. I am just tired from broken nights of sleep and today's outing. You don't need to worry about me."

"I'm glad. You are not one to take naps, so it took me aback to hear that you were upstairs. I rather relish the idea of napping myself. May I join you?"

"Of course, but before you sleep, I want to know what your father had to say about the state of affairs at the estate. Is it truly bad?"

"It is not good, but since he found out about the situation and gave them money to buy seed and feed for the animals, he says things have improved. If he had known earlier, he would have stepped in and given his assistance so that things would not have deteriorated to the point they did before Cassandra left."

"Oh dear, do you think he blames her for how things are?"

"No. He said that all the farms have experienced problems for the past two years. It was not Cassandra's fault. He only wished that she had reached out for help when she first recognized the problem."

"Yes, that would have been best. But Cassandra is not one to burden others with her concerns. She would rather deal with them herself."

"But are we not commanded by God to bear each other's burdens, Beth?"

"We are, but I think all those years of living with an unsupportive husband taught Cassandra to look after all things on her own. Howard was of no help to her."

"Even with the little I know about the man; I can see that he only ever looked out for himself."

"In his later years, yes, but when I was young, he was a much different person. I only wished he'd had time to reform before he died."

"Yes, that was tragic, Bethany. And to think that it all could have been avoided if he had lived a godlier life. But I am only glad it was him, and not you, who died that day. My heart would have broken in two if you had succumbed to a second attempt on your life."

"And if the assassin had killed you, Sam... It does not bear thinking about."

"No, it does not. God preserved us both to live a happy life together. These past years have been the best of my entire life, Beth, and it is all because of you."

"I echo that sentiment, Sam. I could not be happier than I am right now."

"Thank you, love. Now, is there anything else we need to discuss, or can I get down to the business of cuddling with my wife before we sleep?"

"I believe your wife would appreciate some cuddles, sir, and then a time of sleeping in her husband's arms until the baby wakes up."

Sam pulled her in close to his body and tucked her head under his chin. As they settled in, he realized that he could feel their hearts beating as one. *This is marriage ... uniting body and soul,* he thought as he started drifting off. *And I was blessed to find the perfect union with Bethany.* Before his mind fell silent in sleep, he thanked God for His wonderful provision.

***

Cassandra, too, was thanking God. Not for her late husband but for providing her with a means of escape from the boarding house and its responsibilities.

She still could not believe that He had worked in the former housemother's heart to bring her back to this place. It was a miracle. Now, she would be free again. But to do what? And to live where? Could she really go back to the estate and live there without a formal role? If she did so, would she not be seen as someone just living off Bethany's largesse? But if she did not go back, where would she go? She had exhausted her possibilities of work outside the boarding house, and now even that position was gone.

Not that she was complaining, but it did put her back in the same position she had been in when she'd first arrived. And she did not have the energy right now to look for work again. No. Even if it was for only a short time, she needed to go back to the estate. A contented smile stretched across Cassandra's face as she nestled into her bed and reminisced about the joyful times she'd spent there with her sons. *Soon,* she thought, *I will get up and pen a note to Bethany with my decision. It will surprise her to hear about what has happened. Yes, I will do that as soon as I rest my eyes for a bit.* As she felt herself start to drift off to sleep, another thought occurred her. *I wonder what Lord Dudley will think of my return...*

***

Cassandra woke up two hours later. A bit confused, she looked at the tiny watch pinned to the bodice of her gown. *Four o'clock? I slept for two hours! What must the cook think of me?* And then she remembered and relaxed back on her bed. It did not matter. A sennight from now, she would be gone, never to return, so the cook's opinion or anyone else's did not matter. She would only be accountable to herself and God. Of course, until then, she was still the housemother and had a job to do. So, she stood up, tidied her hair, straightened her gown, and left the room to join the others for tea. The time for rest and relaxation was over for the day.

***

While John Dudley was not privy to Cassandra's thoughts, he had spent a great deal of time in the past days thinking about her, wondering about her, and worrying about her. Yes, he had to admit that when he was not busy with estate business, his mind would swing to Cassandra. He still had no idea how to get her back to the estate. Neither had the Kingsleys. But they never stopped trying.

Today, they had other things to attend to. John had received a message from the duke two days earlier, stating that he and the duchess would be stopping by, along with a couple of guests, on their way to their country estate two days hence. If possible, they would like to have luncheon at Stillwater if that would suit John and the Kingsleys. John had sent back an immediate response, saying that they would be delighted to host their Graces and their guests for luncheon on the specified day. And now, as it was nearing noon, John was waiting in the front parlour to welcome them.

And there it was, the ducal carriage coming through the gates, followed by another one of the duke's carriages. *There must be several guests,* thought John. *Perhaps I should alert the Kingsleys that we will have to set more places at the table.* John walked out of the parlour and into the foyer. Seeing Kingsley at his post, he said, "I see the carriage has arrived, Kingsley. But it is accompanied by a second carriage. I was not expecting that many guests. Do you want to alert Mrs. Kingsley now or after we know exactly how many we will seat for luncheon?"

"Perhaps after, Lord Dudley. That will also give us an idea of how much food we need to plate for the meal."

"Good, Kingsley. I'll leave those matters up to you and your wife. Now, let us greet our guests."

"Indeed, sir," said the butler, straightening his livery before pulling open the door. "After you, Lord Dudley."

They stepped out onto the porch just as the first carriage pulled up. A footman jumped down off the high seat, and coming around, he opened the carriage door, put down the step, and reached out his hand to assist the duchess in getting out. Smiling, she thanked him before taking a couple of steps towards John. But before she could even greet him, the duke joined her from inside the carriage, reaching out his hand to grasp his nephew's.

"John, my boy!" he said. "It is good to see you. Thank you for accepting our request. It was rather presumptuous of me, I know, but our guests wanted to see the place. I hope you don't mind."

"Of course not, Uncle Douglas," said John, before leaning over to kiss his aunt on the cheek. "But I was not expecting you to arrive in two carriages. Are your guests in the second one?"

"Yes, they wanted to travel as a family, so they could point things out to the children. You will meet them soon," said the duke, as his carriage pulled away and the other drew up to the porch.

"A family?"

"Yes, parents and three delightful children. I am sure you will enjoy their company," said the duke, as the footman opened the door, put down the step, and handed out a beautiful young woman carrying an infant in her arms. When she saw John, her face broke into a huge smile. "Surprise, John! We are here to visit you!"

John's vision blurred with happy tears. It was Bethany, and soon he could see Sam, and then David and Cecelia. It was his Australian family. He rushed down to greet them, and soon they were embracing in a large huddle. They stayed that way until Douglas complained; then they laughed and broke apart. And John took each of them, except Sam, into his arms individually for more long hugs. A smile spread across David's face as he caught sight of John, but Cecelia hid behind her mother's skirts. Once she saw the joy on her parents' faces as they embraced him, though, her fears dissipated, and she reached out her arms to be picked up. John was glad to oblige her, giving her a small squeeze before putting her back down and turning to Sam.

"Sam, you old dog! I can't believe it's you! I knew you were planning to visit, but I did not expect you so soon. Welcome home, Cousin!" Then he grabbed him in a hug and held on for a long time.

Sam laughed as soon as he could breathe again. "So, our surprise worked, did it? I'm so glad. Just to see the look on your face when you saw Bethany was priceless. You looked like you had seen a ghost."

"I thought for a moment my imagination had conjured her up, old man. I never expected to see the two of you today."

Then a quavering male voice broke into their conversation. "Lord Yardley? After all these years, is it really you?"

Sam turned towards the voice and found Bethany standing beside one of her dearest friends: Kingsley. Tears were rolling down both their cheeks, revealing their joy at being together again.

"It is, Kingsley, and I can tell by my wife's tears that the two of you have already become reacquainted. So, now it is my turn to greet you." Sam took a couple of steps forward and enfolded the older man in his muscular arms. He could feel the frailty that had set in since last he'd seen the butler. Kingsley was growing old, and that brought tears to Sam's eyes as well.

As host, John decided that he needed to do something before the porch was awash in tears. "Why don't we all head inside to the front parlour and find comfortable seating? I'll alert Mrs. Kingsley so she can join us there."

After nods of agreement, the duchess took the infant from Bethany's arms, so that she and Sam could link arms with Kingsley. The duke held out his hands to David and Cecelia, and they all went inside the manor. Once there, the duchess said to John, "I'll go to the kitchen and bring Mrs. Kingsley to the parlour. As she knew I was coming, at least, she won't suspect a thing. We don't want her to see Kingsley in this state; it will ruin everything."

John agreed, and she handed the baby to him. Douglas looked at him as if wanting to cry, and then thought better of it, instead giving him a little smile. The duchess headed down the hall to the kitchen while the rest went into the parlour.

When the duchess reached the kitchen, she found Mrs. Kingsley amidst her luncheon preparations. As she was wielding a knife when the duchess came to the doorway, she waited until the cook had put it down before speaking.

"Good morning, Mrs. Kingsley," she said, walking into the room. "I see you are going to a lot of work to feed us. I hope we are not too much of a bother."

At the sound of the duchess's voice, Mrs. Kingsley looked up. "Oh, my gracious! Good morning, Your Grace. I did not hear you come in. May I help you with something?"

"No, I only came to invite you to join us in the front parlour. I have someone special I would like you to meet."

Looking around at the various foods arrayed across the kitchen and at her spattered apron, Mrs. Kingsley shook her head. "Oh, Your Grace, I am not—"

"Nonsense," interrupted the duchess. "We are all almost family. You do not need to fuss about your appearance. And it is only for a short while. Then you can return."

Realising that one did not argue with a duchess, Mrs. Kingsley took off her apron and hung it over the back of a chair. Then after brushing back a few wayward strands of hair, she shook out her dress and said, "Well, Your Grace, if it is only for a few minutes. I still have much to do before lunchtime."

The duchess smiled, and then waved Mrs. Kingsley out and into the hallway. They walked side by side towards the parlour, from which they could hear multiple voices. The cook frowned. She had understood that their only guests would be the duke and duchess. So, who else was in the parlour with them? And where was Kingsley? He should have come immediately into the kitchen and inform her of the extra guests so she could prepare more food. She hesitated a bit, the need to return to the kitchen and continuing working to feed a crowd of people intensifying.

Seeing her hesitation, and guessing that it had something to do with what she was hearing, the duchess put a hand on her arm and encouraged her to continue walking towards the parlour, and smiled at the woman's questioning look.

"It will be all right, Mrs. Kingsley. I assure you of this. You will be happy to meet our guests and they you."

Uncertain but still aware of her own humble status in the duchess's presence, the cook moved forward and into the parlour. When she arrived, the room fell silent a moment, and then a young woman was rushing forward to pull her into her arms.

"Mrs. Kingsley!" cried Bethany. "It is so good to see you!"

The cook was shocked at the realisation of who held her. "Miss Bethany? My dear child! Is it truly you?"

Through her tears, Bethany laughed and reassured the cook that it was indeed her. Finally, Bethany released the stunned woman, and then Sam's even stronger arms wrapped her up in another hug.

"What a delight seeing you again, Mrs. Kingsley! I hope the surprise will not harm your health."

"I think I will survive, Lord Yardley, though barely. But what a joy to see you. Now tell me, who are these children?" She smiled as she pulled back from his embrace.

"They are our pride and joy, ma'am. Come, let me introduce you to them," said Sam, pulling her over to where the children stood beside their mother. "This is David. He is five years old. His sister, Cecelia, is three, and the baby in my father's arms is our youngest, Douglas. He is eleven months old. Children, this is Mrs. Kingsley. You met Mr. Kingsley a little while ago; this is his wife, Mrs. Kingsley. She is the cook and housekeeper, plus a very dear friend of your mother's. Please say hello to her."

With a little nudge from their mother, David and Cecelia moved forward and took Mrs. Kingsley's hand briefly, before moving back to stand again with Bethany. Then the cook went over and greeted the duke before looking down at the sleeping baby in his arms.

"Would you like to hold him, Mrs. Kingsley?" asked the duke.

She nodded and reached out her arms to take the baby. Once nestled in her arms, Douglas opened his eyes and looked up at her. Satisfied that she meant him no harm; he sighed and closed them again without so much as a whimper. Mrs. Kingsley looked over at Bethany, tears rolling down her face once more. "He has your beautiful eyes, Miss Bethany. I never thought to see this day, especially after you moved to Australia. This is such a special moment for me. Thank you for sharing your children with me today."

Bethany came back over and hugged her once more. "You were a mother to me for many, many years, Mrs. Kingsley, and I now want you to be another grandmother to my children. Will you do that for me and Sam?"

Choked at this request, the cook could only nod and smile while continuing to look down at Douglas. While Bethany had not been a child of her womb, she had always been a child of her heart, and now she would love these little ones as if they were her own as well.

***

The reunion set the tone for the rest of the day. Afterwards, the men headed out to the barns with John in order to see the progress he had been making with the estate, while the women and children went into the kitchen. Mrs. Kingsley gave David and Cecelia milk and cookies at the table, just as she had for Bethany so many years earlier. Bethany insisted on helping her with luncheon preparations. The cook protested, saying it was not proper for her to assist her, but Bethany overruled her protests. She told Mrs. Kingsley that after living on the station for the past number of years, with only limited help, she could easily wield a knife in the kitchen.

So, after handing off the baby to the duchess to hold, and donning an apron, Bethany proceeded to wash, peel, and cut up vegetables that would be side dishes for their meal. The children watched without surprise, making it clear to Mrs. Kingsley that they had seen this side of their mother many times and were quite used to it. The conversation was light and cheerful as Mrs. Kingsley plied Bethany with questions about her new home and their voyage back to England.

***

The men too were having a time catching up on each other's news. After exchanging greetings with Mr. Wiley in the barn, they stepped outside to inspect the livestock in the paddocks, where they observed that all the animals appeared well fed and healthy. Seeing the state of things, the duke turned to John. "It appears you have turned the corner on the estate, John. Are things going well, despite the ongoing drought?"

"Yes, Uncle Douglas. Thanks to your generosity, we have been able to purchase sufficient feed for the animals, and seed for next spring's planting. Hopefully, by then, the drought will be behind us, and the crops will grow well. I have instituted some of your dry-land farming ideas, Sam, such as ploughing irrigation canals between the rows, and setting up large barrels to catch rainwater at the end of each row to water the crops, in case there is still not enough moisture for the crops to grow well next year. Hopefully, God will send plenty of rain next year, but if He chooses not to do so, then we will be more prepared to deal with the drought than we were this year and the last."

"I'm glad you learned something while you were with us, John. I never expected you would have to use dry-land farming techniques here in England, where it is usually so wet. Obviously, God had a plan in you coming to visit us, and that was to help save Bethany's estate."

"I agree, Sam," said his father. "I have also borrowed John's ideas for my estate and tenants. Perhaps you moving so far away wasn't such a bad idea after all."

"I'm glad you approve, Father," said Sam, laughing. "I was not sure I had your blessing when we left for Australia five years ago."

"You did not. All I could think of then was how infrequently we would get to see you and Bethany, and your growing family. I still don't like it but am glad something good has come out of your decision."

"I am glad as well, Sam," said John. "For if you had not moved away, I would have had no place to visit, and I would still be stuck in a rut in England, not knowing what to do with my life."

"Have you decided then, John?" asked Sam.

Eyeing the duke, who was listening intently for John's next words, he nodded slowly, and then took a deep breath. "Yes, I have. I have not yet told my father, so please keep this to yourself, Uncle Douglas, but after I finish my tenure here, I hope to pack my bag and move back to Australia to farm with you, Sam."

Sam reached out and thumped John on the back. "That is wonderful news. I was hoping for that answer. We will look forward to having you join us."

The duke reached out and shook John's hand. "I know this will be hard on your parents, John, but just as I learned to do when Sam told me of his plans, they will come around. Congratulations, son."

"Thank you, Uncle Douglas. Having experienced the same situation with Sam, you will help my parents adjust to my departure. But as I still have months to go and work to do before I leave the estate, I ask you both not to divulge my plans until I have spoken with my parents. Do I have your word on that?"

The men both nodded, and then the conversation reverted to the management of Stillwater Estate. Eventually, they headed back into the house for the noon meal.

***

After a delicious lunch, the children went down for a nap, while the adults continued their visit in the front parlour. The duke confessed to John that they were not actually heading to their country estate. That had been a ruse so they would receive permission to stop at the Stillwater Estate. Both the elder and younger Yardley families were heading back to the city later that afternoon. The duke hoped John would forgive him for tricking him in such a manner.

"Of course I will, Uncle Douglas. It was a joy to have you, Aunt Margaret, and Sam's family here today. You have an open invitation to visit."

"Speaking of returning, John," said the duchess, "have you heard anything from Cassandra Stillwater about a possible return to the estate?"

"No, I haven't. I tried to persuade her to move back here when she visited her boys on their last school break. But I could not do so."

"I saw her recently, John, and also tried, but to no avail," said Bethany. "She said that she could not leave her position as housemother for the YWCA, as she had only recently acquired it."

"I knew she was living there, Bethany, but I was not aware that she was also working at the house. That would make it more difficult for her to leave. How did you find her?"

"Not well, John. She was pale and had large bags under her eyes. She confessed to not sleeping well and that the actions of some residents were quite troublesome."

"I am sorry to hear that. She looked well on her recent visit, but she was only a resident at that time, not the housemother."

"I am sure that would be a wearisome job, looking after all those women," said the duchess. "I would not want to have that responsibility."

"Nor would I," said Bethany, "and judging from Cassandra's words, I think that she is regretting her decision to become the housemother but feels she cannot leave now."

"Aunt Margaret," John said, "if you put a word out through the servant grapevine that the YWCA is looking for a new housemother, perhaps they could appoint a new one, and Cassandra could leave without regrets."

"But what if Cassandra finds out, John? Would she not be upset that we went behind her back to do this?"

"Blame it on me, Aunt Margaret. I am already not favourably seen by Cassandra because of certain actions I took when we first met, so it will make little difference to her opinion of me."

"John, what did you do?" asked Bethany.

"I, uh, looked at the estate books without her knowledge. She was holding onto them so securely, and not letting me see them, that I thought she was, perhaps, tampering with the numbers and using some of the estate funds for herself. When I left to return to Dudley Manor, the guilt overwhelmed me, so as soon as I came back, I confessed what I had done. While she forgave me my sin, from that moment on, she would not give me her trust again, and I fear she never will."

"That was not well done of you, John," said Bethany. "I now see why she does not trust you and is reluctant to return to the estate, even just to live. Perhaps, when we leave for Australia next year, and she knows you are moving there as well, she will come back. But until then..."

"I am sorry, Bethany. I never intended to hurt her. I would do anything to make things right so she would return, but I have yet to come up with any ideas as to how that can be done."

"You don't need to apologise to me, John, only to Cassandra. She is the one you hurt."

"I will keep apologising every time I see her until she finally gives in and forgives me."

"You said that she forgave you at your first meeting after your blunder. Forgiveness is easy to say, but forgetting and learning to trust again is much harder. That will take time, John, and you have little to spare."

John nodded but said nothing more as he had nothing else to say. The conversation soon moved onto other topics, and then it was time for the Yardleys to head back to London. They summoned the carriages. The children were awakened from their naps, and farewells were spoken. Only this time, there were no tears, for they'd promised a return visit soon. And as their carriages rolled down the lane towards the gate, everyone was smiling and waving. After watching them depart through the gate, John and Kingsley went their separate ways, but each was thinking the same thing: The only thing that could have bettered the day would have been if Cassandra had been there as well. They simply had to make that idea a reality.

Chapter 20

The following week flew by as Cassandra anticipated the former housemother's return. And then the day came. She arrived as promised at exactly nine a.m., and after taking some time to unpack, she declared herself ready to resume her former duties. Cassandra spent the next hour with her, reviewing the supplies in the pantry and making a list of needed items. "Is there anything else you need to know?"

The housemother smiled. "No, I don't think so, Mrs. Stillwater. Thank you for looking after things so well in my absence. I feel like I am only returning after a lengthy holiday, so I doubt I will need any further assistance."

"If you do, you know that I am only a few doors down the hall, ma'am."

"Yes, I do. Have you given any thought as to what you will do now that I have returned?"

"Nothing specific. I am going out to my former home in the country for a few days of refreshment. Perhaps that will help me in making future plans."

"Country air is always good to aid clear thinking, Mrs. Stillwater. That is one thing I will miss, now that I've come back to the city."

"Yes, it is. Well, if there is nothing else, I will let you readjust, ma'am. Thank you again for coming back and taking over. You are an answer to my prayers."

"I don't know that I have ever been called that before today, Mrs. Stillwater, but God works in mysterious ways. I am glad He directed our paths in this manner."

"So am I," said Cassandra, before getting up from the table. She nodded to the cook and the housemother before heading back to her room. She was free once more. But what to do with that newfound freedom? That was her next matter for reflection and prayer.

***

The next day, John received a message from Cassandra. She asked if it would be suitable for her to come and spend a few days at the estate in the following week. John hastily penned a note back to her, welcoming her. After giving it to the messenger, he informed Mrs. Kingsley of Cassandra's request. She smiled when she heard the news and said she would start laying in stocks of Mrs. Stillwater's favourite foods to prepare for her visit. She also said that the notice would give her time to air out the bedding in the mistress's room, so it was fresh for her. Kingsley was pleased to hear the news as well. Although it did not affect his role like it did his wife's, he said that he would help his wife in whatever tasks she needed done in order to prepare the house for Cassandra's return.

***

While the Kingsleys and John were preparing for Cassandra, Bethany and Sam were readying their family for an extended stay at the estate. When they had returned from their day at the manor, they had agreed that, rather than live in London for the next year, they would be happier out at the estate. Since it was only an hour from both London and the Yardley's country estate, it would be close enough for frequent visits with Sam's parents wherever they were situated. Bethany was also happy that it would take them out of the city before the next social season. She was still not comfortable with the soirées that occurred during that time, so she was glad of an excuse not to attend any of them.

Once they'd set their plans, and Sam had informed his parents of their move, they sent a message to John, letting him know of their imminent arrival. Although the timing of their move coincided with Cassandra's visit, John did not think he needed to inform her of the Yardleys' plans. Besides, he was in no position to refuse their move; he was only the manager, and it was Bethany's estate. If Cassandra had been strangers to the Yardleys, then he might have put off her visit, but they were her family, and he thought she would appreciate Bethany's company while she was here. That would also give him and Sam more time to talk about their plans as partners in Yardley Downs in Australia. John wanted to invest in the station, rather than just working there as he had on his previous visit. If Sam agreed, they would look at expanding and running more sheep, which would increase the profits for them both. John was eager to talk to Sam about his ideas.

Having had no word about keeping their arrival a secret, John headed to the kitchen to speak with Mrs. Kingsley to make sure that she had enough supplies on hand for the following week. They would have to increase their expenditures on supplies to accommodate the Yardleys, but for now, they only needed to think about feeding everyone while Cassandra was also in residence. The Stillwater Estate was about to become much livelier.

Kingsley was in the kitchen when John arrived, so he received the news at the same time as his wife. It delighted them to hear about the Yardleys' plans; they were looking forward to hearing childish voices echoing through the hallways once more. It had been far too long since a child's laughter had been heard regularly at Stillwater Estate.

***

The next day, Cassandra gathered her small bag of belongings and headed out to the hired hack. She told the housemother that, although she was only planning a visit to the estate, she was uncertain of her plans after that time. So, it was better to free up her room for another boarder, rather than leave it empty on the premise that she would return later. The housemother agreed with Cassandra's plan. There were always young women coming to the house looking for rooms, so she knew she would easily fill the vacancy. She also believed that it would be beneficial for Cassandra to refrain from making plans to return and instead focus on finding another opportunity after her short break. She wished her well as Cassandra stepped into the hack and left the boarding house behind.

It was not a painful leave-taking, as she had never found what she'd wanted when she had returned to London. Perhaps the housemother was right, and it was time for another change, although she was getting weary of moving from place to place. Mayhap the next move would be the last, and she could settle in wherever that was for the rest of her life. But for now, she was eager to get back to the country and breathe fresh air once more.

***

At the same time as Cassandra was on the move, so were Bethany, Sam, and their children. They had a carriage to travel in, plus a large cart that would follow with all their belongings. Bethany was glad to be leaving the city behind, as was Sam. Their lifestyle in the Australian countryside was much more to their liking than living in London. They had grown accustomed to the wide-open spaces, and even the well-spaced townhouses in Mayfair did not suit them. No, it was time to take the children out to the country and let them experience what both their parents had enjoyed while growing up: pastures for riding, streams to fish, vegetables to pick, and space to run and play. The whole Yardley family was looking forward to spending the rest of their time in England outside the city limits.

Ast they had packed up everything the day before their departure, the Yardleys were on the road early the next morning, about an hour before Cassandra left the boarding house. As it was only an hour's ride to the estate, they had no plans to stop for a rest break unless they spotted something interesting along the way. Seeing nothing but deer in far fields, and hares along the roadside, they arrived at the estate well before lunchtime. It gave them time to greet everyone, move their baggage into the house, and have lunch before Cassandra arrived. John informed them of her impending visit on their arrival, which thrilled Bethany. Perhaps now she would have time to talk Cassandra into remaining on the estate and not returning to London. She would do her best to persuade her to come back home.

***

Cassandra arrived at the estate just after noon. She had stopped halfway through her ride at a grassy knoll to eat a lunch that the cook had sent with her and to take in the view. Even though there were still signs of the drought everywhere she looked, she appreciated the sights and sounds. It reminded her of God's continual goodness, even amidst troubles. She thanked Him for the beauty of His creation, even the starkness of the fields, which should have been green, and the trickle of water in the stream, which should have been full of gurgling water. It was a reminder that men should not take the seasons for granted but appreciate everything that God sent them each year. Cassandra breathed a silent prayer of thankfulness for the day, and for the food she had consumed, before continuing on her way.

When Cassandra climbed down from the carriage after arriving at the manor porch, she thought she heard children's voices coming from the barns. For a moment, she thought it might be her sons, but then realised it was too soon for them to have another school break. This was good because she had not yet started making plans for their promised beach holiday. She needed to do that soon, or else the other vacationers would book up all the cottages, and she would be out of luck. But if it was not her children she was hearing, who was it? The only way to find out was through Kingsley, so she hurried up to the door and knocked. Instead of the butler though, a young footman opened the door.

"Oh, hello," said Cassandra, stumbling a bit for words. "I was, uh, expecting to see Kingsley. Is he not here?"

"He is in the kitchen, ma'am. I can get him for you. Won't you come in?"

Cassandra preceded him into the foyer, then shook her head. "No, you don't need to find him. I'll make my way to the kitchen."

"Yes, ma'am. We have been expecting you, Mrs. Stillwater. I will look after retrieving your bags and taking them up to your room."

"Thank you."

She decided then that her ears must have deceived her. The house was quiet; no sounds of children's voices could be heard. *Perhaps there are ghosts in the barns.* As she did not believe in ghosts, she gave her head a shake and headed down the hallway towards the kitchen, where she now heard adult voices. When she arrived, she blinked a few times to clear her vision. The kitchen was full of people. Scanning the room, she saw Bethany sitting at the table holding a baby, a man looking very much like Sam standing behind her, and Lord Dudley and the Kingsleys standing across the table from them. When Cassandra came into view, John looked over at her. "Mrs. Stillwater! Welcome! We did not hear you arrive. Please come in."

The man standing behind Bethany came over and greeted her. "Cassandra! It is wonderful to see you again. How are you?"

"I'm fine." She squinted a bit at the man behind her. "Sam?"

"Yes. I assumed you recognized me from our previous visits, but you were not expecting to see us today, were you?"

"No, but it is wonderful to see you again. You look rather different from when I saw you five years ago. But it is a good look on you."

"Thank you."

"But I have not met your children yet. Would you introduce me to the baby?"

"This is Douglas," said Bethany, getting up to greet her, "your youngest nephew. Would you like to hold him?"

"Perhaps later, Bethany, after I have finished greeting everyone else. For now, I will only say hello to him." Cassandra smiled at the baby and mouthed a greeting to him. He smiled back at her, showing his impressive display of new teeth.

"Eight teeth already, Douglas? You are a handsome young man, aren't you?" she said, before looking back at Bethany. "How old is he now, Bethany?"

"Almost a year. He has been cutting teeth ever since we arrived in England, so he has not been a cheerful boy for the past while."

"I can remember going through that with my boys and having many sleepless nights because of it."

"I remember you looking exhausted during those times, Cassandra. Now, I know what you went through. I am so happy to have a supportive husband to help me. You were on your own. If I remember correctly, Howard provided little help to you."

"That is true. He saw child rearing as women's work and had only brief contacts with his sons. That is why they barely remember him."

"I wish your life had been easier, Cassandra, and your marriage, but at least you have your boys from it. It will be wonderful to see them again. I doubt I will recognise any of them after being away these many years."

"Yes, they have grown up a lot since you were last here. I hardly recognise them myself when I see them at school breaks. I thought I heard their voices when I arrived because of children's laughter drifting up from the barn. But I must have been mistaken."

"You heard our older children's voices. Sam took them down to the barns to see the animals, and Mr. Wiley said he would look after them for us. But he must be tired of entertaining them. Sam, would you mind checking on them? I don't want them to interfere with Mr. Wiley's work."

"You're right, Beth, it has been awhile. John, do you want to come with me to bring the children back to meet Cassandra? It will take more than just me to tear them away from the animals."

"Glad to help, Sam. Haven't had much of a chance to reacquaint myself with them yet. Don't think that Cecelia remembers me, but David does."

"Yes, he does. It devastated him when you left the station, and he spent the next week going around the yard looking for his Uncle John."

John smiled a bit sadly at that. "I missed him too, Sam, especially on that long journey back to England. Not much to do on board except read and wonder what all of you had gotten up to that day."

"Well, when we go back next year, you will have lots of company. You'll be wishing for your privacy some days."

"I doubt that, but right now, we had better get the children if we want to stay in Bethany's favour. Don't want her angry at me."

"No," said Sam, laughingly teasing his wife. "She wields a mean wooden spoon, and I see her looking for one. Let's head out now."

The men left the kitchen, and the women soon heard the back door open, and then close. Bethany smiled at Cassandra. "I'm so glad you are here. It will give us the chance to catch up on each other's lives. Are you staying long?"

"I don't know. I gave up my room at the boarding house because I did not know when, or if, I would be back. But perhaps I was a bit hasty, seeing that you and Sam have taken up residence here. I will be in the way."

"Cassandra Stillwater, don't you even think of such a thing! You are my dear sister, and you are never a bother. There is plenty of room for all of us, and I am sure Mrs. Kingsley does not mind cooking for a large family again, do you?"

"Of course not," said the cook. "I am overjoyed to have all of you here under this roof. It is my pleasure to cook and bake for all of you."

"And I will help," said Bethany. "I have become quite adept at cooking in the past few years."

"I'm glad my lessons helped prepare you for your new life in Australia, Miss Bethany. When you would help me in the kitchen while you were growing up, I never imagined those cooking lessons would be so valuable to you. I thought you would marry a nobleman and have servants to do the chores for you."

"Well, I did marry a noble," Bethany said, laughing, "only he chose to forgo that life and live a rougher one in the Colonies. So, half your prediction came true, at least."

"Do you miss living here, Bethany?" asked Cassandra.

"Other than not being able to see my friends and family, I truly don't. We have a full life in Australia, and I love it there."

"Better than your first months of living there I suppose?" said Mrs. Kingsley with a smile.

Cassandra frowned. "Please, don't even speak of those days, ma'am. I still have nightmares about what I did to Bethany."

Bethany frowned at her. "You are not serious, are you, Cassandra?"

"Yes."

"But ... you know I think of you only with love now. And even when they'd convicted me of stealing your necklace, I knew that Howard had to be forcing you to lie to the judge. I never condemned you for what you did. Not once."

"I lived with enough self-condemnation, Bethany, that it did not matter. It was only once I had confessed my sin to God, and had gone to the judge to tell the truth about what I had done, that I could start to shed that guilty feeling."

"And yet now, after all these years, Cassandra, you still feel guilty? Why?"

"Because I seriously hurt the person I loved most, aside from my sons. And Satan frequently reminds me of my guilt."

"Then the next time he comes around, you tell him that you are cleansed and forgiven and tell him to go back home. The Bible tells us that, if we resist the devil, he will flee from us.[5] He cannot stand against the power of Christ in us. So, remember that the next time he comes calling. All right?"

"I'll try. I don't have your strong faith, Bethany, but I will try."

"That faith only comes from trust, and from seeing God work in your life. My faith was weak when I went to Fremantle Gaol, but I kept trusting that God was still there for me, and that He would see me through my trial. And He did ... in the most miraculous way. I would not be married to Sam and have a wonderful family if it had not been for my ordeal. I am not saying that God has the same plan for you, dear sister, but I know he is working everything out for your good. Don't you agree, Mrs. Kingsley?"

"I do, Miss Bethany. But Mrs. Stillwater needs to believe for herself. We can't do it for her. We can only pray."

"And I will pray for you, Cassandra, that you will leave the guilt in the past and live a life full of hope for the future."

"Thank you, Bethany, Mrs. Kingsley," said Cassandra, reaching out for their hands. "Now, I know why I came out to the estate for a visit; it was to hear God's wisdom from the two of you. I am truly blessed."

The women held onto each other for a moment longer until they heard the men and children come in the back door. Then they dried their tears and smiled as the noisy children burst into the kitchen, eager to share what they had seen in the barns. After that, there was no time for private conversations, only busy preparations for tea and dinner, before settling the children for the night in the nursery next to Sam and Bethany's room, with a young maid watching over them until their parents retired. Then the house was quiet, with only the ticking of the grandfather clock in the front hallway marking off each second.

Everyone slept well that night, including Cassandra, who experienced no guilty nightmares for the first time in many months. Her sleep was tranquil, which would help prepare her for the day to follow.

Chapter 21

Cassandra woke refreshed and ready to face the day. It was the first time in a long while she had felt this good upon awakening. Perhaps it was because of the talk she'd had with Bethany last evening, but she finally felt free of any guilty feelings from the past. Now, if only she could determine what to do in the future. Perhaps God would miraculously show her that path as well, just as He had when the former housemother had showed up at the YWCA, willing to resume her former position. Cassandra knew she needed to trust God more fully and rest in His promise to take care of her, but that was hard for her. She was so used to looking after everyone around her that it was hard to let go of the control. But maybe this was a lesson God wanted to teach her: that He was in control and that she should let Him lead her each day and not look too far into the future. Cassandra resolved to do that, starting with today.

So, she got up from her bed, splashed water on her face, and then dressed in a simple cotton gown before heading down the back stairs to the kitchen, where she found Mrs. Kingsley hard at work, preparing breakfast.

"Good morning, Mrs. Kingsley."

"Oh, good morning, Mrs. Stillwater. Did you sleep well?"

"Very well, thank you. And you?"

"Can't complain."

"I see you are busy. May I help you?"

"No. Everything is just about ready. The others are in the breakfast room. Why don't you join them, and I'll have the food out soon."

"It smells delicious. Looking forward to eating your cooking again. I missed it when I was at the boarding house."

"Did they not feed you well?"

"Oh yes, there was always enough food, but it never had the texture or flavour of yours, Mrs. Kingsley."

"Well, I hope to serve you many more meals in the future, ma'am, starting with today's breakfast. Now, be off with you so I can get the food out to you."

Cassandra took the hint and headed into the breakfast room where she found the rest of the family. "Good morning, everyone," she said as she came into the room.

The assembled group responded with a chorus of good mornings.

"How did you sleep?" asked Bethany.

"Very well. And you?"

"Wonderfully. I always sleep best when I am surrounded by fresh country air rather than city smog."

"Yes. I know what you mean. After living here for five years, and then moving back to London, I noticed the noxious air immediately, not only during the day but also at night. I realised then how fortunate I had been to have had these past years living on the estate with the boys."

"Now that you are back, perhaps you will stay," suggested Bethany. "It is much better for your health."

"I'll have to see where God leads me next. I am giving Him control of my life again, so we will see what He has in store for me."

"I am sure it is only good things, Cassandra. He only looks out for our best."

"Yes, I am sure that is what you thought when you were in the colonial prison, didn't you?"

Bethany laughed. "Not at first. But I did not see what He had planned for my future ... a future with the man of my dreams and three beautiful children. No, I only had to trust Him daily and put my hope in His goodness."

"And that is what I plan to do as well." Seeing the footman put the breakfast foods on the sideboard, Cassandra stopped speaking. John prayed for the meal, and then Bethany and Sam started filling plates for David and

Cecelia before getting their own. After that, Cassandra and John got what they needed from the sideboard, and then seated themselves at the other end of the table from the Yardleys. No one spoke much until the plates were empty and the adults had refilled their cups with either tea or coffee.

"So," John said, "what do you ladies have planned for today?"

"I don't know, John," said Bethany. "I don't feel energetic, so perhaps a walk around the manor grounds will meet my needs. What about you, Cassandra?"

"That sounds ideal, Bethany. I am not up for much else today either. Perhaps tomorrow, if the weather is fine, we could plan a picnic down by the creek. I am sure the children would love to paddle in the water, wouldn't you?" she asked David and Cecelia, who nodded in agreement. "So, I suppose that today, Bethany and I will rest while the children play in the barns. What about you gentlemen?"

"We will watch the children, so you don't have to, Beth," said Sam. "It will also give John and me a chance to talk about our plans for the future."

"You and Lord Dudley have mutual interests?" asked Cassandra.

"Yes. As you may have heard me say yesterday when you arrived, when my tenure at Stillwater is complete, I plan to travel back to Australia and share a sheep station with Bethany and Sam."

"I knew you were only planning to be here for a year, but I thought you would stay in Britain to manage your family estate. Are your parents aware of your plans?"

"Only my aunt and uncle, as well as Sam and Bethany. My parents are unaware as yet. I plan to tell them soon."

"I am sure your news will disappoint them."

"Perhaps, but they only want me to be happy, so their disappointment will be short-lived."

"I can't imagine how I will feel if any of my sons gave me that news, sir. But fortunately, they are still young and have schooling yet to complete before they go out into the world."

"You would deny them the opportunity to explore and find a new home elsewhere, Cassandra?" asked Sam.

"Not if they had set their hearts on it, but like most mothers, I will discourage them from thinking that way. I want to keep my sons close, so that when I am old, I will have their love and support."

"As you say, the boys are young, but it won't be long until they are grown men. Perhaps by then, you will have reconsidered. Why, you may even have another husband and family."

"That is not in my plans, Sam. I have been married once, and though I love my sons dearly, I would not put myself in that position again."

"Even for love?" asked Bethany.

"I am too old for love." She shook her head. "No, the love of my boys will suffice."

"No one is ever too old for love, Cassandra. Perhaps that is in God's plans for you."

"Then He needs to change His plans because that is something I will never agree to," said Cassandra plainly.

"Perhaps not. But wait... What did you say a bit earlier? I believe it was, 'I'll have to see where God leads me next. I am giving Him control of my life again, so we will see what He has in store for me.' Isn't that correct?"

"Yes, you have caught me out, Bethany. But knowing how I feel about marriage, I doubt He has that in mind for me."

"We will see, my sister. We will see. But in the meantime, why don't we get our walking shoes on and take a stroll around the grounds?"

"I agree," said Cassandra, pushing back her chair and standing up. "I will meet you at the front door in a few minutes."

Bethany nodded before herding the children up the back stairs for a wash. Then Sam could take over, and she could work on getting Cassandra to see her point of view about love and marriage. That was her plan for the day.

***

A few minutes later, Sam and John ushered the children out the back door, while Bethany and Cassandra left through the front door to stroll around the grounds. When they were several yards away from the manor, Bethany again broached the subject of remarriage.

"I noticed you were quick to dispel any notions of getting married again, Cassandra. Did your life with Howard really put you off even considering having another husband?"

"Yes."

"But you know that there are many men who would make you a wonderful husband."

"If there are, I have not met them. The only men I know are already married."

"What about John?"

"Lord Dudley?"

"Yes. He is still single."

"And planning to leave for Australia within the next year."

"Would you be averse to moving away from England?"

"My boys are here, so why would I want to leave and live half a world away?"

"So that you could have a life of your own."

"It is right for you, Bethany. After all, you found the man of your dreams in Sam, a man who adores you and would do anything to make you happy. You also decided together to move back to Australia and raise your family on a sheep station. But it is different for me. Lord Dudley has already made his plans to join you, and even if I desired a life with him, which I do not, I don't want to leave the only love I have, which is that of my sons. It is enough for me."

"I am sorry to hear that, Cassandra. You are still young and healthy. True, your boys love you, but before you know it, they will be young men and leading lives of their own. Why, how old is Peter now?"

"He is sixteen, almost seventeen. He plans to attend university next year and study law."

"Seventeen. How quickly time passes... And his brothers will soon follow him out into the world. Do you truly want to live alone on the edge of their lives?"

"No, but I could stay here, and they could come and visit me whenever they had the time. I am sure they will not neglect their mother even when they reach adulthood."

"I am sure they won't either, Cassandra, but they will have their own lives and interests, and perhaps families of their own soon. You don't want them to stay tied to you forever, do you?"

"No, of course not."

"So, would they not be happier knowing that you are moving on with your life, while they are finding their own, instead of always being concerned about your wellbeing?"

"I suppose so. But this conversation is pointless, Bethany. Lord Dudley has shown no interest in me as a woman since the day I met him. His only concern has been my management of the estate."

"I disagree. Why would he have shown up at the boarding house the day you were attacked if his only care was for the way you had managed the affairs here? He had already taken over the estate management, and so he had no reason to seek you out; did he?"

"I believe he was in the city conducting business that day and was only being courteous in coming to see me."

"Cassandra, do you not think John's main purpose was to visit you and not to attend to business? I do not know how to make you see yourself the way others view you, as a lovely woman who has much to offer a new husband. I am sure John would see that as well if you gave him a chance."

"Perhaps all my years of feeling worthless, Bethany, have made me hesitant to accept any compliments as to my value. I was of so little merit to my father that he basically sold me to Howard. And Howard, well, you are aware of what he thought of me. When I became the estate manager, I thought it would lend credence to my worth, but I failed to keep it viable. And now I am out of another job because I could not handle the affairs of a few young women. I came out here for a few days to sort out my life and find someplace where I can fit in and be productive. Please don't ask me to do more than that, I beg you."

"My heart aches to hear those words, my dear sister. It is certainly not how I see you, nor how anyone else around here does. But I have said my piece, and I will be quiet. Only know this: I will be in constant prayer for you, asking God to reveal to you the precious woman that you are in His sight and ours. Until then, let us talk about other things, shall we?"

Cassandra agreed, and the two women linked arms and strolled around the grounds, speaking only of happier times they had experienced in the past.

***

Meanwhile, Sam was having a similar conversation with John about his need for a wife. They were in the barn, leaning up against the railing of an enclosure while they watched the children playing in the straw. Sam turned to Joe. "So, are you planning to get married before you accompany us back to Australia next year?"

Joe laughed. "What brought that to mind, Sam?"

"Don't really know, but it would be good for you to give it some serious thought. After all, there are few single women in our part of Australia."

"Do I need to be married? Is that required for our partnership?"

"Of course not, but as our property increases in size, you will want to establish your own home on the station."

"How long do I have before you and Bethany will no longer accommodate me? Six months? A year?"

"You know you are welcome to stay with us as long as you want to, John. But you may also like some privacy, which is hard to find in a household of children, unless they are your own."

"I quite enjoyed my time with David and Cecelia, Sam. They are wonderful children."

"They are, but they are getting to be more of a handful as they grow older. And we have Douglas as well now. Our home is getting noisier by the day."

"And knowing you and Bethany, I don't expect Douglas will be the last child added to your family. You plan to have more, do you not?"

"If Bethany is agreeable to it, yes, we will."

"So, not only will your home be noisier but it will be fuller as well. Do you plan to expand the house?"

"Yes, Bethany and I have already talked about adding more rooms to meet our needs. But that is not an immediate priority."

"Perhaps I should think about establishing a home for myself once we get back."

"If you do, you will need someone to care for you and your home, John. A wife would meet those needs."

"As you have appeared to have thought this through, Sam, whom do you suggest I marry?"

"Uh... What about Cassandra?"

"Mrs. Stillwater?"

"Yes. Is that an abhorrent idea?"

"No, of course not. But I doubt she would have me, Sam. And besides, you heard her thoughts about leaving England and her sons behind. She has no intention of doing that."

"Perhaps, for love, she would think differently."

"Love? Where did you come up with the notion that I love Mrs. Stillwater?"

"Only from the looks you give her when she is not gazing in your direction."

"You are mistaken, Sam. I respect her and care for her, but I cannot say that I love her. And as to her feelings for me, well, she certainly does not love me. I don't even know that she likes me."

"A marriage built on care and respect could also be a good one, John. Love can grow out of that state."

"I concur, but do you think she would even consider it?"

"I don't know, but I think it may be worth your while to try courting her and see if she responds to your overtures."

"And how do you propose I do that with us both living on the estate, or even worse, her moving back to London in a few days?"

"You have courted women before, John. Don't you remember how to do it?"

"My courtships were brief, Sam, as you will remember. Besides, they were all young, silly, society girls who had no thoughts in their heads besides what dress they would wear to the next party. I don't think Mrs. Stillwater is that type of woman."

"No, I agree. So, you need to work harder to find out what interests her and speak to those pursuits. I can speak with Bethany if you like. She and Cassandra have been friends for many years, so she must have some ideas."

"You want to involve Bethany in this endeavour? Won't she tell Mrs. Stillwater what we are about?"

"No, she won't. Bethany wants Cassandra to be happy, and if she thinks this will help her, she will be glad to assist us."

"Well, talk to Bethany and see what she says. If she has any ideas, please let me know. But if not, please let it go. All right?"

"All right. Now, let's round up the children and take them inside for their naps. They will be tired enough to sleep for at least an hour. I will use that time to speak with Bethany."

"And I need an hour to work on the estate books, Sam. After all, while you are a man of leisure, I am still a working man and must prove myself to your father as being worthy of my pay," said John as he moved across the barn to help Sam corral his offspring.

***

After an awkward lunch, during which Cassandra and John meticulously avoided looking at or speaking to each other, John went back to working on the books, while Cassandra settled in to read a book in the morning parlour. Mrs. Kingsley promised to keep David and Cecelia entertained, having them help her make biscuits. So, Bethany and Sam headed upstairs to their room for a moment of privacy while Bethany fed Douglas. When they settled down beside the fireplace with Douglas contentedly nursing, Bethany said, "Did you notice the strain between John and Cassandra at lunch, Sam?"

"I did. I hope it had nothing to do with my conversation with him while we were in the barn this morning."

"What did you talk about?"

"His need to get married before he leaves England because of the lack of single women in Australia."

"What was his response?"

"My statement had surprised him, but he said he would think about it."

"Does he have anyone in mind?"

"No."

"That could be a problem with him living out here and not in London."

"I did, uh, suggest a candidate for him to consider."

"Oh? And who might that be?"

"Cassandra."

"Ah... No wonder they were so ill at ease with each other during the meal, Sam. I also talked to Cassandra about the possibility of getting married again and suggested John as a potential groom."

"How did she respond?"

"In the same manner she had at breakfast. She is not looking to remarry, and the love of her sons is enough to sustain her for the rest of her life. Also, she is not keen to move away from England, especially to a country halfway around the world."

"So, she is reluctant to consider him? I told John I would ask you if you knew of any particular interests of Cassandra's that he could use in courting her. Are you aware of any, Beth?"

"Well, she is fond of gardening and riding, Sam. I know she used to lament to me she had neither the space nor the time for either when she lived in London. She was looking forward to doing both when she and the boys moved out to the estate."

"I don't know how keen John is on gardening," Sam said, "but he is an excellent rider and loves the sport. Perhaps he could take her out riding while she is visiting, and she can increase his knowledge about the different flora on the estate. When he goes out with Mr. Wiley, I doubt they discuss that aspect of the farm."

"That is an excellent idea. Please mention it to John. Other than that, I do not have any other suggestions at the moment. If I think of anything else, I will let you know."

"I will tell him. Now, I am going to stretch my legs a bit with a stroll around the grounds. Would you like to join me?"

"No, if you don't mind, I am going to put Douglas down for a nap, and then lie down myself for a bit. I don't know why I am so tired, but I am. An afternoon nap might restore my energy. Have a nice walk, love."

"I will do that," Sam said, then got up and walked over to kiss Bethany and brush a hand over Douglas's head. "I'll let Cassandra and Mrs. Kingsley know too so that they can entertain our older children for the next hour. Have a good rest, Beth." Then he left the room, while Bethany continued to feed Douglas and mull over ideas as to how to get Cassandra and John together. They were a perfect match in her eyes. If only they saw it the same way...

***

Sam was also thinking about their conversation as he left the house. He'd already informed the ladies downstairs of Bethany's plans to nap for a bit. He'd also heard from Kingsley that John had headed back to the barn a few minutes earlier. So, Sam walked briskly in that direction, armed with a book about English flora that he'd tucked under his arm. Perhaps it was time to give John a lesson in botany before he accompanied Cassandra on a ride in the pastures.

***

Days turned into weeks, and before Cassandra knew it, she had been back at the estate for an entire month. Looking back over that time, she wondered what she had done to make the time pass so quickly. After an initial reluctance, she now enjoyed going with John for morning rides. He had turned out to be an agreeable companion, and she had taught him a lot about the local plants whenever they stopped for a rest break. She would miss those hours with him when her visit to the estate was over. But having had no insights from God about what she should do next with her life, she was content for now to rest in His presence and let each day roll into the next.

Soon, the boys would have another school break. She was looking forward to having them with her and spending more than just a few hours with them. She regretted not having kept her promise of booking a holiday at the seaside for them, but she knew they loved being at the estate. Perhaps, after they left to go back to school, she would find the energy to look for a new position in the city … or perhaps not. Country life was so much more relaxing. Did she truly wish to leave it behind again? Cassandra laughed as she realised that she was once again planning for the future instead of living for the day. She shook off her thoughts and focused once more on her joy of living moment to moment.

***

John, too, was enjoying his morning rides with Cassandra. She was an excellent rider, which complemented his style of not walking the horses through the meadow but rather taking them for a brisk gallop whenever he sensed their desire to run. They usually ended up by the creek, where they would dismount and let the horses have a drink while he and Cassandra noted the nearby flora. John had not thought he would be so interested in learning about a single flower or plant, but the way Cassandra described them had caught his attention. She became quite passionate about certain types of flora, her voice rising and her face lighting up when she saw a new bloom. Her passion for riding and plant life caused John to wonder what else might excite her to this degree. He was keen to find out but did not want to disrupt their present relationship with probing questions. He would have to make those discoveries on his own.

***

It thrilled Bethany and Sam to see the relationship between Cassandra and John develop. It gave them hope for the future ... if only they could break down Cassandra's barriers to finding a new life for herself outside of England. They were careful not to probe for details either, wanting the relationship to grow without interference. But one afternoon, while sitting with Cassandra in the back parlour, listening to her describe her morning ride with John and what they had found, Bethany could hold back no longer.

"It sounds like you are enjoying your morning rides with John."

"Yes, I am enjoying my time with him, Bethany. I did not expect it to be this way."

"Oh, and why is that?"

"I don't know. Perhaps it was my previous experience with him, or perhaps I prejudged him before I knew him."

"Yes, sometimes first impressions are not the best. Often people are nervous and not themselves when they meet."

"That is true, but there was also his deception. That did not sit well with me."

"No, that was poorly done of John. But he has apologised for his behaviour, and you have forgiven him, have you not?"

"Yes."

"Forgive me for asking, but will you miss John when he leaves with us next spring?"

"If I am not engaged somewhere else and still living on the estate, I believe I will, Bethany. Lord Dudley is companionable."

"Why do you still address him so formally, Cassandra? By now, I would have thought you would have progressed to calling each other by your first names."

"He has suggested that, but I am reluctant to do so for a couple of reasons. First, because it implies a certain intimacy, which we do not have, and second, because I fear that, if we had so close a relationship, it would make things harder next spring when you all depart. No, it is better that we maintain a certain distance between us, so as not to get too involved with each other."

"I see," said Bethany. "But I must say that it sounds like John would be amenable to a closer relationship with you. Do you truly have no desire for that?"

"It is not a matter of desire but of practicality. As I have said, my life is here in England, and he is looking forward to a new life in Australia. Thus, there is no reason to seek out a closer relationship."

"And you are still averse to perhaps coming with us to Australia?"

"Yes. I have not changed my mind in that regard."

"Well… I will speak no more of it. Now, when do you expect the boys to join us for their school break?"

***

Sam was having a similar conversation with John as they watched Mr. Wiley take first David, and then Cecelia, on pony rides around the paddock. "Seeing the children enjoying their first pony rides reminds me of your morning rides with Cassandra. How are those going, John?"

"Well, Sam, thank you. We are both having a good time, both riding and exploring the ever-changing plant life. I did not know there was so much variety in the plants and flowers around here."

"Yes, God's creation is amazing, is it not? I am glad you have found interests in common. Has your relationship changed in the past weeks?"

"We are friendlier to each other, Sam, but other than that, I would have to say no. Mrs. Stillwater always maintains a certain distance from me, even when we are strolling by the creek, looking for new flowers."

"Are you still addressing her so formally?"

"Yes. I proposed we use our first names, but she declined. She said that it would not be proper."

"Surely, after all this time, and our family connections…"

"I agree, Sam, but I do not want to push her beyond where she is comfortable. I am letting her set the limits on our friendship."

"That is wise, John. However, I had hoped that she would warm to you once you were enjoying similar interests."

"I had hoped so, too, but I see no signs of that. Perhaps I will travel to Australia as a single man and live with you and Bethany for the rest of my life."

"There are always housekeepers for hire, John," said Sam, laughing. "Remember that, please."

John laughed as well. "I will. I can see the idea of having a permanent house guest does not sit well with you, my cousin."

"Only for your sake, not for ours."

"Then let us pray that a suitable candidate for marriage is released from Fremantle Gaol soon after we arrive. After all, isn't that where you and Bethany met, and your friends Joe and Joann as well? Seems that it is a good place to look for a bride."

"Good luck with that, John. But Bethany and I knew each other from Britain, so seeing her as an ex-convict wife does not count. Joann, on the other hand, had never met Joe before her release, so they might give you some tips on how to choose a bride from the jail. And Sally also. She visits the prison regularly for Bible studies and would know which women might be suitable for you. Yes, I think you had best talk to Sally once we arrive. She can steer you in the right direction, and perhaps, help you with your courtship, as she did with Bethany and I."

"I will keep that in mind, Sam, if my courtship of Cassandra does not progress. It is always good to know there are other options. Now, it is almost time for tea. Shall we gather up the children and take them inside? I am sure Jack is tired of walking the pony round and round the paddock."

"Good idea," said Sam, before hailing Jack to bring the pony and its riders over to where they were standing. Once David and Cecelia climbed over the fence, they walked with their father and John up to the manor, all the while asking how soon they could return for more rides.

***

When they arrived at the house, Sam took the children to wash their hands before sending them down to the kitchen for their tea. He found Bethany napping on the bed, with Douglas contently sleeping in his crib. The children's voices woke Bethany, and she sat up to listen to their riding tales before they ran down the hallway towards the kitchen stairs. She told Sam that

Douglas had finished eating and should sleep for an hour while they had their tea. She would send Molly up to watch him.

After rinsing her hands and splashing water on her face, she straightened her hair, shook out her gown, and then accompanied Sam out of the room. They headed down the front stairs to the parlour, where they found Cassandra and John waiting for them. Spying Molly in the foyer, Bethany asked her to sit with Douglas, which she assented to, and then headed upstairs. Comfortable knowing that her children were in good hands, Bethany looked forward to having tea.

***

About an hour later, Sam was surprised to find Bethany napping in their room. Douglas had been sleeping through the night for the past week, so neither of them had needed to get up with him. He wondered why Bethany continued to be so weary. If she did not improve in the next week, he was going to take her into London to see Dr. Harrington, their long-time family physician. Until that time, there was no point in worrying, though he would be keeping a close eye on her in the coming days.

***

The next week passed much the same as the previous ones. John and Cassandra continued their morning rides, and then separated after lunch until teatime, where they convened with Sam and Bethany for an hour's chat. Sam continued his close scrutiny of Bethany, who caught him observing her but said nothing, only raising an eyebrow at his scrutiny. Sam was now convinced that something was wrong with her. She took a nap every afternoon and was ready to retire soon after they put the children down for the night. Usually, she remained upstairs to feed David after settling David and Cecelia. She seldom came back downstairs for evening tea, only telling John and Cassandra after dinner that she would see them in the morning. And often when Sam came up to bed, he found her already asleep.

Finally, one day, he said, "Bethany, I am worried about you. You are sleeping a lot, and yet you do not appear rested. I would like to have Dr.

Harrington see you. Perhaps he can give you a tonic of some sort that will help how."

"I am not ill, Sam, so I don't think I need to see a doctor. I am just rather tired."

"Yes, but this is not normal for you. You were not like this after David and Cecelia were born. That is why I want you to be examined."

"All right. Yes, this is not normally how I am after giving birth, especially after so many months. Perhaps my blood is lacking something. I will see the doctor, but if he finds there is nothing wrong with me, will you please stop worrying?"

"I will try, Beth, but I cannot guarantee it. You mean so much to me that I will do anything to keep you by my side for as long as I can."

"I love you too, Sam, and because of that, I will consent to your wishes. Would you arrange the appointment? If possible, I would rather not worry your parents by staying in London overnight. Plus, if we only are away for a few hours, we can leave the children here. It would be nice to have you all to myself for a bit." She smiled at her husband.

"I'd like that too, Beth. Time alone is scarce when you have three children. So, even a carriage ride to town and back is worth it. I'll send a note to Dr. Harrington and find out when he can see you. All right?"

"Yes. Now, speaking of sleeping, I would like an afternoon nap, Sam. Would you care to join me?"

"Much as I would love to, it is safer for you if I don't. You know what happened the last time we took a nap together, just after we arrived in Britain. Neither of us got much sleep, did we?"

Bethany blushed. "No, we didn't. You are a hard man to resist, my husband. Perhaps it would be better if you did something else while I slept."

"I'll listen for the children and take Douglas downstairs with me, so you aren't disturbed. Have a good sleep, love," he said, before picking up Douglas and walking out of the room. He headed down to the front parlour, knowing Molly was in the nursery watching over the other two children. Douglas was still sleeping, and Sam hoped he would remain in that state for at least the next hour. But he was sure that if he woke up, the adults on the main floor could cope with his needs, unless he needed to eat. Then, unfortunately, he would have to return to his mother.

Sam found John in the parlour when he walked through the door. John looked up at him. "I'm surprised to see you, Sam. I thought you were with Bethany."

"No, she needs to take a nap, so I've brought Douglas down with me. Hopefully, he won't wake up needing his mother for a while."

"Bethany is sleeping again? Seems to me she is sleeping a great deal, Sam. Is anything wrong?"

"Not that we are aware of, John. But I am concerned enough that I want her to see a doctor. May I borrow some parchment and an inked quill so I can send a message to Dr. Harrington in London?"

"Dr. Harrington? We have an excellent physician in the village, Sam, by the name of Dr. Wild. I could send for him. He is much closer than Dr. Harrington."

"Thank you, but no, John. I will feel more comfortable with a physician I know and trust. Dr. Harrington has been our family physician for many years, so I would rather have him examine Bethany."

"I understand. Here is some parchment. You are welcome to use my quill and desk while you write your message. I will let Kingsley know that a message needs to go to London this afternoon. He will send a groom in with the note. I'll leave it up to him who takes it to the city." John got up from his chair at the desk and gestured Sam to replace him there. Then he walked out into the foyer and spoke to Kingsley, returning a few moments later just as Sam was sealing the note.

"Kingsley will have Michael come up. Apparently, he rode into London to fetch Dr. Harrington when Joann was ill, so he knows the doctor's address."

"Thank you, John. It is not urgent, but I would like Bethany to be seen as soon as possible. She and I will hopefully travel into, and back from, the city in one day. We would like to leave the older children here if you are agreeable. We will take Douglas with us, as Bethany will need to feed him during the day."

"I'm sure that won't be a problem. Mrs. Kingsley and Mrs. Stillwater adore your children, as do I. We can keep them fed and entertained for one day. It will also give you and Bethany some time alone, something I know you get little of now."

"That is true, John. We cherish every moment we can steal. But neither of us would give up having a family just for more time alone. The children are too precious to us."

"Perhaps someday I will experience the same. But for now, I'll enjoy my bachelorhood."

"You have enjoyed it for too many years, John. It is time to experience the other side of life."

"Perhaps. Now, if your message is ready, I'll give it to Kingsley, and it will be on its way."

Sam handed him the note, and John took it to the foyer. Soon, Sam heard the door open and close, and then the sound of hooves clattering down the cobblestone lane towards the gate. Hopefully, Dr. Harrington would clear up the mystery of Bethany's ongoing fatigue.

Chapter 22

Bethany awoke about an hour later. Glancing toward the window, she could see that the sun had moved slightly lower in the sky but was still streaming brightly into the room. She noted the empty crib beside her. *Sam must still have Douglas with him.* Closing her eyes again, she listened for any sounds of the baby crying. There were none. Relaxing back against the pillows, she wondered what was wrong with her. She agreed with Sam that wanting to sleep all the time was not normal for her. Even when she had been pregnant, she had not experienced this kind of lethargy. She'd had nausea every morning for the first few months, but after that, she had been well until the babies were born.

In any case, there was no way that she was carrying another child. Even though she had had one small monthly since David's birth, she did not consider pregnancy to be a possibility. It had to be something else. It would be good to have Dr. Harrington examine her and determine the cause of her fatigue. Then whatever the outcome, she could deal with it and get on with her life. She might have to adjust things in her lifestyle and hire more help at the station, but they could do that.

She thought of women she had met in London over the years who'd had several children and looked decades older than they actually were. Would that be her fate? Bethany laughed to herself. Thank goodness Sam loved her as much for her inner beauty as her outward appearance. Or at least, that is what he told her. She knew that, someday, if she lived long enough, she would have wrinkles and grey hair, just like her beloved mother-in-law did. And the Duchess's inner beauty still shone through, and no one ever even noticed the changes of time in her outward appearance.

Determined to shake off her lethargy, persistent even after her nap, Bethany got up, went over to the basin, and splashed cold water on her face. It helped. Then she donned her gown again and fixed her hair before heading out of the room. Still not hearing Douglas, she decided to check the front parlour to see if he and his father were there. When she walked into the room, she found John holding the baby. Douglas was cooing and smiling until he caught sight of his mother. Then he reached out his arms towards her, and Bethany moved forward to take him.

"Where is Sam?" she asked.

"He went to check on the other children and make sure that they were not annoying anyone. He will be back soon."

"I am glad he is keeping an eye on them and Douglas. Has the baby been fussing while I have been napping?"

"Not at all. He only woke up a few minutes ago, and I agreed to hold him while Sam went to the kitchen."

"He looks content in your arms, John. You must have a knack with infants."

"Don't know that I do. I've never been around too many babies, being an only child."

"Would you like to be a father someday?"

"If God so wills it, yes. But I am also getting past the age of having children, so it will need to be soon."

"Nonsense," Bethany said. "I know of children whose fathers were much older than you are when they were born. You have plenty of time."

"Thank you for that encouragement. Perhaps the age of the mother is more of an issue than that of the father."

"Perhaps, although women can bear children well into their late thirties, at least according to my friend Sally. You remember her, don't you?" Bethany asked. "She and her husband run the boarding house in Fremantle, and she also assists the local midwife with births in the area."

"I remember her. They are great friends of yours, aren't they?"

"Yes. Sally and Nick are wonderful, and she helped me birth all of my children. I would not have it any other way."

"So, an older woman can have children?"

Knowing his mind had moved to Cassandra, Bethany nodded. "Yes, and without complications, especially if she's already had children when she was younger."

"Thank you for that information, Bethany. I was not aware of that fact."

"You are welcome, John. Now, I hear Sam returning, so I will take Douglas and head to the kitchen to supervise my older children. I will see you at teatime." John nodded, then looked up as Sam came into the room.

"Oh, you are up, Bethany. I checked on our offspring. They are making biscuits with Mrs. Kingsley. They appear to be behaving themselves. Did you want me to take Douglas again?"

"No, that's fine, Sam. I'll head down to the kitchen to watch over the children for the next while, and I'll take Douglas with me, in case he needs to eat. You enjoy yourself with John. I'll see you both later."

"Well," said Sam, brushing a kiss across her cheek. "Let me know if you need my help."

"I will, love," she said, while heading back out the door. "Enjoy your afternoon, gentlemen."

Once Bethany had left the room, Sam and John settled into a couple of large, leather-upholstered chairs. Their conversation comprised of estate management and plans for their mutual future in Australia. They made no further mention of marriage, although it was never far from John's mind now, especially after what Bethany had so recently disclosed to him. If they were to marry, would Cassandra even consider having more children? He wanted to have a family, so that was something he would need to think about.

***

Bethany found Cassandra in the kitchen as well, reading a story to David and Cecelia. She had found some books she used to read to her sons when they were young and knew that Bethany's children would also enjoy the stories. It was keeping them entertained, so Mrs. Kingsley did not have to worry about them being burned by the pans of biscuits she was taking out of the oven. The aroma of freshly baked biscuits filled the kitchen.

Bethany could not resist taking one off the cooling rack. It was still hot, so she blew on it to cool it down before taking a nibble. It brought her back to her childhood when she would visit Mrs. Kingsley and steal biscuits, just as she was doing today. The cook smiled when she saw Bethany's action.

"Teaching your children bad habits, are you, Miss Bethany? Took me back many years just now when I saw what you were doing."

"I couldn't resist," said Bethany. "They are just as delicious as they were when I was a child."

Cassandra laughed. "At your trial, I remember Mr. Damon joking with Kingsley and the vicar's wife about your habit of stealing biscuits. Looks like you have not got over the habit."

"I am surprised you remembered that, Cassandra."

"I remember most of the trial, Bethany, especially my part in it. I can't ever forget what I did to you."

"Some memories are hard to erase, but I am so glad we are back to being what we were before my trial: sisters and best friends."

"I agree. A lifetime without your forgiveness and love would have been almost too much for me to bear, Bethany. I, too, am much happier now that we can be sisters once more."

David and Cecelia listened with interest to their mother and aunt. Seeing their attention, Bethany motioned Cassandra to continue reading the story while she turned her back on them to finish her biscuit and visit with Mrs. Kingsley. The children were too young to hear the story about Bethany's conviction for theft and subsequent jail time. Someday, when they were older, they would hear it. But not today.

**

Michael, the groom, arrived back at the estate later that afternoon with a return message from Dr. Harrington. Kingsley brought the note to Sam, who quickly read it:

Dr. Harrington would be pleased to see Bethany at 1:00 p.m. in two days' time.

That was good. Hopefully, he could help Bethany get back to her normal self. Seeing as it was almost teatime, Sam held onto the note until the ladies joined them in the parlour. Then he gave it to Bethany, and after reading it, she nodded and slipped it into her pocket. They would discuss it later.

***

Two days later, Bethany and Sam were just on their way to London, accompanied only by Douglas. The Kingsleys, Cassandra, and John had all assured them that they would look after their other children for the day. Despite having no doubts of that, it was still hard for Bethany not to agree to David and Cecelia's demands they go to London as well. But Sam had stood firm, telling the children that this was not a pleasure trip, and that it would bore them to accompany their parents. And then Bethany had closed her ears to her children's pleas and looked straight ahead as they departed from the front porch, so as not to see their weeping faces.

Once they were outside the estate gates, she breathed a sigh of relief. "Thank you, Sam, for being firm. If it had only been me, I would have listened to their cries and given in. I was thankful I only had to support your decision."

"You're welcome, Beth. It was difficult for me too, but they have to learn that they cannot always get their own way, especially when they are carrying on in such a manner. Learning these lessons while they are young will help them adjust more easily as they grow older."

"Did your parents instruct you in that way?"

"Yes. There were many times when I wanted to do exactly what Rupert was doing, or go where he was going, but my parents told me no, just as I did with David and Cecelia today. I was not happy either, but I learned to respect and obey my parents at an early age. I hope our children will as well."

"With you as their father, I am sure they will. I have to admit that I am soft and give into their demands more often than I should. My father spoiled me as a child; I don't remember either him or anyone else ever denying me anything. Perhaps that is why I can't deny David or Cecelia what they ask for. From now on, if I feel myself softening when I know I should be firm, I will send them to you. All right?"

Sam laughed. "As long as you are agreeable with whatever decision I make, Beth, that is fine with me. We need to stand as one, otherwise our children will outwit us both."

"I will, Sam. We are one."

He pulled her in close to his body before leaning down to kiss her. "For which I am ever grateful."

Bethany blushed, and then kissed him back. "Me too, my husband. Me too."

They spent the rest of the journey cuddling, revelling in their alone time. Even Douglas cooperated and gave his parents the time they needed to reconnect. While awake, he kept himself occupied by playing with Bethany's old toys, which they had found in the attic. He had no time to fuss while he was having such fun.

***

Soon they arrived in London, and after a delicious luncheon at a well-known pub, they headed over to Dr. Harrington's. The purpose of the trip began to affect Bethany, and she found her hands shaking, wondering what the doctor would reveal to them. Sam noticed her movements, reached over, and grasped her hands. "Are you nervous, Beth?"

She nodded.

"Then before we get to the office, why don't we pray? Would you like that?"

She nodded again, so Sam began: *"Dear Heavenly Father, we are coming to You now, thanking You for creating and sustaining our bodies. Lord, we are concerned about Bethany's health. We don't know what is going on in her body, but You do. You even count the number of hairs on her head. So, we ask that You calm our nerves and help us rest in You. Give Dr. Harrington wisdom as he examines Bethany. Help us accept whatever he tells us, whether good or bad. Bethany is in Your loving hands, and I pray she will know Your peace, even at this moment. In Jesus' name, I pray this. Amen."* Concluding his prayer, Sam squeezed her hands. "Better now, love?"

"Much better, thank you. That was exactly what I needed."

"Good. Now, I see we have arrived at our destination. So, let's go in and see what Dr. Harrington has to tell us."

Dr. Harrington's surgery was on the first floor of his home, with him and his family living above the office. Sam and Bethany walked in the front door, and his assistant greeted them before taking Bethany into an examination room. Sam was about to say that he would wait out front, but Bethany took his hand. "I need you with me, Sam. I don't know Dr. Harrington well, but you do, so won't you please stay with me?"

He agreed and followed her into the next room. The assistant helped Bethany climb up onto the examination table and ushered Sam to a nearby chair, before saying that the doctor would be with them shortly. Then she left the room.

Dr. Harrington arrived just moments later. "Lord and Lady Yardley. How good to see you. How are you both faring?"

They greeted him; then Sam said, "Bethany is having trouble getting enough sleep, Dr. Harrington. We are wondering if there is something ailing her, as she has never had this problem before now."

The doctor then asked Bethany to describe her sleeping habits and how she felt when she woke up. He also asked if they had any children yet. When Bethany told him that they had three, the youngest being about a year old, he laughed. "No wonder you are tired, Lady Yardley. Three children under five would tire anyone out. Are you still nursing your youngest?"

"Yes," said Bethany. "But he is weaning himself. He doesn't nurse as often now that he is eating solid foods."

"That sounds appropriate for his age," said the doctor. "But you may need a tonic to help build up your blood. How are your monthlies?"

Bethany blushed at the intimate question. "I have only had one since Douglas was born."

"And how often is he nursing?"

"About every four to six hours, and then he sleeps through the night."

"Lord Yardley, have you and your wife resumed an intimate relationship since the baby was born?"

Sam laughed. "A month after Bethany recovered from the birth, we were on a ship headed to England. We all stayed in one cabin. So, at night, we were too exhausted from looking after the children, Bethany feeding Douglas, and me keeping our other two from falling overboard to even think about let alone share any intimacy. It was only once we got back to England that we have been able to relax and enjoy each other's company again."

"And when did you get back?"

"A couple of months ago."

"I see. I think I know the answer to your problem, Lady Yardley, but I would like to examine you first before I say anything. Do you mind?"

"Not as long as Sam can stay with me."

"Of course he can. But I need you to take off your shoes and stockings. I can have my assistant come back in and help you if you like."

"No, I can manage with my husband's help."

"Good. I'll be back in a few minutes," he said before leaving the room.

"What do you need help with Beth?" asked Sam once the doctor was out of the room.

"My shoes and stockings, Sam," she said, tears spilling from her eyes.

"What's wrong, love?"

"Sam, I think there is something wrong with my woman parts. Did you hear the questions the doctor asked? I think he suspects something but won't say anything yet. I'm so frightened, Sam."

"Beth, remember what we prayed about before we came in? We don't know that there is anything wrong, so concentrate on filling yourself with God's peace. Can you do that for me?"

"I'll try, Sam. I'm sorry to be like this. I don't know what has come over me."

"I know, love. But Dr. Harrington will give us answers soon, so let's focus on getting you undressed. All right?"

Beth nodded and wiped away her tears, rolling down her stockings after Sam had taken off her shoes. A minute later, there was a knock on the door, and then Dr. Harrington came back in.

Noting Bethany's tear-washed face, he said, "Don't be worried, my dear. Please just lie back and let me examine you."

Bethany did as he asked, and after a moment of discomfort, he assisted her in sitting back up, until her legs were dangling over the table's edge. Then with a broad smile, he said, "I have confirmed my diagnosis. Congratulations, Lady Yardley. You are going to have another baby."

Chapter 23

Sam and Bethany's mouths dropped open. Another baby? That was not what they had expected to hear. "Are you sure?" asked Sam.

"Absolutely. And it explains why Bethany is so tired all the time. I will give her a tonic for her blood, but rest and good food are my main prescriptions for today."

Bethany finally found her voice. "How far along am I, Dr. Harrington?"

"I'm not sure, but because you haven't started showing yet, I'd say you were only a couple of months along."

Bethany thought back over the past two or three months and realized that this would have been just when they had arrived in England. But how could it have happened? She was still nursing Douglas, and she had had one monthly. She voiced her question to the doctor, who assured her that such circumstances were no guarantee against pregnancy, despite popular belief.

Satisfied with his answer, Bethany turned again to Sam. "I'm not dying. I'm having another baby!"

Sam was just starting to get over his shock. "Yes. We came expecting the worst and are going home with the best news of all. We're going to be parents again… But how will we manage four children on the voyage back south? It was hard enough with only three."

Bethany smiled and patted his hand. "We'll figure it out, my love. We have many months before the baby arrives. Let's just rejoice that God is blessing us with another child."

Smiling at the pair, Dr. Harrington nodded. "While you process everything, I'll get your tonic ready, Bethany. Once again, congratulations." With that said, he left the room.

Sam helped Bethany get dressed, and then they headed out to the waiting room where the assistant gave them the bottle of tonic, along with his best wishes. They left the office then with considerably lighter hearts than they had carried in with them, revelling in the good news all the way back to Stillwater Estate.

And when they got back, they found that they had even more reason to celebrate: Cassandra's sons had arrived for their school break.

***

Cassandra was thrilled when her sons had tumbled out of the carriage. She had already informed them of the recent changes to her life, and that she was back at the estate, not wanting them to seek her out at the YWCA and find that she was no longer there, having left with no forwarding address. Even so, it was a truly joyous moment when she met them on the front porch.

"Mama, you're here!" said Arthur, running up to throw his arms around her.

"Yes, my darling, I am, and now so are you."

"Are you here to stay now, Mother, or are you still visiting?" asked Calvin, next in line to hug her.

"I don't know. I am waiting on God to give me direction, and until He does so, I will be remaining here."

"That's good," said Wendell, when it was his turn. "This is where you belong. You should resume your old position of estate manager when Lord Dudley leaves."

"No, Wendell, I will not be doing that. I have no desire to resume that position."

"Then what will you do, Mother?" asked her eldest, Peter, looking down at her from above.

"Peter, you are so tall! You must have grown three inches in the past couple of months."

"At least two, Mother. But you did not answer my question. If you stay on the estate, what will be your role?"

"I do not know, Peter. Bethany assures me that I don't have to do anything. So, perhaps I will live here as a long-term guest and do nothing."

"Aunt Bethany? When did you speak to her about this?"

"On the day I arrived for my visit."

"I don't understand. Did you have a letter from her?"

"No, we spoke in person. Oh, you don't know! She is here in England! She, your Uncle Sam, and your three cousins came to London awhile back. But after living in Australia, they could not stand living in the city. So, they packed up and came out to the estate. They got here just prior to my arrival."

"Aunt Bethany is here?" said Arthur, pulling on his mother's arm. "Is she inside? Can we see her now?"

"Arthur, control yourself. No, she and Sam went to the city for the day. They will be back before dinner. But they left the children with us. Would you like to meet your cousins?"

"Yes, please, and then could we have a snack? I'm—"

"Starving," his brothers finished for him, in perfect unison.

Cassandra laughed. Nothing had changed. Arthur was still begging for food, as though he had not eaten in days. She hoped he did not have his father's metabolism, or else he would develop a belly as massive as Howard's one day. Right now, Arthur was a growing boy, and as skinny as a rail, so he could eat as much as he wanted, but later on... No, she would not dwell on the future. Only the present. And in the present, she had her four sons all within reach once more. What a day it was!

***

Bethany and Sam arrived back at the estate. After greeting her nephews, and checking on her children, Bethany headed upstairs to feed Douglas and take a nap before dinner. Sam remained downstairs to answer all the nephews' questions about their trip and to keep an eye on David and Cecelia while they had their tea. Then he, John, and the boys, along with David and Cecelia, headed back to the barn to see the horses.

Two hours later, Bethany descended the stairs with Douglas in her arms and headed to the kitchen to find her family. She was surprised to find only Cassandra and Mrs. Kingsley there.

"Sam and Lord Dudley took all the children out to the barns after tea," said Cassandra. "My sons were restless after their carriage ride, so John—I mean, Lord Dudley—was kind enough to take them out to stretch their legs. And of course, as soon as your children heard the words 'barn' and 'horses,' they wanted to go as well. So, they are all out at the barn."

"That is why it is so quiet," said Mrs. Kingsley. "Now, can I get you a cup of tea, Bethany? You must be thirsty after your day's activities."

"Yes, thank you, Mrs. Kingsley. That would be greatly appreciated."

While the housekeeper bustled around getting Bethany's tea, Cassandra asked, "So, what did the doctor say? Are you ill?"

Chapter 24

Bethany blushed. She had planned to wait and announce their good news at dinner, but it seemed there was no real reason to so. "No, I'm not ill. He did give me a bottle of tonic to build up my blood, but other than that, I am fine."

"So, why are you so tired all the time? You seem to need a lot of sleep."

"I guess that happens when you are nursing one baby and expecting another," Bethany said with a smile.

Cassandra gasped. "You are having another baby? Already?"

"Yes. It should arrive about a month or so before we leave for Australia."

"Congratulations! But four children on a long sea voyage... How will you manage?"

Bethany laughed. "Those were Sam's words when we found out too. But we have time to figure it all out. I'm sure God will give us a plan."

"I'm sure He will. Oh, I am so happy for you, Bethany! This is wonderful news!" Cassandra moved over to give her a big hug.

Mrs. Kingsley abandoned the tea to join the hug. "Oh, Miss Bethany! I agree with Mrs. Stillwater. This is marvellous! And this time, Mr. Kingsley and I will be with you to experience your joy! I can't wait to tell him!"

"Go ahead, Mrs. Kingsley," said Cassandra. "I'll finish fixing Bethany's tea."

Bethany nodded her approval, and Mrs. Kingsley rushed out of the room, calling for her husband as she went.

Cassandra got Bethany's tea ready, and then she and Bethany started talking about everything they would need to prepare before the youngest Yardley made his arrival in several months' time. After they had exhausted that topic, Bethany reverted back to speaking about John and how good he had been with David on his visit to Australia. She hoped to spark an interest in Cassandra about his potential as a future husband and possible father to her sons.

"John is kind," she was saying. "I remember, when David would get fussy, he was always there to take him out to the yard and play with him. I did not allow David to go out without adult supervision because of the risk of snakes or spiders, but I was comfortable in letting him go with John. He formed a close bond with him while he lived with us and was desolate when he left for England. It took a long time before he stopped looking for his playmate whenever he got up from his naps. It overjoys us that John is coming back to live in Australia."

"Does he not plan to have his own home?"

"Not right away. But eventually, he would like to establish his own place, marry, and have a family."

Cassandra felt another pang in her heart at Bethany's words. John was going to be married after he went back to Australia. She wondered why that should bother her so, but it did. She shook off the feeling. "How delightful. I am sure he will make a wonderful husband and father."

Bethany looked at her closely. Was that pain she was seeing in Cassandra's eyes? Were her feelings for John deeper than just friendship? If so, that pain would be a sign. Now, they just needed her to get over her barrier of not wanting to leave England and her boys. That was the next hurdle, and one, perhaps, that her sons could help her overcome.

Then, the sound of children filled the kitchen, as Sam and John returned to the house with all of them. This was what the Kingsleys had wanted when they'd said they were looking forward to hearing the halls filled with the laughter of children again. It was a happiness no one could deny.

***

That evening after dinner, the adults and Peter gathered in the front parlour for their final tea of the day. Peter watched his mother interact with the others. She appeared much happier than the last time he had seen her here. It pleased him that she was staying at the estate again, and not planning to leave it again for a long time ... if ever. He also watched her interactions with Lord Dudley. Was there something going on between the two of them? The last time he had seen them together, he had wondered about their relationship, and Lord Dudley's intentions towards his mother in particular. But now, even though nothing had been said, there was a companionable warmth between them. They even shared brief glances and smiles as they refilled teacups over and over again. Could it be that they were falling in love?

Peter was not sure how he felt about that. He wanted his mother to smile again, but was Lord Dudley the man to make that happen? Wasn't he planning to leave the estate within a few months to manage his father's affairs? Where would that leave his mother? Content or heartbroken? Peter decided he needed to look more deeply into their relationship while he was here. The last thing he wanted for his mother was for her to live another unhappy life with a man. She'd already had too many years of sadness with his late father. Peter was determined that it would not happen again. So, tonight, he would watch, and tomorrow, he would speak to his mother about her heart's desires.

***

The following morning, Peter put action to his thoughts. Saddling his horse for a ride with his brothers, it surprised him to see his mother come into the barn.

"Mother," he said, "what brings you out to the barn this early in the morning?"

"I, uh, have been in the habit of taking morning rides with Lord Dudley," said a blushing Cassandra. "Do you mind if I join you?"

"Of course not. Your appearance just surprised me. I did not know you rode."

"While we were living in London, I had no opportunity to do so. And when we moved out here, I was too busy raising you and your brothers, as well as looking after the estate, to have time to ride. But now I find myself much more at leisure and am enjoying my rides with Lord Dudley."

"The two of you?"

"Yes. Are you upset about that?"

"No, but I did not realise you were on such friendly terms with him."

"We have put aside our past differences and now have a companionable friendship. I will miss him when he leaves for Australia."

"He is moving to Australia?"

"Yes. Oh, I should not have said anything, Peter. It is not common knowledge outside the estate. Even his parents are not aware of his intentions yet. Please do not tell anyone his news."

"I won't, Mother. I will keep his secret."

"Thank you. It is not ours to tell."

"Agreed. But I am surprised. I thought he would go back to his family home and manage that estate."

"I believe that is what his parents were hoping for, but it is not in Lord Dudley's plans. He became enamoured with Australia, when he lived there with your aunt and uncle, and desires to return with them when they go back next year."

"How do you feel about that, Mother?"

"I will miss him, but my place is here in England with you and your brothers."

"Has he asked you to join him?"

"No, but your Aunt Bethany would like me to come with them."

"But you are not considering it?"

"No."

"Why not?"

"Because I aspire to be here with my sons, not halfway around the world."

"I see."

Then John arrived with Cassandra's saddled mare, so their time for speaking was cut short. Peter mounted his horse while John helped Cassandra mount hers, and then the three of them rode out to join the other boys for a brisk canter in the meadows.

***

Seeing Peter speaking with his mother, John had actually delayed bringing Cassandra's horse to her. She seldom saw her sons, so he wanted to give her every opportunity to spend time with them, either singly or as a group. He loved the fact that she was so devoted to her sons, and knew that if given the opportunity, she would be just as devoted to any future children she might have. Even though she was still resisting his attempts to court her, he wished her well in the future, and hoped that she would find a loving husband in England with whom to spend the rest of her days.

That thought, of Cassandra finding a husband other than himself, did not sit well with John. He realised then that he did not want to share her with anyone else, and that if she was to have another husband, it should be him. But how to convince Cassandra of that? Perhaps he could enlist Peter as an ally in his quest. The other boys were too young to see that Cassandra needed more than just their love and companionship for the rest of her life, but Peter was almost a young man. He would see things differently than his brothers. *Yes, it would be good to see how Peter feels about his mother's happiness, and whether he would be amenable to her moving away in order to find that joy. I need to speak with him.*

With that decided, when they all dismounted by the creek, and Wendell and Calvin were watering the horses, and Arthur was strolling along beside his mother, John stepped up beside Peter. "Did you enjoy your ride?"

"Yes, sir, I did. Even when I can secure a horse in the city, there are few places to ride quickly, so you end up walking alongside all the other riders."

"Yes, I know. That is the reason I love living in the country. There are no restrictions on how fast or how far you can ride."

Feigning ignorance of John's plans for the future, Peter said, "Are you looking forward to taking over your family's country estate when your tenure here is complete?"

"I plan to move to Australia with Sam and Bethany and live there, rather than take over the family holdings."

"Are your family aware of your plans to leave?"

"Not as yet. I need to tell them soon, though, so that they have time to digest the news and get over their sadness before I depart."

"It is hard for families to be apart, especially with so many miles separating them and little chance of meeting again for a long time."

"That is true, and I will miss my family, but I would be miserable if I did not follow my dreams."

"I understand," said Peter. "I, too, have dreams, though not of such adventure as you desire. Rather, I would prefer living in the country and managing an estate such as Stillwater."

"Do you not wish to travel and see the world?"

"Not particularly. I love England and desire to live here, not anywhere else."

"How old are you now, Peter?"

"Seventeen."

"And are you planning to further your education at university when you finish your time at Eton?"

"That is my mother's wish, but I am not sure. I like school but not enough to want to spend several more years expanding my already sufficient education."

"Does your mother know this?"

"No. She wants me to continue my schooling, and I don't have the heart to disappoint her with the news."

"Just as I am planning to tell my parents my wishes and plans, Peter, you will need to inform your mother of your desires. I am sure that, once she knows how you feel, she will accept whatever you choose to do with your life."

"You are right, Lord Dudley. I will try to tell her while we are here on school break. Then she will not press me to apply for entrance to a university."

"That's a plan, Peter. Only please, do not tell your mother that I put you up to this. It will create more ill will between us."

"I do not see any evidence of ill will, sir. In fact, you and my mother appear to be on much friendlier terms than you were when I was last here."

"We are, Peter. But it is a tenuous relationship, which could easily break down again if I said the wrong thing to her."

"Such as?"

John thought for a moment, then decided to test Peter's feelings: "Such as suggesting that she marry me and come to Australia to live." He held his breath as he awaited Peter's response and was surprised when it came.

"Do you love her, Lord Dudley?"

"I care for her and will miss her tremendously if she does not accompany me to Australia. I truly do not know if I love her, though, as I have never been in love."

"My father did not love her and treated her badly, sir. I do not wish her to experience that again."

"I would never hurt your mother, Peter. I respect and care for her too much to do that to her."

"That is good. If I ever heard that you had... Well, you would have to watch your back, even in Australia. I was too young to do anything about my father's treatment of my mother, but I would not tolerate another man abusing her. Do you understand?"

"I do, Peter, and I feel the same way. Husbands should love and care for their wives, not abuse them. God tells us that in the Bible, and I try to live the way He wants me to in all aspects of my life."

"Thank you for your honesty, Lord Dudley. I perceive you are speaking the truth about your feelings for my mother. Though you do not yet profess to love her, I believe you would treat her well. Does she feel the same way about you?"

"I don't know, Peter. I believe so, but I think her love for you and your brothers is holding her back. She thinks that will suffice her for the rest of her life, and that she needs nothing else."

"I see. Perhaps I can talk to her, Lord Dudley, and support your cause. It will not be long until my brothers and I are men. Even though we will always love Mother, we will have divided attentions once we are married with families of our own. I do not want to worry about her being lonely out here."

"She needs to hear that from you, Peter. I certainly cannot suggest that to her, but you can. And I believe you should, for how else can she make the best decisions for her own life moving forward?"

Peter nodded. "You are right. I'll speak with her about it while I am here on break, as well as about my own future plans. It was good to talk with you, Lord Dudley, man-to-man."

"And with you, Peter. And I am glad you and your brothers have gotten past your efforts to drive me away from the estate. I checked my bed carefully each night for snakes and frogs the last time you were here. Perhaps I can relax during this visit."

Peter laughed. "Sir, there will be no snakes or frogs placed in your bed. We are beyond that stage, except perhaps for Arthur. But we can control him."

John clapped Peter on the shoulder as they neared the others by the creek. He was elated to know that Peter was firmly on his side. Now, he only needed to wait and see how Cassandra would react to her son's words.

***

Cassandra wondered what had changed between Peter and Lord Dudley. When she had last seen them together, they were barely speaking. And now they were joking and laughing, almost like father and son. So, when they returned to the manor, and after they had dismounted and left the grooms to care for their horses, Cassandra lagged behind so that she could walk with Peter. John noticed her efforts, and so he walked ahead with the other boys to give them some privacy.

"So, what were you and Lord Dudley talking about when you rejoined us at the creek, Peter? It looked as if you were enjoying his company."

"I was, Mother. I have changed my mind about him. He is a good man."

"How did you determine that?"

"Oh, I don't know how, but he talked to me like an adult, rather than a child. I like being treated in that manner."

"I know, Peter, but I struggle to think of you as anything other than my little boy. I have difficulty realising you are almost a man."

"I understand, Mother, but I am almost finished school and need to think about my future."

"Aren't you going to start university next fall?"

Peter took a deep breath. It was time to tell her the truth. "Mother, I don't want to go to university. I want to come back to the estate and learn about managing it. Then, perhaps, Aunt Bethany will hire me to replace Lord Dudley as the new manager when he leaves for Australia."

"You are too young to manage the estate, Peter."

"Father was almost the same age as I am when he took over, Mother. If Aunt Bethany does not think I am ready to handle it on my own, perhaps I could apprentice with someone for a year, until I am fully comfortable in the role."

"I suppose I could supervise you for a couple of years, Peter. I was not planning on resuming the role when Lord Dudley leaves, but if it is of benefit to you—"

"No, Mother, I was not thinking of you. Perhaps one of the other estate managers connected to the Yardley family. I don't want to put you in that position again for my sake. You need to live your own life."

"My life is you and your brothers, Peter. I have no other reason for living."

"Then you need to find another reason, Mother. My brothers and I all love you dearly, but we are growing up and will soon be young men with families of our own. I don't relish the idea of dividing our attention between them and you ... and always feeling that we are neglecting one or the other."

"But if you move out here, even with a family—"

"Mother, you have done your job and done it well. It was a hard life for you, raising us both with and without Father. You deserve to find some happiness for yourself, rather than solely continuing to care for us."

"I wouldn't even know where to start, Peter. My happiness is so entwined with your lives. Perhaps there is no happiness for me without you."

"There is, Mother, and if you open your eyes, I think you will see it. But you have blinders on right now that are only allowing you to look straight ahead, and not to your sides. You need to take them off and look around you. Happiness is right beside you ... just waiting for you to notice."

"You are speaking in riddles. Please tell me what you mean."

"All right. Lord Dudley is standing by your side, Mother. He wants to make you happy. But he can only do that if you agree to marry him and move to Australia. Is that plain enough for you?"

"You want me to move to Australia?"

He shook his head. "I want you to find joy and happiness, and I believe that you would find it there with Lord Dudley."

"I cannot believe the words you are speaking to me, Peter. Did he put you up to this?"

"No. These words are my own. But I believe him when he says that he cares for you and wants to look after you for the rest of your life."

"Did he say he loved me?"

"I asked him that question, but he said that since he has never been in love, he is unaware of the feeling. But he does know that he will miss you dreadfully if he leaves you behind."

"I will miss him too, Peter, as I have grown fond of him. But I am no more familiar with that sort of love than he is. There was never any love between your father and me. Ours was a business arrangement. Perhaps I am too old to learn to love, and if I am, I would hate to disappoint Lord Dudley. I seem to fail at everything I do." She sighed and shook her head. "No. Even if I seldom see you and your brothers, he is better off without me. I would only ruin his life."

"Mother—"

"Enough, Peter. Thank you for enlightening me. I shall have to be cautious in my dealings with Lord Dudley from now on, so I don't raise his expectations." Cassandra picked up her pace then and marched into the house, leaving Peter behind, wearing a frown as he watched her go. How could he convince her of anything when she saw herself only as a failure? He needed guidance and wisdom, so he took his petition to his all-knowing heavenly father.

Chapter 25

Cassandra flopped down onto her bed. Everyone was conspiring against her. First Bethany and Sam, then Lord Dudley, and now her own son. Why wouldn't they leave her alone? Closing her eyes, she took some deep breaths and tried to calm down. It worked, though perhaps too well. She was soon fast asleep and dreaming of a place that was filled with light, a place called Heaven, where the voice of Love began to speak softly to her:

"Cassandra, my child, do not be afraid. It is your time to experience the blessing of love I have kept in store for you. Reach out and take it."

"Father God? Is that you?"

"Yes."

"You are saying that Lord Dudley loves me?"

"Yes. He does not recognise it, but he does."

"So … should I leave everything I know behind and follow him halfway around the world to start a new life in Australia?"

"That is up to you, my child. Only you can make that decision. Remember that I love you with My all-encompassing Love. That will never change, no matter where you live."

"But Father, what if I fail again as a wife? I do not think I could bear that misery once more."

"You may fail at tasks, but you are not a failure, Cassandra. My Son's blood has washed and sanctified you. You are perfect in my eyes."

***

A peace washed over Cassandra as she contemplated these words. God was not concerned about her mistakes or failures. He saw her only as His daughter ... in Christ's redemptive white robes. He wanted her to step out confidently and follow her heart, rather than her head. And as her heart was leading her towards a new life in a new country with a new husband, how could she say no?

Slowly, her eyes opened, and she looked around her. Nothing had changed but her heart. In God's strength and love, she could now move forward and stop looking back. It was time to put her thoughts into action.

Even with this new sense of purpose, Cassandra wondered how she could approach Lord Dudley and let him know of her change of heart. *It is not as if I can just walk up to him and say, "Excuse me, sir, but I had a chat with God recently, and He told me that you love me, even if you don't know it yet. As I have the same feelings for you, I would like to marry you and move to Australia as your wife. When do we leave?"*

Cassandra laughed to herself as she thought about such a scene. No, even with this new intention in mind, she could never gather the courage to be so daring. Lord Dudley would also have to hear the voice of God and approach her. She could not take the first step in changing their relationship, but she could go back downstairs with a different attitude. Perhaps that would be enough to spark an interest in Lord Dudley. And then if the opportunity arose, she could start calling him by his first name. That would catch his attention after all this time of addressing him as Lord Dudley. She laughed again, then began fixing her hair and shaking out her gown. Finally, after a last look in the mirror, she straightened her shoulders and marched downstairs.

***

John was also receiving the counsel of God, though not quite so directly as Cassandra had. His was coming to him with the voice of his friend Sam Yardley. They were talking about John's recent conversation with Peter, and his approval of a potential marriage between John and his mother.

"So, Peter approved of your intentions, John?"

"Yes, he did. After how he viewed me the last time he was here, it came as a total surprise."

"Perhaps he had a change of heart over these past two months."

"Perhaps, but whatever happened, his attitude is totally different now."

"That is good. It means that you have an ally in the Stillwater camp. Maybe Cassandra will listen to him."

"Perhaps."

"Are you still of a mind to marry her?"

"If she will have me, yes. But I do not know what else to say to persuade her. I have run out of words."

"Perhaps, you should pray then, Cousin, and ask God to lead her to you. If this is in His will for you and Cassandra, then He will work out the details."

"That is a good idea, Sam. And I will ask Him to give me a sign that I am moving in the right direction, just as Gideon did in the Bible."

"There is one slight difference, John. Gideon already knew what God wanted him to do. He just needed the reassurance of God's leading and power. Still, even though you are only looking for direction, I am sure that God will honour your request."

"Thank you, Sam. Please add your prayers to mine."

"I will. Now, I hear footsteps coming down the stairs, and knowing that Bethany went up to feed Douglas, it can only be one other lady, so I will leave you to your quest. Good luck," he said, before clapping John on the shoulder and exiting the room. John heard him greet Cassandra, so he breathed a prayer for courage as Cassandra walked into the room.

"Hello, Mrs. Stillwater," he said as she walked over to him.

Cassandra took a deep breath and let it out slow. "Hello, John."

John took a step back. Cassandra had called him by his first name, not Lord Dudley, as she'd always insisted on doing. Was this God's sign to him? He decided to test her further by saying, "You are looking lovely, Cassandra. Is that a new gown?"

She blushed and looked away for a moment before bringing her gaze back to his face. "No, you have seen this dress many times, John. I only changed from my riding costume."

Hearing this response, John knew that she had not simply misspoken. Something had changed with Cassandra, and it gave him hope for the future.

"Uh... Perhaps, this is a bit forward, Cassandra, but has something changed since our ride this morning? You seem different."

"Perhaps I am. I have had an interesting conversation, and it has greatly enlightened me."

"Oh, as to what?"

"As to how I see myself, and how God sees me."

"And how does He view you?"

"As His perfect child."

"Indeed, He does. Through our redemption in Christ, we are all perfect, or sanctified, in God's eyes. Even when we see ourselves as failures, He never does."

"I see that now. I have always thought of myself as a failure, and that this was why everything I did turned out badly. But I have a new perspective now. Whatever I have done, even if it did not go correctly, is not a reflection on who I am. And as such, I can live free of the guilt of my past missteps."

"That is an excellent way of viewing things, Cassandra. I have certainly never thought of you as a failure, only someone who's had to cope with difficult circumstances. I admire you for what you have done not only for yourself but for your sons as well."

"You do not think less of me because of my past, John?"

"Certainly not. Why would I do that?"

"Because my marriage failed, and my work as the estate manager failed, and—"

"Stop right there, Cassandra. Your marriage failed because of your husband, not you. And as far as the estate goes, without the duke's financial backing, it would be failing under my management as well. Neither of those things were your fault."

"But what about my failure to tell the truth at Bethany's trial?"

"That was sinful, Cassandra, but both God and Bethany have forgiven you, have they not?"

"Yes."

"Then let it go, dear lady. It is in the past and should not continue to haunt you. The devil would like to keep you down by repeatedly bringing it back up, but you must resist his attempts to do so. Take those thoughts captive in Christ and let Him take them from you any time the devil comes around to torment you with them."

"I will try, John. Thank you for your counsel."

"Anytime. I am always available to you."

"Well, for the next while at least. Then you will be off to Australia with Sam and Bethany. Who will I turn to then for wise advice?"

"God will always be there for you."

"I know, but sometimes it is helpful to speak with a human friend. Bethany has always been that friend, but I don't have any others like her."

"I would like to continue as your friend, Cassandra."

"I would like that too, John. But like Bethany, the only way I can talk to you will be through letters, and that will mean months between such interactions."

John decided it was time to find out just how far their relationship had progressed. "Not if you moved to Australia with us, Cassandra. The door is still open for you to join us."

"Really?"

"Really. In fact, I would like you to come."

"You would?"

"Yes."

"But why?"

"Because I hate the thought of leaving you behind and not knowing if I will ever see you again."

"I hate that thought too, John, but what would I do in Australia? I do not want to impose on Bethany and Sam."

"You could be my housekeeper."

"Your housekeeper? I thought you lived with Sam and Bethany."

"I did. But now I need a place of my own, and I will need someone to take care of it."

"So, you are looking for a housekeeper then. Not a wife."

"No," said John. "I need a wife more than a housekeeper, and you are the only one I can see in that role."

"You wish me to marry you?"

"Yes."

"I am flattered by your proposal, John, but having had one loveless marriage, I do not want another."

Seeing the disappointment in her eyes over his distinctly underwhelming proposal and wondering if he was going to lose her because of it, John finally realised his feelings for what they were. He loved Cassandra, more than anything, and wanted to spend the rest of his life making her happy. He stepped forward then and went down on one knee, taking her hands gently in his.

"My dear Cassandra," he said softly, "that was the worst proposal of marriage a man could ever offer a woman. Please forgive me. My thoughts for you are far from loveless; I am in love with you and wish to spend the rest of my life making you happy. Would you please reconsider your answer?"

Seeing him there, down on one knee in front of her, Cassandra realised that his words were true. John did not want to marry her for her dowry or to act as his housekeeper. He wanted her, Cassandra, as his bride. He loved her. She had never heard those words before, but with them said, her doubts vanished.

"I reconsider, Lord Dudley, and my answer is now yes."

John smiled, got quickly back to his feet, and took her into his arms. "Thank you for making this the happiest day of my life. I will do everything in my power to make you happy from this day forward. Even if you do not love me, I will—"

"Wait," she said. "You think that I don't love you?"

"I have not heard those words from your lips, so I can only assume—"

This time Cassandra cut off his words with her actions, doing something that she had never dreamt of doing: She reached out with both hands and placed one on either side of John's face, pulling it down to her level and kissing him.

Surprised at her sudden action, but not unhappy, John soon took control. He wrapped his arms tightly around her and deepened their kiss, which did not end until their need for breath gave them little choice but to pull slightly apart and stare into each other's eyes.

Blushing wildly, Cassandra smiled. "I am sorry if I was too forward, but I—"

"You are free to be forward like that any time, my love," he said quickly. "I quite enjoyed the interaction."

Cassandra continued blushing at his words. "I don't know what came over me, but it seemed easier to show my love than to say it. But just so you have no further doubts about my feelings for you, John Dudley, I will speak my truth as well: I love you."

John sealed those words with another kiss. Their commitment was now complete. Nothing else needed to be said. Soon, they would repeat those words of love and commitment before a minister, but for now, they would simply revel in their feelings and look forward to a lifetime of happiness.

Trusting in God's plan had finally turned Cassandra's failures into a success beyond her wildest imaginings, and for the first time in her life, she was happy to follow wherever it might lead.

Epilogue

Nine months later...

Cassandra could hardly believe it. She was standing at the rail of a three-masted ship that would take her to Australia. She was beginning a brand-new life—a life of adventure with her husband of five months. A year ago, she would never have dreamt of such a thing happening to her. It was amazing how utterly her life had changed.

***

The months after John had proposed had flown by. They had resisted the pressure from their families to have a large society wedding. Instead, they'd agreed to a small ceremony with only family and friends, and then a large reception the following day. Cassandra had not wanted to be on display, but Bethany had convinced her that she would survive the ordeal, just as Bethany had done several years ago when she'd married Sam. For her friend's sake, and so that her boys would have memories of her wedding and happiness with John, Cassandra had agreed. The two days of wedding celebrations had gone off without a hitch. Cassandra had few memories of the celebrations, only of saying her vows, and then the bridal kiss after the minister had proclaimed them man and wife. Everything else was a joyful blur.

In the intervening months between their wedding and departure for Australia, Bethany had delivered another healthy baby, a little girl they'd named Amanda Margaret. Her grandparents had been thrilled to witness the birth of their second granddaughter but saddened to know that the family's departure was rapidly approaching. And then the day had come that they'd all been dreading. The Yardleys were heading home.

It had thrilled Cassandra's sons to hear that she was going to marry John, but less so when they'd realised that this meant she would be moving to Australia. Peter had told his younger brothers that their mother deserved a chance at happiness after everything that she had endured for their sakes while they were young. They had agreed and put on brave faces during the wedding and celebration, so as not to dim their mother's happiness.

Since the wedding, it had been determined that Arthur was too young to stay in Britain without Cassandra, so he was accompanying her and John to Australia. He would be schooled at the station along with Bethany and Sam's children until he was ready to go to Eton. That would coincide with the fulfilment of Peter's promise to his mother that he would bring his other brothers to Australia for a visit. Then Arthur would travel back to England with them to attend secondary school.

So, the tears on the departure day were a mix of both joy and sadness. Peter's promise was enough to wipe away some tears during Cassandra's leave-taking, but not all of them. Other than in boarding school, they had never been apart from their mother for more than a day, so even the promise of a visit in a couple of years was hard for them to bear. But regardless, it was now time to let her go.

"I love you all," said Cassandra, not bothering to stem her tears as she stood with John's supportive arm around her shoulders. "And I'll expect you to write often and tell me of all your adventures. I can't wait until the day I see you again."

The boys chorused their agreement to write her frequently with the promise that she would do the same. Then John gently turned her, walked her over to the carriage, and helped her inside to join Arthur, already seated inside. Cassandra sat down and turned to look out the window. Then John climbed in after her, and the footman closed the door and climbed up beside the driver. After one last wave of her hand, the driver clicked the reins, and they followed Sam and Bethany's carriage down the street. Cassandra watched until they turned a corner, and the boys were out of sight. Then she settled back into John's tender embrace and let her tears flow freely. Her new life had already begun.

***

As the ship left the harbour, Cassandra was startled when John moved up behind her and drew her back against his chest, wrapping his arms around her.

"I didn't hear you coming," she said. "My thoughts took me into the past."

"To happy moments, I hope," he said, leaning down to kiss her upturned face.

"Mostly. I still miss my boys, but I am so happy to be here with you that my joy overshadows any lingering sadness." She smiled up at him over her shoulder, inviting another kiss.

"I can't imagine how hard this must be for you, love, but I am so thankful you married me and are joining me in Australia. I don't know what I would do without you."

"Oh, you would have married an ex-convict just like Sam and Joe did, and I would have been left alone to live out the rest of my life as a lonely widow," Cassandra said teasingly.

"No woman, even an ex-convict, would ever bring me the happiness that you do, Lady Dudley. I am so blessed to have you as my wife."

"No more blessed than I am, Lord Dudley. I have a new lease on life and look forward to spending the rest of my days with you."

"And I with you, love. A year ago, I wondered what God had in store for me, but I never could have imagined the blessings He had planned for me. My success and happiness are now complete."

"Mine too, John. He took my failures and turned them into the greatest possible success: a lifetime of serving Him by your side. God is good."

"I could not agree more, my love," said John, before turning her around into his full embrace and leaning down to kiss her again. The time for words had ended.

The End.

End Notes

All citations are from the King James Bible:

1. Psalm 118:24
2. Philippians 4:8
3. Romans 8:28
4. James 4:13-15
5. James 4:7
6. Psalm 127:5

Coming Next...

ADELAIDE'S DILEMMA

Summer 2025

Adelaide's Dilemma

Adelaide Wintry was a lady by marriage but not by character. Her husband, Edward, heir to the Barony of Wintry, had died in a riding accident just after their only son had died at birth, leaving Adelaide a widow with two young daughters to raise. When her brother-in-law Joseph had arrived from Australia, two years after Edward's death, Adelaide had been sure that he was the answer to her prayers for a new husband. She had used her outward beauty to try and compromise Joseph into marrying her, but he'd been alert to her ways and had not fallen into her trap. Instead, he'd left her on the doorstep of the Wintry townhouse with these words:

"This is where we part, Adelaide. I do not know if we will ever see each other again as I have no plans to return to England, and I doubt you could endure a trip to Australia. I would like to see my nieces again some day, so perhaps that could be arranged when they are older. My best wishes in your search for a new husband. But if I may give a bit of brotherly advice? Don't try so hard, Adelaide. It will only put men off. Instead, let God take control of your life. You are a beautiful woman on the outside, but your inner self needs improvement. Someday, your outer beauty will fade, but a lovely spirit never does. That is also something you can teach your daughters. I look forward to hearing how they fare in my letters from Father. Think on my words as you begin your new life without Edward. Goodbye and fare thee well, my sister." And then he had left her, hoping never to encounter her again.

Adelaide had heard him, thinking this would be their last time together. She had acknowledged his words, and to Joseph's surprise, when they had met a final time at his wedding, Adelaide had been demure and silent, a sharp contrast to her previous behaviour. But would his words make any difference in Adelaide's life? Would she make a conscious effort to change who she was?

Stay tuned for the rest of her story; to learn Adelaide's fate.

It might surprise you…

Author's Notes

Have you ever felt like Cassandra did, as though you were a failure and had been one your whole life? That nothing you ever did turned out right, whether it was at school, at home, at work, or in relationships? I can certainly relate. I would try different things and yet never achieve my goals. I always fell short of my expectations, and it left me feeling depressed.

But one day, after a significant "failure," I realised that I was too often running ahead of God, just as the women in these last two books have done. I was in places, or situations, that He did not want for me, but I had plunged ahead without seeking His wisdom before diving in and starting to swim. Taking my eyes off God, just as Peter did when he jumped out of the boat in the sea of Galilee, meant that I too started to sink. It was only when I looked up at Jesus, and He took my hand once more, that I came out of the waves and directly into His arms.

I am still guilty of running ahead of God at times, but more and more, I stop and ask for His guidance before I leap into the water. That process has served me well in the past several years, including when I started thinking about writing and publishing these books. God blesses me abundantly when I follow His will with the encouragement that comes from my readers and friends.

If we are children of God, we may fail at things, but we are never seen as failures by God. God loves each one of us and desires the best for each of His children.

I pray that you enjoyed this book, and that God used it to touch your life in some way. If so, I'd love to hear from you. You can contact me through my website: **www.nancyireneyoung.com**. I look forward to hearing from you.

God bless you in your journey with Him.

Nancy

Other Books by
NANCY I YOUNG

VIKING SERIES

Home: A Viking's Heart

Alva's Redemption

VICTORIAN WOMEN OF FAITH SERIES

A Journey to Joy

Freed: To live or …